Negative Image

Books by Vicki Delany

Constable Molly Smith Series
In the Shadow of the Glacier
Valley of the Lost
Winter of Secrets
Negative Image

Other Novels
Scare the Light Away
Burden of Memory

Negative Image

A Constable Molly Smith Novel

Vicki Delany

Poisoned Pen Press

Poisoned
Pen
Press

Poisoned Pen Press
6962 E. First Ave., Ste. 103
Scottsdale, AZ 85251
www.poisonedpenpress.com
info@poisonedpenpress.com

Printed in the United States of America

For Gail Cargo. Thanks, Mom

Acknowledgments

As I have no experience in law enforcement whatsoever, it would have been impossible to bring Molly Smith, John Winters and the Trafalgar City Police to life without much help from various police officers, in particular Detective Paul Burkart, Constable Janet Scott-Pryke, and Brita Wood of the Nelson City Police, Constable Nicole Lott of the Prince Edward County OPP, and Staff-Sergeant Kris Patterson of the Belleville Police Service. I have the good fortune to belong to a wonderful critique group consisting of Dorothy McIntosh, Madeleine Harris-Callway, Donna Carrick, Jane Burfield, and Cheryl Freedman, who helped enormously. Thanks also to Verna Relkoff of the Mint Agency for editorial help.

Advice on medical matters was provided by Doctors C.J. Lyons, Peter Duffy, and Dan Kalla. The tireless Cheryl Freedman put me in touch with the proper learned people.

Thanks to my colleagues and friends at Type M for Murder (http://typem4murder.blogspot.com) always ready with support, advice and friendship.

Chapter One

Rachel Lewis knew she was pretty, but she also knew that being merely pretty wasn't good enough.

You needed a substantial dose of luck.

There were plenty of models and no-talent celebrities who were nothing special when you saw them without make-up, lighting, tousled hair arranged exactly so. They were simply women, ordinary women, whom the camera, with the right photographer behind it, transformed into something extraordinary. Rachel worked hard at keeping her body lean and in top shape, and although she was only five foot seven, short in the modeling world, she could walk with grace, and sex appeal, in the highest of heels. Her hair was mousy brown and thin, as common as dirt, but that's what wigs and extensions were for. All she needed was to be photographed by the right photographer, someone who had not only skill behind the camera, but who also had fame, a reputation, contacts, and she'd be heading straight up the ladder, on her way to the big-time.

At last Rachel Lewis' luck had turned. She'd found him.

She parked her cart in the hallway, and knocked loudly. When no one answered, she opened the door with her key. Tucking the small folder containing her even-smaller portfolio under her arm she eased the door open.

If the boss found out she'd approached a hotel guest on a personal matter, it would be enough to get her fired. To Rachel, that was a risk worth taking. She was tired of working here, anyway; the skiing season was over and she had no other reason to hang around.

"Housekeeping," she called. Still no answer. She walked into the room. It was a pig-sty, but then again, it always was. It didn't matter to her if he was a pig, all that mattered was that he was a fashion photographer and he'd agreed to look at her portfolio.

She'd been lucky, yesterday, to catch him coming out of his room. Although luck had little to do with it: she'd been waiting next door, listening to the sounds of a man getting ready for his day. When she heard the door open, she'd run into the hallway, and made her pitch.

She'd studied acting in school, and had rehearsed her lines as if she were going to be on the stage. He looked her up and down, with a lazy eye. The light in the hotel hallway wasn't good, much too bright, illuminating every flaw, but she'd put on a cap that came low over her forehead and designer sunglasses that cost three hundred bucks. She might look strange, a hotel maid wearing sunglasses indoors, but figured it was worth trying for the effect. Same with the four inch heels she'd stuffed into a pocket of the housekeeping cart for just that purpose, and the belt that cinched the waist of the hideous black and mustard uniform.

He'd moved his eyes up and down her body, while she posed, one leg in front of the other, hip slightly forward. He told her he was in a hurry, but she had good lines and he'd look at her portfolio. If he liked what he saw, he said, he'd invite her for a…drink, and discuss her prospects. Leave it in his room, sometime. He walked away, and she'd gone back to the room she was supposedly cleaning and let her knees collapse underneath her. Today she'd brought the portfolio on which she'd spent every last penny of her savings with her to work.

Room service dishes. The food, cheese and pâté, bread and crackers, grapes and slices of melon, was untouched. She lifted the uncorked champagne bottle out of the pool of water in the silver bucket and was surprised at its weight. She held it to the light streaming in through the open drapes. Almost full.

Lifting the bottle to her mouth she took a deep drink. Delicious. She held the champagne, bubbles gone, in her mouth for a few moments as she flicked through the detritus on the desk. Computer printouts, photographs of the mountains, tops still covered with snow but grass and trees coming back to life in the spring sunshine, shaking off the memory of a harsh winter. A few shots of people in town, women, young women, with jackets unzipped and pockets bulging with gloves and faces turned to the sun. Nothing, no one, special, she thought.

One old picture, yellowing and turning up at the edges, was pure porn, and not a very good photograph at that. She dropped it back on the desk. You saw a lot of secrets cleaning up after people. Her own portfolio, she would lay out carefully on the bed after making it.

Clothes littered the floor. Underwear, socks, a thick hand-knit sweater. No women's clothes. His wife—at first the staff thought she must be his daughter, perhaps even a granddaughter—had another room. Rachel took a quick glance at the door to the adjacent room. The lock was turned. Interesting that he'd shut his glamorous young wife out at night.

What did they say: *the rich are different than you and me.*

She popped a couple of grapes into her mouth and took another swig of champagne, *Moët et Chandon,* before settling down to work.

Someday she'd be the one discarding underwear on the floor for someone else to pick up, and leaving full bottles of *Moët* for the trash.

She took her cloths and bottles of cleaning supplies and pushed open the bathroom door.

The champagne and grapes rose up in her stomach.

Chapter Two

"What have you got, Dave?"

"Man dead upstairs. Hotel guest. The maid found him when she went in to clean."

"Have you seen him?"

"Yes."

"Is this likely to be our business?"

"I'd say so, Sarge. Shot in the back of the head."

A small crowd had gathered in the lobby. Staff and hotel guests stood in silence, watching the police. Two paramedics stood by the elevator with their stretcher, the sheets clean and crisply folded.

Sergeant John Winters recognized the hotel manager. "I'm going upstairs for a quick look, Peter. Can you and your people remain here?" It was phrased like a request. It wasn't.

He headed for the elevator. Constable Dave Evans followed.

"Is anyone upstairs?"

"Molly's guarding the door."

"Who was first on the scene?"

"Molly."

"You stay here. No one in or out of the hotel, and no one unofficial upstairs until I get back. When Detective Lopez and the coroner arrive, send them up."

He nodded to the paramedics. The elevator door opened as soon as he pressed the button.

The Hudson House Hotel was the best hotel in Trafalgar, British Columbia. It was an old building, old by western North

America standards, built in the late 1800s. For most of the twentieth century, it had been lodging for itinerant loggers and miners. It turned into a backpackers' hostel when young people discovered the area's skiing and climbing opportunities. At the beginning of this century, as tourists got older and more affluent, less inclined to rough it, the hotel attached a new wing, underwent major renovations, and the old building was refurbished to a degree of luxury it had never before known.

Sergeant John Winters of the Trafalgar City Police looked at himself in the spotless glass paneling of the elevator. He and his wife had been reversing down the driveway, heading for a much-needed few days of hedonism in San Francisco, when his cell phone rang. He'd taken the call, and driven back up the driveway. Eliza had not been pleased at this change in plans. She'd taken it quite badly, and that surprised him. It wasn't as if this was the first time in their long marriage plans had been canceled at the last minute. She was scarcely mollified when he said it would probably turn out to be nothing important and they'd catch the next flight. She slammed the door getting out of the car and dragged her suitcase to the house with shoulders set in anger while her boots, and the wheels of the suitcase, made the ground shake. He made a mental note to call her once he'd seen the body. Young police officers had been known, in their enthusiasm, to mistake an accidental death for a deliberate one. Nevertheless, he'd already called the forensic guys.

He stepped out of the elevator. The thick beige carpet muffled his footsteps.

Constable Molly Smith looked up at the sound of the elevator doors opening. Her face was pale under her skier's winter tan, and she looked pleased to see him.

"Anyone been in there?" he said, without a greeting.

"The chambermaid, the hotel manager, me and then Dave, but no one else, far as I know. I took the call. All I was told was that someone was dead. Soon as I saw him, I shut the door behind me and called for backup."

"Who found him?"

"A hotel maid. She ran out of here screaming her head off and the manager came up and went in. He's the one who called us."

"Where's the maid?"

"Taken to hospital. Shock."

"Let's see it then."

"In the bathroom."

The room was beautifully, and expensively, decorated in shades of green and peach with heavy wooden furniture, thick drapes, deep carpet. Winters noted the disarray, the uneaten food, the dirty clothes, papers scattered across the desk and spilling onto the floor.

Smith didn't need to tell him where to go. The scent of death, of blood and bodily waste and vomit, came from the bathroom.

The man was kneeling over the toilet, his face planted into the bowl. *Worshiping the porcelain god*, some people called throwing up into the toilet after a night's drunk. The back of the head was matted with dried blood and gray matter. Blood had spattered across the walls around him. About a foot inside the door a puddle of vomit, fresh by the look and smell, lay on the floor.

"Whose is that?" he asked Smith, without turning around.

"Maid."

"You touch anything?"

"Only the side of his neck, not that it was necessary to check if he was dead, but, I thought…I guess I thought I should."

"Not a problem."

"That footprint there, I think it's mine." The faint marks of the edge of a boot tread were beside the body.

"Okay," he said, "I've seen enough for now. Let's wait for Ron."

As they left the hotel room, the elevator bell pinged and the doors opened to let out Ron Gavin, the forensic investigator, with his partner and their equipment. The Trafalgar City Police was small, and Winters relied on the RCMP for forensic assistance in major cases.

"You stay on the door," Winters said to Smith. "Keep the log. Ron, Alison, we've got work for you. This way."

Molly Smith pulled out her notebook, and jotted down the time and who had gone into the room.

The elevator pinged again. This time it was a Mountie in uniform. He was tall and handsome and the edges of his mouth turned up when he saw her standing in the hall.

He sauntered toward her. She bent her head back to her notebook.

"Guys inside?" he said.

"Yes. Wouldn't have thought this would need the dog."

"It doesn't. Norman's in the car. Thought I'd drop by, see if anyone needs a hand, or something."

The door to the hotel suite was open, low voices came from inside. Winters laughed. The Mountie grabbed her arm and pulled her to one side. He bent and kissed her, full on the mouth, and his right hand grabbed the seat of her uniform trousers.

She pulled away, both angry and pleased. "Adam. Stop that."

He reached for her again, and she swatted at his hand. "I mean it."

"No one's watching," he said with a wicked laugh.

"The sergeant catches us having a grope, I'll really be in for it."

"The sergeant should be so lucky." He ran one finger down the length of her nose. "I can't stop thinking about that thing you do."

He jumped back at the sound of footsteps.

"Molly, have the station contact Doctor Lee at KBRH and tell her we're bringing someone for her careful attention." John Winters looked at her. "Your hat is crooked. Straighten it. Adam, if you're not here to see Corporal Gavin, get back downstairs."

Hot flames rushed up Smith's neck into her face. *Goddamnit*, no one would think anything less of Adam for fooling around on the job; they'd probably give him a wink and a nudge. But her, they'd say she was too unprofessional, too wrapped up in emotions. She lifted a hand to her hat. It was not crooked.

"Thought I'd see if you need a hand, Sarge," Adam said.

"I don't. Molly, contact Ray and ask if he's got the coroner yet."

"Catch you later." Adam headed for the elevator.

Everyone knew they were dating, Molly Smith and Constable Adam Tocek of the RCMP, nothing wrong with that. Many, if not most, police women dated and married fellow officers. Men outside the job just didn't understand. But to be caught in public, it would be the woman who was called on the carpet. Why if…

The door at the end of the hall opened. The heat rose again in Smith's face. If that woman had been two minutes earlier she would have gotten a nice picture for the front page. Constable Smith necking while supposedly guarding a murder scene.

Meredith Morgenstern, reporter with the *Trafalgar Daily Gazette*, pasted on a smile as fake as her boobs and marched down the corridor as if she had a right to be here. The photographer, a weedy young guy, working part time while finishing college, slunk along behind her. He lifted his camera to take a picture of the constable guarding the scene.

"I don't think you're allowed up here, Meredith," Smith said.

"Sure I am. The people want to know."

"Constable Smith," said a voice from behind the door. "This is a restricted area. If Ms. Morgenstern won't leave, she will be escorted out."

"Once you've made a quick statement, Sergeant Winters, I'll leave you to your work."

"Constable, call a car to take Ms. Morgenstern to the station." He stood in the door, blocking the way.

"All right, all right. We're going."

The photographer took another picture. Fortunately there was nothing to be seen from the doorway. All the action, past and present, was in the bathroom.

"Christ, I can't stand that woman," Winters said once the stairwell door had closed behind the reporters. He spoke into his radio as he returned to the room. "Evans, if I'd wanted you to let people up the back stairs I would have told you."

Smith let out a puff of air. Winters' attention was shifting to Dave Evans. That was good.

This time the elevator doors opened to reveal Detective Ray Lopez, Winters' partner, and the coroner.

Smith wrote their names in her notebook.

◇◇◇

"She ran into the hall, screaming and crying. Maria, who was working the other end of the corridor, along with a good number of guests, came to see what was wrong. Maria ran downstairs and got me. When I arrived, people were standing around outside the door. Two women were trying to calm Rachel. I don't think anyone else went into the room, but I can't be sure. I…" He turned away and swallowed. "I went inside. Took one look and called 911. Then, or maybe it was before I made the call, I shut the door, and told everyone to go back to their rooms. I doubt if anyone did."

"Probably not," John Winters said. They were in the hotel manager's office. Splotches of bright red covered Peter Wagner's normally ruddy face, his ample jowls shook, and he tugged at the wedding ring, buried in fat, on his left hand. Upstairs, Ron Gavin was hard at work, itemizing everything in the dead man's hotel room while his partner crawled around the bathroom floor. The coroner had declared the death, and the medics had been allowed to remove the body. It would be taken to Kootenay Boundary Regional Hospital in Trail for autopsy. The cause of death couldn't be much clearer, single gunshot to the back of the head, but the formalities had to be followed. You never knew what stories that gunshot might hide unless you looked. Winters had immediately ruled out suicide. Not only was the wound at a bad angle, there was no sign of the gun.

"What can you tell me about the dead man? Is he staying here alone?"

"Name's Rudolph Steiner. He's with his wife and assistant. I don't know where they are. I went to their rooms but no one answered, and I checked the restaurant and gym." Wagner was hugely overweight and breathing much too heavily. Rivers of sweat poured down his cheeks and forehead. Winters hoped he wouldn't have to call the ambulance back. Wagner held his hand to his mouth. "Oh, no. Do you think…?"

Winters pulled out his cell phone. "What room numbers? Send someone with a set of keys to meet Detective Lopez there. Steiner's wife doesn't share a room with him?"

"Mrs. Steiner has the adjoining room, and his assistant is at the end of the hall." He reached for his phone and gave the order before dabbing at the sweat on his face with a cheerful yellow polka-dot handkerchief.

Winters asked Ray Lopez to check that the rooms were indeed empty and put his own phone away.

"Fortunately, it's the end of the season," Wagner said. "I've been able to get all the guests off that floor. The ones who want to stay, that is. We've had several premature check-outs. You'll let us know when people can go to their rooms and get their things?"

"Yes. I'll need a list of the premature checkouts." Winters checked his notes. "The maid who found the body. Rachel Lewis. She been with you long?"

"Came at the beginning of the season. She's a ski bum, working to make money to stay in Trafalgar and ski on her days off. I'm expecting that she, along with several others, will be quitting soon. Moving on."

"You have any reason to think she knew this Steiner guy?"

"No. Although…"

"Although?"

"I'll check with the head of housekeeping, but I seem to think she was assigned to the top floors. Not the second."

"Find that out, will you? Anything else you can tell me about Steiner?"

"He was a photographer, a big name apparently, although I've never heard of him. Not that I would. Good clothes, expensive watch. In the company of a wife who probably needs fake ID to drink in the bar and a personal assistant, female. That's about all I know."

"Where's he from?"

"I checked the register. Address in Vancouver."

"You ever see him with anyone other than the wife and assistant?"

"I don't live here, John, I just work here." Wagner cracked a weak smile. His breathing was starting to settle down, and his color was already looking better. "I'll ask the staff, if you like."

"Please."

"He used room service a lot, and all the restaurant charges to his account were for one person at a time."

"When did they check in?"

Deep in his pocket, Winters' cell phone rang. He checked the display: Ron Gavin, the forensic investigator. "Excuse me a moment," he said. "Yes?"

"John, I'm taking a break. Need to stretch my legs, get a coffee. Come with me."

What? "I'm sort of tied up, Ron. You can't be finished already?"

"Still plenty to check out." Gavin's voice was low and tight. "I *need* a break, John. And I'd *like* you to come with me."

"Okay. Give me half an hour."

"*Now* would be good. There's a back door next to the kitchen leading out to the service area. Take it." Gavin hung up.

Winters stared at the phone in his hand.

"Problem?" Wagner asked.

"Something I have to check out. I'd like to speak to anyone on your staff who was on the second floor last night or this morning. I'm guessing your night manager is home in bed. If you can get me his address, I'll go around later."

"Okay, sure."

"And the guests. Prepare me a list, please, particularly of those on the second floor. And then, if I can give you some advice, you'd better go home and have a rest. You don't look too well."

Wagner shook his head, and the bags of fat under his chin wobbled. "Too much to do."

The lobby was quiet when Winters crossed it. The desk clerk watched him with wide, curious eyes. Dave Evans was at the front door, and almost snapped to attention when he saw the sergeant approaching. Winters ignored him, and headed out the back.

If someone didn't stand up and confess soon, this would take a lot of time and effort. A hotel full of staff and guests. It would be a nightmare to interview them all.

Nestled deep in the mountains of the southern interior of British Columbia, Trafalgar was a small, low crime town. There was no security, not even a doorman, at the hotel entrance; the upper floors were open to anyone who wandered in off the street. As soon as he saw the body, Winters had called his boss, the Chief Constable, to suggest he contact the RCMP Integrated Homicide Investigative Team, which helped with major crime cases in the small towns and rural areas of British Columbia.

That reminded him, he'd forgotten to phone Eliza. Something was bothering her lately, and he'd thought a few days in San Francisco, one of her favorite cities, would cheer her up. He'd been working a lot, with a rash of break and enters around town, and she'd been left at home, moping and restless, waiting for a spring that was taking a long time to arrive.

Gavin stood by the service door, waiting, and Winters decided to call Eliza after he'd discovered what the Mountie was in such a knot about.

Gavin didn't say a word, just held the door open and let Winters through. The alley was dark and narrow and thick with mud after days of melting snow and last night's rainstorm. Gavin walked away from the door, his hands in his pockets and his head down. The yellow stripe on his uniform pants shone faintly in the gloom. Winters followed, puzzled at his friend's strange behavior.

"We go back a long way, John," the Mountie said, coming to a halt about halfway between the back door and the street corner.

"Yeah, I know. What are you on about?"

"First time in all my years I've ever done this."

"Done what? Spit it out, man. Are you in some sort of trouble?"

"No. But I might be."

He reached into his pocket and pulled out a piece of paper. "Found this upstairs. Figured you'd want to see it. You can decide what you want to do with it."

"What the hell?" Winters snatched the paper. "You removed evidence from a crime scene. Are you nuts?"

"Look at it, John."

It was a photograph, about four by six inches, the color faded, the paper worn, one corner torn. It showed a woman, a young woman, naked, sitting on the floor with her knees bent and her legs parted, holding her small breasts toward the camera like an offering.

"So the guy was a pervert."

"That picture was taken with film, not digital. I'd say it's about thirty years old. They haven't made a carpet like that since the 70s, and her hair's cut in that shaggy mess you don't see any more."

"So he's been a pervert for a long time. I don't see…"

"Look at it, John. Look again. *Look* at the woman."

He looked. Her lips were moist, her mouth partially open, the tip of her pink tongue trapped between her small white teeth. The pupils of her eyes were large, the gaze unfocused. Cocaine probably.

She was young and beautiful, with thick dark hair, long slim legs, and a narrow waist. Her eyes were the color of olives in a very dry martini.

Those green eyes. The first thing he saw every morning.

His whole body shuddered.

The woman in the picture was Eliza, his wife.

Chapter Three

At the small office in the back of Mid-Kootenay Adventure Vacations, Lucky Smith whacked at the letter 'e'. Miserable computer. Something was stuck in the keyboard and the 'e', the most used letter of them all, wasn't responding properly.

"*Eeeeeee*", the screen screamed, and Lucky swore with gusto. She'd been told many times not to eat at her desk, or at least to put a plastic screen over the laptop's keyboard. She was normally too busy to take a meal break, and she didn't have a plastic screen, or know where to get one. She eyed the keyboard, wondering how hard it would be to lift up the keys and clean underneath.

"I'm going for lunch, Lucky, want me to bring something back?" Flower stood in the door to the cramped office that was little more than a closet in the back of the store. She'd done half her brown hair in cornrows, tight braids with colorful beads at the ends, and left the rest hanging straight. She looked like an interrupted vacation, which Andy complained wasn't exactly the impression they wanted to give at Mid-Kootenay Adventure Vacations. Lucky reminded her husband that this was Trafalgar, where individual expression was the rule rather than the exception. He still muttered under his breath whenever Flower's beads swung. Lucky suspected that the hairstyle would be gone by now, if not for Andy's obvious disapproval.

Now that Lucky and Andy no longer had children living at home, they still had petulant young employees to deal with.

"If you're passing Eddie's, I'd like a slice of carrot cake."

"Back soon."

Flower told Andy she was off, and he said, "See you." The bell tinkled over the door to the street.

Lucky made a tentative stab at the 'e'. Only one letter appeared on the white page of the screen. The computer beeped to tell her she had an email. She pulled it up, grateful for the chance to delay writing her letter to a wayward supplier. The message was from the young man Andy had hired to work as a kayaking guide over the summer. She read quickly. The letter mumbled something about "opportunities" and "career goals", and Lucky suspected he'd got a better offer. Andy would not be pleased.

She heard a loud noise from the storefront as something heavy fell over. One of the advantages of owning an outdoor adventure store: very little they stocked was breakable. Then crashing and banging as a pile of what were probably skis and poles clattered to the floor.

"If you've got a minute, can you come in here, dear," Lucky called. "I have to show you something."

No answer.

Lucky listened. All was quiet. If the shop was empty perhaps Andy had followed Flower onto the street and was exchanging the time of day with passersby. It was early April, a slow time for business as the ski season had ended and the summer tourists were yet to arrive.

A moan, full of pain, had Lucky jumping to her feet and running.

Andy lay face down in the middle of the floor, in the midst of a jumble of reduced-rate skiing equipment. He moaned again as Lucky fell to her knees beside him. "Andy, are you all right?" She shoved the skis aside and rolled him over. It wasn't easy with all the weight he'd put on over the years. His face was horribly white and drenched in sweat. Round frightened eyes looked into hers.

She jumped to her feet. She ran to the counter. Couldn't find the phone. It had to be here somewhere. She tossed papers and tourist info pamphlets and Flower's mountain bike magazine into the air. She knocked a stack of B&B brochures to the floor.

"What's happened? Can I help?"

Lucky whirled around to see a man standing in the shop doorway. He had a cell phone in his hand.

"My husband. 911. He's fallen. Please." She ran back to Andy. She felt the man cross the floor, heard his voice. He put a hand lightly on her arm. "They're on their way," he said. "Try to stay calm."

It was only later that Lucky found her own cell phone in her sweater pocket.

◇◇◇

Molly Smith shifted her feet. It was quiet in the hotel corridor. The coroner had been and gone, the body following; the RCMP forensic team was busy inside. Detective Lopez had left the room in a heck of a hurry, but was soon back, and gave her a shake of his head, although she didn't know what that meant.

Occasionally she heard people on the stairs, but no one tried to come through the door. Meredith had retreated, ready to pounce at the next opportunity. Smith knew Sergeant Winters was questioning the hotel staff, and phone and computer lines were no doubt burning up as they tried to get background on the dead man and everyone who knew him.

She studied the painting on the wall opposite. It was an old painting, of some old guy, all whiskers and starched shirt and arrogance. She stuck her tongue out at him, wondering if anyone would notice if she lay down on the nice thick carpet for a nap. That made her think of Adam and she grinned. The old guy in the painting did not return her smile. They'd been together since New Year's Day. They'd spent the winter skiing Blue Sky, although she was a far better skier than he, and snowshowing on the old railroad trail in the woods behind his property, while Norman, Adam's police dog, ran on ahead. They watched the Space channel on TV, ate bowls of stew and crusty, rustic bread in front of the big fireplace in his house, or Thai take-out in the small kitchen of her apartment. And they made love. A lot. She grinned again.

The old guy in the painting didn't look as if he ever got any.

They were happy, she was happy, but one small cloud lingered on the horizon: Adam simply didn't seem to understand how much it mattered to Molly that their relationship be kept out of her professional life. He was always dropping around where she was working and trying to grab a quick kiss or whisper lewd suggestions into her ear.

Her little toe throbbed, and she shifted her feet again. God, but this was boring.

Her cell phone vibrated, and she checked the display, glad for something to do. "Hi, Mom, what's up?"

The voice at the other end was so full of tears, it was difficult to understand.

"I'll get there soon as I can. Try and stay calm, Mom, you know Dad's a tough old bugger."

"Problem?" Ray Lopez stood in the doorway. Despite his surname, the detective was red-haired and freckled, and very fond of a pint of Guinness.

"That was my mom. Dad's had a serious fall; they're at the hospital. She said it's really bad, but I'm hoping that's just her being scared."

"Go," he said. "I'm in the way in there anyway. Call the office and tell them I'll watch the door until someone can get here to take over."

"Thanks, Ray."

◇◇◇

John Winters stared at the photograph. The empty-eyed woman looked back.

Eliza. This couldn't be Eliza.

But if it weren't she had a twin.

The picture looked to have been taken twenty-five, thirty years ago, when Eliza would have been in her late teens. The woman in the picture was around that age, certainly not much over twenty.

They'd met when she had a break-in at her home. The young uniformed Constable John Winters had taken the call. She had been beautiful, extraordinarily beautiful, confident and poised beyond her twenty-two years. She lived in an apartment that he first assumed belonged to her parents. But it was hers, as were the expensive, although not ostentatious, furnishings, the original watercolors on the walls, the Haida yellow cedar carving on the coffee table, the designer clothes in her closet.

She was a model, had been since she'd been discovered as a sixteen-year-old in Saskatoon, Saskatchewan. She'd had some big contracts, major magazine covers and European runways, and made a lot of money. Any randy young cop would have wanted her, but what made John Winters love her, and had kept him in love with her for over twenty-five years, was her strong, down-to-earth streak of Prairie common sense. Even back then, she was rational and pragmatic and managed her money with great care. She took courses in finance, invested well, and resisted the urge to spend-spend-spend. To friends and family on both sides, theirs seemed a strange relationship, but they each went about their professional lives knowing they had love and support behind them. They'd always spent a lot of time apart, as Eliza continued to travel for work, but the marriage had worked out well. Perhaps because neither of them felt obliged to make sacrifices in their careers.

Eliza, their marriage, was the foundation of his life.

These days she worked when it suited her, although as she approached fifty good jobs were getting increasingly hard to find. They'd moved to remote Trafalgar less than a year ago, his career choice, not hers. She bought a small condo in Vancouver to use when she needed the bright lights and the big city, to meet with her agent, to go to stockholder meetings, to work.

He thought he knew her.

Stunned into silence by the photograph in his hand, he looked at Ron Gavin.

"You don't want that thing being passed around the station, John."

"Were there any…other pictures?"

"The guy was apparently a professional photographer. Lots of shots of mountain ranges and the river. Pretty girls in town going about their business. Nothing else like that one." Ron gestured in disgust. "No more porn, and nothing that old either. It's one of a kind, unless there's a drawer I haven't found yet. Do what you want with it, but I never saw it." He eyed Winters. "I'll be ready for a meet around five. We getting any help?"

"What?"

"Is anyone coming to give us a hand with this?"

"Chief called IHIT. They're sending a couple of guys tomorrow."

Gavin went back to the hotel, leaving Winters alone in the alley.

His first instinct was to rip the picture up, toss the pieces into the wind and the hotel refuse. Instead he put it in his pocket, and went to get his car.

◇◇◇

A magazine lay open on Lucky's lap, but she hadn't read a word. She looked up as footsteps stopped in front of her cubicle.

"Where's Dad?" Moonlight, Lucky and Andy's daughter, asked.

"They've taken him for some tests."

Lucky stood up and let the girl envelop her in a deep hug. Andy was tall, Lucky short. The children had inherited their father's height and towered over their mother. Moonlight wrapped her arms around Lucky.

Lucky broke the hug and stepped back. Her daughter had come straight from work. She was blond, like her father, and slight, definitely not like her father. To Lucky she always looked intimidating, alien, in the blue police uniform.

"What have they told you?"

"Pretty much nothing."

"Sounds normal. Is someone at the store?"

"Flower had gone for lunch when your dad…when it happened. I left a man I've never seen before minding the place until she gets back. I hope we don't find he's stripped the store down to the walls."

"Mrs. Smith?" A man in a white coat stood in the door.

Lucky's heart leapt into her chest. "That's me."

"Hi, Molly," he said.

Moonlight said, "Hi," and for some reason Lucky thought of the night her daughter was born. It had been winter, and a full moon bathed the snowy woods, and Lucky knew that Moonlight would be the baby's name. Twenty years later she rejected the hippie name and started calling herself Molly. Lucky hated it.

"I'm Doctor Singh," he said. "We're going to be admitting Mr. Smith."

Lucky put her hand to her mouth. She felt Moonlight touch her arm.

"Your husband broke his hip when he fell. It looks as if he fell against several objects?"

"Yes. I think he tripped and crashed into some skis and poles. They were all over the floor."

"It's possible he had a very minor stroke that brought the fall on and we will be looking into that."

"A stroke?"

"That's just a possibility we'll be investigating. However, we will have to operate on the hip."

"He's going to be all right?"

"He's resting comfortably at the moment, and you can go upstairs. We have tests to run and should be able to operate on the hip in a day or so."

"And then he'll be back to normal?"

"A broken hip requires a fair amount of recovery time, so Mr. Smith will be laid up for a while."

"His hip," Lucky said. "That's something that happens to old people. Andy's only fifty-seven, same age as I am."

The doctor gave her a sad smile. "Bones can break at any age. But your husband is considerably overweight, Mrs. Smith, and I suspect he doesn't get much exercise.

"Why don't you let Molly take you upstairs? The nurse will tell you which room."

His footsteps sounded on the floor as he walked away. In another alcove a child cried.

"I'll call Flower," Moonlight said, "check everything's okay. You'll need extra help in the store until Dad gets back, so I'll call that friend of yours who helps out when you're busy. What's her name?"

Lucky couldn't remember the name of the woman who'd been her friend for almost twenty years. She shook her head.

"Never mind. Have you told Sam?" Moonlight asked, referring to her older brother.

"I don't want to worry him."

"You're worried, so I'd say he can start worrying. Let's go see Dad and then you can call." Moonlight took her mother's arm, and gently guided her out of the emergency room cubicle.

◇◇◇

John Winters didn't make it home. He'd intended to. He'd run back to the station to get his car, and headed out of town, at a speed that should have had patrol officers pulling him over. Fresh snow had fallen high on the mountains, but in the valley it was all turning to slush, and everything, snowbanks, cars, boots, even peoples' pant legs, were brown and dirty. What a photographer would find to take pictures of at this time of year, he didn't know.

Pictures. One picture. He slowed down as he came to a side road, and turned into it. The road was plowed, although no one lived on it. It ended at a construction yard.

Once he was out of sight of the highway, Winters pulled over, and rolled down the window. The forest was dark and wet from last night's rain, the air full of the musty odor of decaying leaves soaked by snow melt. The deciduous trees were stark and naked. Long strands of pale green lichen hung from the branches of the firs. It was very quiet.

He held his hand over his jacket pocket and touched the spot where the photograph lay. He imagined it felt hot beneath his fingers.

Ron Gavin had removed evidence from a crime scene. And John Winters had taken it. He tried to convince himself it wasn't really evidence—just an insignificant bit of flotsam found amongst the dead man's possessions.

Imagine telling that to a judge.

Imagine the judge showing the photograph in open court.

It wasn't as if the picture had been taken yesterday. It was old enough that a lot of people wouldn't recognize Eliza. Most men wouldn't—they wouldn't be looking at the face. His stomach clenched.

What was it doing in Steiner's room anyway? Had the man carried it around for thirty years? Porn wasn't exactly hard to come by these days, most of it a lot more explicit than this single shot of a drugged-up teenager. A drugged-up naked teenager.

According to Gavin, it was on its own. Not part of the guy's collection to peep at on cold nights in strange hotel rooms.

What was Steiner doing with the picture? Did the man know Eliza lived in Trafalgar? Had he brought it with him for some purpose?

Blackmail? To remind her of the fun times they'd had in the good old days?

The guy was a professional photographer, from Vancouver, and looked to be in his fifties. It was entirely possible he knew Eliza. Professionally as well as...*personally.*

Winters pounded his fist against the steering wheel.

Just because Steiner had a picture of Eliza in his possession didn't mean Eliza had anything to do with him. Barb Kowalski, the Chief Constable's assistant, kept a picture on her desk of Brad Pitt dressed up like a Greek god and looking a total fool. If Barb were murdered in the office, they wouldn't be dragging Brad Pitt down for a line-up.

Eliza Winters was hardly on the Brad Pitt scale of celebrity, but she did have some fame in her own world.

He tried to tell himself he felt better about having the picture removed from the scene: it was of no more significance to the investigation than Brad Pitt in a leather skirt.

Slowly, he pulled the offending item out of his pocket. He closed his eyes, took a breath, and looked at it.

She was probably being coerced. Drugged up and didn't know what she was doing. She'd told him that the agent her mother hired had chaperoned the wide-eyed innocent from Saskatoon around the fleshpots of Europe, watching out for her like a eunuch guarding the Sultan's harem. Perhaps on one occasion Eliza escaped from the over-zealous supervision of her chaperone and some bastard fed her drugs and abused her.

Good thing Steiner was dead. Or John Winters would kill him.

He put the picture away, and put the car into gear. He'd been heading home, ready to demand his wife tell him what was going on. Instead he'd assume she knew absolutely nothing about it.

But his mind couldn't let go of one niggling thought: how uncharacteristically edgy and bad tempered Eliza had been over the last few days.

Chapter Four

Meredith Morgenstern stared at the most famous woman in Canadian journalism. "You can do this," she said, her face set into determined lines. "You will do this. You have the stuff." She nodded firmly, then looked away from the washroom mirror, turned on the tap, and poured soap into her hands. She believed in being positive: to achieve something, you had to visualize it happening.

Easy enough to visualize success, but she was a discouragingly long way from achieving it. She needed a break. A big story, a juicy story, a story that would hit the pages and the screens of the big media. She needed attention.

To Meredith's eternal disappointment she was still working here, in her home town, on the exceedingly thin, one-section local newspaper. When she'd been studying for her journalism degree the *Trafalgar Daily Gazette* had offered her an internship. She accepted the position because she could save money living at home for the summer. When she graduated, she found herself being hired on full time, and figured it would do as a stop-gap until something better came along. It was now two years later and absolutely nothing better had come along. She was beginning to lose hope. It was not a good time to be trying to get established as a newspaper reporter: all over North America papers were cutting staff or shutting their doors permanently. She needed a big story, on which she could make a big splash, something, anything, to bring her to the notice of the city papers, or, dare she hope, TV.

The chances of getting such a story in Trafalgar B.C. had seemed remote. An American TV anchor had come to town last summer, trying to stir up trouble he could then report on, and strung her a line about a job opening at his cable network. Jerk. He'd scurried home soon enough with his tail between his legs, and was now looking for job openings for himself.

It didn't help that the local police, in the person of Sergeant John Winters, weren't exactly enamored of her.

At least Meredith had that to be proud of—she wasn't any police patsy, to be used to plant information or avoid unfavorable stories as and when it suited them. She tried to use her local contacts, she'd been to school with Moonlight Smith after all, but Molly was too junior, too afraid of the brass, to be of any use as a source.

Meredith was the only child of elderly parents. Her mother had been the advanced age of forty-four when she got pregnant, finally giving up after years of trying, and her dad fifty. People had always mistaken her parents for her grandparents, something her father in particular seemed to be quite proud of. For a teenager, it was plain embarrassing.

Being an only child, Meredith had grown up with all her parents' expectations resting on her shoulders. Being a daughter of old-fashioned parents who thought they were modern those expectations had consisted of having a promising career yet also staying in Trafalgar and settling down with a "nice young man". They wanted grandchildren. And as her mom was now 71 and her dad 77, they wanted them soon!

Well, that wasn't going to happen. She'd miss her parents, and knew it would break their hearts when she moved away, but that was life. She had plenty of time to think about getting married and having children and it wasn't her fault her parents were so darn old. But she didn't have plenty of time to get ahead in her career. Some of her J-school classmates had already landed positions in major media. One woman who, probably not incidentally, was the niece of some bigwig in the Prime Minister's office, was reporting the Calgary news for the CBC.

Meredith's teeth gritted at the thought. If she was ever going to get out of Trafalgar, and be rid of the *Trafalgar Daily Gazette,* she had to do something to make someone of influence notice her.

Now she just might have her chance. A prominent fashion photographer, murdered.

Yippee.

She gave herself a wink and a thumbs up, and left the washroom. The paper's staff photographer was stuffing his phone back into his pocket and the last of his bagel into his mouth.

"Let's head back to the hotel," she said. "We need to get a picture of Steiner's widow. I'm going to call up and ask if she'll see us."

"Why?"

"Because she's the widow, that's why. We need a picture to run alongside a piece on the guy's history." Meredith was hoping for an interview with Mrs. Steiner. It would be nice, although she didn't say so out loud, if the wife had done the deed and Meredith Morgenstern had all her thoughts on tape.

"Won't that be intrusive?"

Meredith rolled her eyes.

"Tomorrow, maybe."

"What do you mean tomorrow? This is a hot story, we need to move fast."

"Joe just called. Reminded me to get over to the Catholic Church. They're having a reception for a visiting missionary family."

"You are kidding me, right?"

"Why would I do that?"

Joe Gessling was the editor and owner of the paper. He had such a poor instinct for news Meredith wasn't at all surprised to hear that he wanted pictures of the congregation eating dry cookies and drinking overly-stewed tea rather than a possible breaking development in a celebrity murder.

The photographer said, "Catch you later."

She watched him walk away. It wasn't much of a problem. Meredith figured she could take better pictures with her own camera than that juvenile hack did.

She needed to interview Mrs. Steiner, but first she had to go to her car and get her camera.

◇◇◇

Winters' phone rang as he headed back across the big black bridge into town. Strands of mist, as thin as gossamer, spun webs around the mountains and stretched down into the river valley. A single patch of black cloud covered the sun.

"Where the hell are you?" Ray Lopez asked.

Winters didn't answer the question. "What's up?"

"Mrs. Steiner waltzed up to the hotel about fifteen minutes ago, and Dave Evans told her she couldn't come in. She started making a fuss. Fortunately, Peter was in the lobby and recognized her. He's put her in a conference room, with a cup of tea, and I've been looking all over for you. No one saw you leave."

"I'll be there in five." Winters snapped the phone shut.

◇◇◇

Josie Steiner was an attractive young woman—if you liked them overly-made up, skeletal thin, nervous and edgy. Her cheeks were gaunt, and her heavy eye make-up had run, making puddles under the sharp, piercing eyes. Her fingernails were long and painted bright red, but one was broken, and she chewed at the ragged edge. He found himself wondering if that was all she ever ate. What with the claws, the bony face, and hard eyes, she brought to mind a hawk. She looked to be in her early twenties and he shuddered to imagine what she'd look like in middle age.

Lopez had informed the woman of her husband's death before Winters arrived.

"I'm sorry for your loss, Mrs. Steiner," he said, offering his hand. Her grip was not that of a hawk, more like a sparrow. She studied his face, sizing him up, but didn't say a word. A tray of tea, small sandwiches, and pastries was on the table. There were definite advantages to conducting an investigation in a nice hotel.

"Mr. Steiner has been taken to the hospital," he told her. "Detective Lopez will accompany you to see him shortly."

She nodded, picked up her tea cup, and put it back down without tasting it. A damp, torn tissue was on her lap. Her blond hair curled around her shoulders, well cut, expensively colored, and fashionably disheveled.

"But first," Winters said, "I'd like to ask you some questions. If that's all right with you?"

Not waiting for her to agree, or not, he began. "Can you tell me the purpose of your visit to Trafalgar?"

Her eyes narrowed with suspicion, and what might have been a trace of hostility. "Why do you want to know?" She spoke with traces of a Quebec accent. A strange response, he thought, to a routine question.

"This is a police matter, Mrs. Steiner. Are you here for business or pleasure?"

"My husband is doing a story for *Mountain Traveler Magazine*." She dug in her cavernous bag, all leather and chains and buckles and zippers, and pulled out a packet of fresh tissues. She wiped at her eyes. "I suppose I should say he *was* doing a story."

"I wouldn't have thought there would be much to take pictures of at this time of year. Everything's brown and dirty."

"*Professional* photography is not about *beauty*, Inspector," she said. "It is about truth."

It was a poor attempt to put him in his place, and he let it go.

"Sergeant," he corrected her. "Have you been to Trafalgar before?"

"No."

"To the Kootenays?"

"The what?"

"This area? Trafalgar, Nelson, Castlegar?"

"No."

"Has your husband been here before?"

"He might have," she admitted with a shrug. "Before we met. We've only been married a short while."

"You and your husband don't share a hotel room?"

The tears had stopped, but her eyes glistened with moisture. "Is that any of your business?"

"Just asking."

"It's none of your business."

"Did you see your husband, or speak to him this morning?"

"No."

"You didn't have breakfast together?"

"No. We normally do our own thing in the morning. I don't eat breakfast, and I always go to the gym first thing."

"Did you do so this morning? Go to the gym?"

"Yes. I was there until around nine. After, I returned to my room, showered and changed, and went shopping." She nodded toward a pile of bags stacked in the corner.

"Did you hear any sounds coming from your husband's room?"

"No."

"You didn't check on him? Pop your head in to say good morning?"

"I told you I didn't." She grabbed a sandwich and bit into it as if she were biting Winters' head off.

"You're traveling with a woman by the name of Diane Barton?"

"Rudy's assistant."

"Do you know where Ms. Barton is?"

A shrug of thin shoulders. The sandwich, with just one bite out of it, was put back on the tray. "Scouting locations, perhaps. That's her job."

He was getting a bad feeling from Josie Steiner. Grief was a difficult emotion both to conceal and to pretend. Grief, he had found, was either all encompassing or it was not. Granted, Mrs. Steiner had only been told the news a short while ago, but she seemed to be going through the motions, expressing sorrow, dapping her eyes, letting the occasional tear fall. She watched Winters from behind those tears, calculating what she was going to say, more concerned with his reactions than her own feelings. Her attitude to the police seemed to be more suspicion and hostility than wanting to help them find the person who murdered her husband.

Highly unusual for an affluent woman.

"Have you seen Ms. Barton this morning?"

"No, and I wouldn't expect to."

"Do you know where she might have gone?"

"No. I don't involve myself in my husband's profession."

"Is she likely to be in a car?"

"She can't walk into the mountains, you know. Rudy rented a car for their use."

Winters turned to Lopez. "The registration book will have a record of the plates. Ask our people and the Mounties to be on the lookout for it, and to escort Ms. Barton back to the hotel."

Lopez slipped out.

"When did you last see your husband?"

"Yesterday around six, six-thirty. He invited me to come to his room and have a look at the day's shoot."

He *invited* her?

"And then?"

Mrs. Steiner got to her feet. She was much taller than Winters expected, and he looked down to see leather boots with heels like skyscrapers. Beige woolen pants, showing thin legs and lack of hips, were tucked into the boots. A tailored blue jacket nipped in at the thin waist covered a red blouse with shiny gold buttons straining to contain her more-than-adequate breasts. He knew, because his wife had told him, that women's breasts were largely composed of fat. A large bosom on a thin body were rarely a natural phenomenon. A pair of small diamond earrings was her only jewelry.

"I have nothing further to say to you at this time," she said.

"A few more questions, if you don't mind. After you saw these photographs…"

"I do mind."

"Did you and Mr. Steiner go out to dinner?"

She remained on her feet. "Rudy didn't like to eat in restaurants. He preferred to have something sent up to his room."

"Did you have dinner with him in his room?"

She headed for the door. "I do not have to answer your questions. I am calling my lawyer, and he will advise me further. He'll make arrangements to take me to see Rudy and do whatever needs to be done." She smelled of something vaguely familiar, and now that she was moving he recognized it. It was the same perfume Eliza used. On Eliza the scent drifted behind her, so you weren't quite sure what you were smelling, only that it was wonderful. Josie had splashed it on like a five-year-old playing dress-up at her mother's dressing table.

She reached for the handle of the door, and jumped back as it swung open.

Ray Lopez looked startled to see her, but he spoke to his boss. "Message from Gavin. They've found a gun in a dumpster out back."

Mrs. Steiner ducked past him and left the room. Winters hadn't been able to see her face when she heard the detective's news.

Chapter Five

Molly Smith's father looked awful. Just awful. His skin was more yellow than white, his normally cheerful plump cheeks sunken, his blue eyes flat. She'd gone up with her mother to see him settled into a bed. He was in a room for four; only one other bed was occupied. At least he got a place by the window. He couldn't see outside, the mountains in the background, the gardens in the foreground, brown and dead after the long winter, but it was someplace for the visitor to stand and look out, when it all got too much.

Lucky had fussed and fluffed pillows and chattered cheerfully, while Molly looked out the window and watched a gray jay searching for seeds under a pine tree.

Andy lay there, and let his wife fuss.

Hospitals, Smith thought, watching a hawk circling high overhead, were horrible places. She'd spent plenty of time in emergency, it was part of the job after all. Bringing in drunken adolescents, attempted suicides, transients off their meds, battered wives. By the time she'd heard about the attack on Graham, her fiancé, and made the frantic journey from Victoria to Vancouver to the hospital, he was dead. They'd cleaned him up and laid him out, and taken her to a nice confortable room to say good-bye. She hadn't come with anyone, and the hospital staff had been so kind.

The memories of the day their dreams of life together died were largely a blur, and Smith sometimes wondered what was real and what wasn't.

Upstairs in the adult wards it was darned depressing. Couldn't they paint the walls something more attractive than industrial beige, or hang some modern photographs? Even a mass-produced print of sunlight on the mountains or a field of wildflowers would go a long way. The children's wing managed to look bright and cheery. Maybe hospital administrators didn't think adults needed cheering up. The machine hooked to Andy's roommate beeped at regular intervals, and the room smelled of disinfectant, body fluids, sickness and fear, all overlaid by a thick, but not thick enough, layer of disinfectant.

The jay took flight and Smith turned and gave her parents a forced smile. "It's almost six, Mom. I have to go back to the station and close out my shift. Then I'll go down to the store and relieve Flower and lock up." She looked down at her uniform. "I'd better go home and change first. Neither the city nor the customers want me running the cash register dressed like this. Did you hear what I said, Mom?"

"Yes, dear. Would you like a drink of water, Andy?"

"No."

"Is there anything I can bring back?" Smith asked.

"Get some granola bars," Lucky said, "and some fruit and nuts so your father can eat when he wants and not at whatever ungodly hour they bring in the meals. Take some of the water bottles from the store and fill them. You know I can't abide bottled water, but your father needs to be able to have a drink whenever he wants."

"Don't talk about me as if I'm not here, Lucky. I am capable of asking for a glass of water." His words were slightly slurred around the edges and his eyes didn't quite focus. Pain-killers probably. An analgesia pump was beside Andy's bed; from now on he'd be able to manage the pain himself.

Lucky walked to the bottom of the bed. "Do you want me to crank your head up a bit higher, dear?"

"If I wanted you to crank me up, I would have asked you."

It was unlike Lucky to be making such a fuss over him. Lucky firmly believed that adult men were capable of looking after themselves.

"I'll be back later," Smith said. "Mom, have you called Sam?"

"Not yet."

"Do it, or I will." She kissed her father on the top of his head, the way he always did to her. As she left the room, the other patient lifted his hand in greeting, and a nurse bustled in, all crisp efficiency, needles, and bottles.

She went back to the station, accepted everyone's kind wishes for her father, finished some paperwork, went home to change, and then to the store to help Flower close up. It was early for closing, but Flower said business had been slow all week, and no one was likely to come pounding on the doors for some last minute, much needed item.

Trafalgar was a small town and everything from the police station to the store to Molly's apartment was only a few minutes' walk.

She was trying to remember if there was a pizza in the freezer or if she should stop and get something when her cell phone rang. It was her brother, Sam. Lucky had called him. Sam was, not surprisingly, full of excuses as to why he wouldn't be able to make it down right away.

"Up to you what you do," Smith said. "I think you should come. He's going to be okay, but Mom's worried and it would make her feel a lot better if you're here."

He muttered something about speaking to his secretary and rearranging his schedule and checking to see what his wife had on this week and hung up. She wondered when her fun-loving, free-wheeling older brother had become such a stuck-up prick. About the time, she reminded herself, that he became a lawyer, a corporate lawyer for an oil company, which upset Lucky even more than Molly becoming a police officer, and married a social-climbing, rich-bitch wanna-be.

She wanted to talk to Adam about her dad, to tell him that she was worried about him. A bunch of the Mounties had gone to a bar to watch the hockey game on the wall-sized TV. If she called him, said she needed him, he'd come. But he'd tell all the guys where he was going, make a big deal of being *needed*, wink, wink, and they'd grin at her next time they saw her.

Perhaps she was over-sensitive, but she couldn't bear the idea that people were gossiping about her.

She checked the door to the alley and the single window in her mom's office, switched off all but one light in the front window display, and flipped the sign to closed. She locked the door behind her and stepped into the street. The temperature had fallen below freezing and what had earlier been the run-off from melting snow made for treacherous going.

A man stepped out of the dark doorway of Rosemary's Campfire Kitchen, the shop next door. He was dressed all in black, with a toque pulled low over his forehead. "Evening, Molly." He stood in front of her, blocking the sidewalk.

"Fuck off."

"Nice night, eh? Can I walk you home?"

"No."

He stepped aside and she passed. He fell into step behind her. She stopped and turned. "Go away, Charlie."

"Or what, Molly? Not so tough when you don't have your gun, are you? I know you're not allowed to carry it when you're not in uniform. Not like in the movies, eh? Do you find that's a problem?"

"Are you threatening me, Charlie?"

"Of course not, that would be a crime. I'm just having a friendly chat. Telling you what I think. When you're out here, on the streets, you're no different than the rest of us." He looked her up and down. "In running shoes and jeans and a long scarf. You might wanna be careful wearing that scarf, it might get caught on something. Without all the gear, you know what you are, Molly? You're just a woman." He cracked his knuckles. "See ya around."

He walked away. She watched him go, a swaggering bundle of muscle and hatred. Although it was early evening, the streets were suddenly deserted. Lights shone inside the restaurant *Fleures des Menthe*, but no one was coming in or out. A single car drove past, the driver staring straight ahead, isolated in a world of glass and steel and engineering. Her heart was beating very fast.

Charlie Bassing. He'd beaten up Smith's friend Christa, been charged and convicted, spent four months in jail. He was out on parole, under an order to stay away from Christa. But he'd lost interest in Christa: he now blamed Molly Smith for all his problems. He'd approached her over the winter, and let her know that as far as he was concerned they had unfinished business. Since then he'd been watching her, making childish gestures such as aiming and firing a gun, occasionally following her, never more than a block or two as if he happened to be going in the same direction.

Not wanting to look as if she were overreacting, she hadn't done anything about it. She hoped he'd give up and go away. Tonight, for the first time, she felt vulnerable. Scared. Here, in her hometown, the place she loved and where she belonged, less than a block from her own apartment, less than two blocks from the police station.

Tomorrow, she'd have a word with Sergeant Winters, ask his advice. She'd also, she decided at last, tell Adam. It would hurt her pride, but perhaps Charlie would think twice if he knew her boyfriend was looking out for her.

She walked home, feeling a good deal better.

◇◇◇

"IHIT's arriving tomorrow, first thing," Paul Keller, the Chief Constable, said. "What have we got to tell them?"

Ron Gavin stared at the table top and said nothing.

Keller had come to the hotel for a meeting to go over what preliminary evidence the forensic team had uncovered. Winters and Lopez were there, along with Gavin and his partner Alison Townshend. The conference room in the hotel was larger and much more comfortable than any office in the police station. The kitchen had provided more drinks and sandwiches.

Townshend shot Gavin a look, waiting for him to speak. She was new, recently transferred from Yellowknife. In her early forties, short and stout, she was perpetually cheerful. Her gray hair was a wild mop, and the edges of her mouth were always turned up, as if she were remembering a private joke.

When Gavin didn't say anything, she selected a ham and cheese croissant and began. "It's pretty certain Steiner died in the bathroom. Probably right over the toilet where he was found. Blood spatter is fairly conclusive about that. No signs of injury or damage in the main room. Getting identification out of a hotel bathroom, as you can imagine, Chief, is a nightmare. Hundreds of people could have been there in the past year."

"And they all leave something behind," Keller said.

"That floor was renovated about three years ago, which means that maybe a thousand people have pissed down the toilet. Tomorrow, when we have some more manpower, we'll be digging out the drains, which is gonna be a lot of fun." She wiped crumbs off her chin.

"What exactly will you be looking for?" Lopez asked.

"There was plenty of uneaten food in the room," Winters said. "Along with unused place settings and glassware for two." The photograph continued to burn a hole in his pocket. He had not called his wife to tell her the trip to San Francisco was off. He still didn't know what he was going to say to her, if anything, about the picture. "Mrs. Steiner said she didn't have dinner with her husband, but before I could ask if she knew who he was planning to entertain, she walked out and has confined herself to her room, awaiting the arrival of her lawyer. It's possible Steiner invited a friend up for a drink and a snack, they had an argument, and the friend offed him. If we're lucky the shooter dropped his wedding ring or high school graduation ring, maybe a cigarette butt brimming with DNA, in the toilet."

"Champagne, cheese, stuff like that," Lopez said. "Doesn't suggest to me an old high school buddy. Sounds like what you lay on to impress a woman."

"Sounds like what you lay on, Ray," Townshend said. "The sort of guys I used to date think a six pack and left-over pizza's enticing."

The men laughed.

"What do we know about the guy?" Keller sipped at his tea. "Steiner. German?"

"Just pretentious," Lopez said, checking his notebook. "Born Albert Jones in Sydney, Nova Scotia. Rudolph Steiner is his professional name. *Nom de* something-or-other. Fifty-six years old, lives in Vancouver. Married for the fifth—note that's fifth as in five wives—to the former Josephine Marais. He's a photographer, apparently some kind of hot-shot in the world of glamour. High fashion stuff. You know, skinny women who never learned how to smile wearing clothes that make them look like they crawled out of a dumpster."

"Or failed clown school," Townshend added.

Winters shifted in his seat.

"I'll start digging into his finances. And his wife's," Lopez said.

"At a guess," Winters said, "the former Josephine Marais doesn't have much in the way of finances to investigate. She looks like a gold digger, and my impression is that she was trying to put on a show of grief, but not feeling much emotion."

"Think she might be behind it?" Keller asked.

"Not ruling her out," Winters said. "The first person she wanted to speak to after getting the news was her lawyer. He'll be here tomorrow, probably on the same plane as the IHIT guys."

"Money, then," Keller said. "If the lawyer's rushing right over. Always complicates things. No one suspicious seen hanging around the hotel?"

"I want to speak to the person Steiner ordered the champagne for," Winters said. "The chambermaid who found the body confessed that she had a couple of good slugs before going into the bathroom."

"I can testify to that," Townshend said. "Found it all over the floor. Some cheese and little green grapes too."

"Point is," Winters said, "the bottle was open, but either nothing was drunk or only a very small amount. Same with the food. The person Steiner was expecting might have failed to show, or, if he did come, he might have not wasted time on pleasantries. So far, no one's come forward to say they saw anyone in the room, heading for it, or wandering around reading the door numbers. Mrs. Steiner has the room next door, and she says she didn't hear anything. I think she didn't hear a lot of things."

"Steiner was kneeling over the toilet," Keller said. "Was he sick into it?"

"Doesn't look like it," Townshend said. "His stomach might not have gotten the message to upchuck before his brain ceased to compute."

"You have such a lovely way with words, Alison," Lopez said. "The maintenance man was apparently on the floor late afternoon or early evening, something about a broken lamp. That room is at the other end of the hall from Steiner's, but he might have seen something. He's not working today. I'm trying to track him down."

"The gun?" Keller asked.

"It was wiped clean," Townshend said, swallowing the last of her sandwich. "No surprise there. Unregistered, which is definitely not a surprise. It's the type used to kill Steiner. We'll run tests, of course, to ensure it's the actual one."

"Not much doubt," Keller said. "Guns are not in the habit of showing up in Trafalgar garbage."

"For now," Winters said, "my money's on the assistant. She seems to have done a runner. I've issued an alert for her, across the province and at the borders with Washington, Idaho, and Montana."

Lopez's phone rang. "Yeah? Escort her to the hotel right away. Someone will meet her at the front." He put the phone away.

"Speak of the devil. The assistant, Diane Barton. Horseman stopped her heading toward town on Highway 3. She'll be here in about ten minutes."

"Drat. If that's it for now?" Winters looked around the table. They all nodded. "I'm meeting IHIT at the Castlegar airport at noon tomorrow. We'll come straight here. They'll want an update."

"I love drain day," Townshend said.

◇◇◇

Diane Barton was in her mid-twenties. She was tall, lean and fit, brown hair cut short with no attempt at style. She wore loose chinos, pockets everywhere, and a baggy Toronto Maple Leafs sweatshirt. Brown eyes blinked behind thick glasses and a broad silver ring circled every one of her ten digits. She wore no make-up and walked with long strides and her handshake was firm.

"Gee," she said, when Winters told her of the death of her employer, "that's too bad."

The dirty plates in the conference room had been cleared in the few minutes since the police meeting, and fresh tea was ready. Winters could get used to working in this environment.

Diane dropped into a chair. "What happened?"

"When did you last see Mr. Steiner?"

"Last night. Around five, I guess. We'd been out shooting most of the day, and went over the pictures."

"Where was this?"

"In his room. He didn't like them."

"Didn't like what?"

"The pictures. Said they were crap. Which they were. He figured it was the light and wanted to go someplace different. That's what I was doing today. Looking around for the right place."

"All day?"

"I've been sitting in the damn car all day. There was an avalanche on the pass. Dumped a shitload of snow all over the highway. I had to wait for freaking hours. I tried to call Rudy, but," she shrugged, "there's no reception up there. Do you think they allow smoking in here?"

"I doubt it."

"Me too." She eyed the tray of sandwiches. "Are those for us?"

"Help yourself." Her story about her phone was probably right. In these mountains you didn't have to move far from the center of town to lose the signal. "How long have you been working for Mr. Steiner?"

"About six months. It's my way of trying to get my foot in the door. I'm a crackerjack photog myself, but it's tough to get a break. I lug his stuff around, scout locations, admire his crap pictures, and hope to hell to get someone to look at mine."

"You don't think he was a good photographer?"

"He was on the way down, and let me tell you, it's a long way down. But he still has the connections, you know. Had the connections, I guess. I'm sorry he's dead, but he was just a job to me." She shrugged and took a bite of a thick sandwich, roast beef on whole wheat.

"Tell me about his wife."

Diane laughed around a mouthful. "She married him because she couldn't get anyone with real influence. She married him because it beats working on your back."

"Are you saying Mrs. Steiner was a prostitute?"

She threw up her hands. The rings reflected light from the lamp on the table beside her. "No, I'm not. Sorry. I don't know much about her. She did some modeling—Wal Mart flyer type of stuff. Crotch shots of sturdy white cotton underwear. She wanted to do better, hell we all do. Sometimes a girl's gotta sleep with the movers and shakers, or so they tell me. Which is why I prefer to be behind the camera, not in front of it."

"You don't like her?"

"I can't stand the freakin' bitch. Knows nothing about photography but is always sticking her surgically-altered nose in and telling me what would look good. He was loaded and connected, I'll tell you that. Can't imagine that had anything to do with her 'falling in love' with him." Diane wiggled her fingers in the air to make quotation marks around the words.

"What about him? What did you think of Mr. Steiner?"

"I didn't like him or not like him. He was the boss. I did my job." Sandwich finished, she studied the array of food again, and settled on a Nanaimo bar.

"What time did you leave Mr. Steiner's room?"

"Five-thirty, probably. Around then. It hadn't taken long. Rudy hated the pictures so there wasn't much to discuss. I told you that."

"Did you see him again?"

"No."

"What did you do after leaving him?"

"Went to my room for a while, read. About eight I went out to eat. Had dinner, by myself as per normal, and then back to my room."

"What time did you get back?"

She looked toward the window. "Ten-thirty, eleven maybe. I had nothing better to do, so had a couple of beers with my dinner, and went for a walk."

"Which restaurant?"

"Something Thai." She shrugged again. "They might remember me, it wasn't busy."

"Did you see Mrs. Steiner at any time?"

"Nope. But I wouldn't expect to see her hanging around any place I might frequent."

"I've been told he rarely went out to eat."

"Oh, yeah. He was a weirdo all right."

Winters' ears pricked up. "In what way?"

"Scared of germs, like that millionaire guy who never left his hotel room, but not so bad. Rudy didn't eat in restaurants because who knows what germs are floating around and landing on the food. He didn't like ordering from room service, but he had to eat when he traveled, didn't he? It was better than going out. I'd been here a couple of weeks before they got here, scouting out locations mostly, and picked them up at the airport in a rental car. Before he got into the car for the first time, I had to wipe the whole interior down with disinfectant. While he watched me doing it." She snorted. "He didn't trust me not to say I'd done it when I hadn't. It was always like that, some things he'd freak over. I suspect that's why Josie had a separate room. Women are okay for, you know, sex, but you don't want them spreading their yucky female germs around. Just my opinion, mind, he never said that."

"Sounds like an interesting man."

She popped the last bite of the square into her mouth and wiped her fingers on her thighs. "He was that."

"What are your plans now?"

"Now as in right now, or for the rest of my life? I'm going upstairs to clean up and grab something to eat. I hope to hell the hotel bill's covered. Tomorrow I'll ask Josie what she wants me to do with Rudy's stuff. Then I'll probably go back to Vancouver and wait for another job." She looked at him. "I can go home, can't I?"

"I don't see why not. Give Detective Lopez your contact information in case we need to be in touch."

Chapter Six

Barb Kowalski leaned back in her office chair and stretched. Things were happening, and although she wasn't an officer and not directly involved in the investigation, it was hard not to get caught up in the flurry of activity and the tension a murder always caused.

The CC had drunk so much Coke yesterday, owing to pressures of the case, he'd run out. On a good day he went through about ten cans. On a bad day, when the stress level was up, it could be twice that. The drink was his indoor tobacco substitute. Between the amount he smoked and the quantities of pop he consumed Barb hated to think what his lungs looked like and what his dental bill must be.

She eyed the French press at the side of her desk. Half a cup left, but she needed to get up and move. She felt like she'd been here all day although it was only ten o'clock. She decided to have the yogurt and apple she brought for lunch, and pop out later and buy a sandwich. Maybe a bag of Doritos for an afternoon snack. She could start her diet tomorrow.

She headed for the lunch room. Jim Denton, the dispatch officer, was on the phone; the legal clerk walked past with a pile of folders, and the by-law officer came through the door. The monitors showed that the cells downstairs were all empty. Molly Smith had gone to career day at the middle school, John Winters and the Chief were preparing for the arrival of IHIT,

Ray Lopez was at the Hudson House Hotel, sifting through clues probably. Barb thought she'd like to follow them around one day, see what the police actually did out there.

She rounded the corner to see a Mountie standing in the hall, reading the staff notice board outside the lunch room. Brad Noseworthy had put up a sheet asking people to come to the car wash to raise money for his daughter's hockey team. Barb pointed at the picture of the smiling girls posing for the team picture in their heavy gear. "She's very good," she said to the Mountie, "Brad has high hopes for an Olympic star one day."

"Worth getting the car washed then," he said. It was Adam Tocek, the one dating Molly Smith. They made a nice couple, Barb thought.

Inside the lunch room a man laughed. "Can't imagine fucking a cop. Might as well be fucking a drag queen."

Tocek's face hardened. He walked into the room.

"You guys talking about someone in particular?"

Barb followed him. Dave Evans was sitting at the table, his legs outstretched. The man who'd spoken was Jack McMillan, a long-time retired officer who hung around the station sometimes, remembering the days when he'd been useful.

Evans looked at Tocek. "Nope. General chit-chat."

"That's what you get when you let girls do a man's job. I wouldn't want to go with a girl who could beat me up," McMillan said with a laugh and a spray of spittle.

"Most *women* don't want to either," Tocek said.

You tell 'em, Barb thought.

"Does she let you play with her gun, Tocek?" Evans said. His voice was low and very tight. "Or do you prefer her truncheon?" He looked at McMillan, fishing for a laugh. "That's if you can find a place to put it."

"You fucking prick." Adam Tocek crossed the room in one step, and before Barb knew what was happening Dave Evans was on the floor, blood pouring from his nose. She yelled.

"Hey." McMillan jumped up. "No need for that."

Evans leaned on the counter and pulled himself to his feet, bright red blood streaming down his face. He swung at Tocek and the Mountie ducked. Tocek punched Evans in the stomach and he grunted and staggered backwards. He fell against the water cooler, but came back fast. Barb heard the blow strike Tocek's jaw. "Help!" Barb cried. "Someone help."

"Break it up, break it up." John Winters was between the two men, his arms outstretched to separate them. Evans moved as if to go around him.

"I said break it up. Next one to throw a punch is up on charges. McMillan, get out of here."

"You got it, Sarge." He walked past Barb, chuckling. "Just like the old days."

"He came out of nowhere and took a swing at me." Evans wiped the back of his hand across his mouth and looked at it. He spat a lump of bloody phlegm onto the floor.

"Too bad I didn't break your fucking mouth," Tocek said.

"You want to tell me about it," Winters said, "we'll go to the Chief's office for a formal chat and call in a lawyer. Otherwise, Evans, get back on the street. Tocek, what are you doing here anyway?"

"Just paying a visit."

"Visit's over. Get lost."

Tocek turned and walked out of the lunch room, rubbing at the knuckles on his right hand. Barb stepped aside to let him pass.

The commotion had drawn everyone out of their offices, and they were standing around the dispatch desk watching. Jim Denton was on his feet and Al Peterson, the Staff Sergeant, was there. Molly Smith clutched her hat in her hands and her blue eyes were large and round in a pale face. Tocek stepped toward her. She said something Barb didn't hear, but she caught the tone easily enough. Tocek turned and walked out the door.

"Some guys can't take a joke," Evans said to the crowd.

"Not another word," Winters said. "You people have nothing to do? Crime has stopped in our fair town, has it?"

People slipped away. No one said anything.

Dave Evans didn't look at Smith as he passed.

"I need a ride to the airport," Winters said. "Al, if you don't need her, I'll take Molly."

"Okay," Peterson said.

"Meet me by the cars in five." Winters walked down the hall.

Barb touched Smith's arm and gave her a small smile. She looked shell-shocked, and Barb was sure she must have heard some of what had been said in the lunch room. Everyone else in the place probably heard it as well. "I have some cookies in my drawer, if you want to talk."

Color, too much of it, flooded back into Smith's pretty face and her eyes blazed. "Talk?" she said. "Oh, yes, I want to talk. But not to you. Thanks anyway, Barb."

◇◇◇

Molly Smith clenched the steering wheel. She'd been sitting in the damned van for fifteen minutes and Winters hadn't bothered to show.

Perhaps he didn't need a ride to the airport; he just wanted to get her out of there before everyone broke into gales of laughter.

She'd programmed her phone with a special ring for Adam. It rang. She didn't answer.

She'd walked through the front doors of the station, feeling good after talking to the kiddies about a career as a police officer. They were young enough to still think being a cop was neat and peppered her with questions. She'd been pleased to see that almost as many girls as boys had come to her presentation. She'd been able to forget, for a while, about her dad, about Charlie Bassing.

Then she'd walked into that. It had given her a jolt of pure pleasure to see Adam standing in the hall, talking to Barb, and she'd been about to walk over and say hi. She heard something of what Evans and McMillan were saying, but before she could react Adam threw himself into the middle of it.

Jack McMillan was a misogynist pig, bitter that the world had moved on and left him behind. He hung around the station and the coffee shop where the staff usually went implying things about her and Dawn Solway, the Trafalgar City Police's only other female officer. Most of the younger guys paid him no attention. Evans didn't like her, that wasn't news, and no doubt happy to talk to someone who felt the same, but she knew Evans was first of all a cop. She never thought his personal opinion about her would get in the way of doing the job.

What the hell was Adam thinking? Or rather not thinking. Did he think he had to fight her battles for her? *Screw that.*

For a moment she thought about talking it over with her mom. Then she remembered that Lucky had more important things on her mind right now than her daughter's love life.

The passenger door opened, and Winters got into the van. "Sorry to keep you waiting. Last minute call from Ray."

"Did he find something?"

"The occupant of the room next to Steiner's says he might have heard a gunshot. He said he was watching TV and didn't pay much attention. He remembers what program he was watching at the time. It was on from eight-thirty to nine and was almost over. If he's right, it gives us a good idea of the time Steiner died."

"The grieving widow has condescended to make an appointment with us for this afternoon. I might bring you along, Molly. The INIT people are both men, it might be good to have a woman there."

"To comfort the poor dear? Make tea, maybe. Pat her hand if she gets distressed."

He looked at her. "No, Molly. To see her from a different angle. She looks to me like a woman who knows how to manipulate people."

"Oh. Sorry." Her face burned and she pulled out of the parking lot.

She waited for him to say something about what had happened in the lunch room. He didn't.

"I heard about your dad. How's he doing?"

"I spoke to Mom this morning. They're hoping to operate tomorrow. The operation's not a big deal, but he'll need a lot of looking after for a while."

"How's your mom taking it?" Winters knew Molly's mother well. Lucky had a tendency to be at the center of whatever trouble was brewing in Trafalgar.

"Hard. She's all fuss and bother, fluffing pillows and doing everything short of feeding Dad with a spoon. Not like her normal self at all."

"Let me know if I can do anything. Or Paul. You know he and your mom go back a long way."

She actually laughed at that. Political agitator and environmental activist verses small town constable and later chief of police. Lucky Smith and Paul Keller had eyed each other over the battlements, only sometimes rhetorical, for many years. "I was surprised he hired me, considering the history those two have."

"You never know what people are thinking, Molly."

"What's that mean?"

"Nothing. IHIT's sending us two guys. I need more, but that's all they can spare right now. What with hotel guests, staff, tradespeople, and those walking in one door and going out another, we could be interviewing people until the cows come home. My prime suspect turned out to have been stuck in a road closure rather than fleeing the scene, and the widow is calling in her lawyer. Which I suspect isn't because she's about to confess, but wants to make sure she's not caught up in legalities when she should be making sure her inheritance is secure. If she'd done it, I don't think she'd have called the lawyer. She'd be wanting to play the grieving innocent. But I've been wrong before."

He looked out the window and watched the scenery pass. The mist hung low over the mountainside, occasionally moving aside to grant a glimpse of brown, dark forest. Dirty snow filled the shadows and crevices at the side of the road. Impromptu streams poured down the hills, carrying snow melt. The river was below them, cold and black, and moving fast. Winters rubbed his thumb over the face of his watch.

Smith remained quiet, knowing he only wanted a sounding board, not her opinions.

"I need to talk to the room service waiter who made a delivery to the room that night, not long before the estimated time of death. So far we can't find him."

"You think that's suspicious?"

"No. He isn't scheduled to work, and his roommate said he's gone hiking with his girlfriend. There's no answer at his cell phone, which, if he's in the mountains, will be because he's out of range."

His own phone rang. He glanced at it, hesitated, and then answered. He sounded weary.

"I was late. Didn't want to disturb you. Well, there's always a first time. No, that's not a good idea. I'll be tied up all day." He hung up without saying goodbye. A fight with the wife, Smith assumed.

He looked at his watch. "The plane had better be on time. I don't intend to hang around waiting."

◇◇◇

It was, and the two Mounties were the first passengers off. They didn't have any checked bags, and the van was back on the highway less than fifteen minutes after their arrival at the airport. There was one corporal by the name of Kevin Farzaneh, young and friendly. The sergeant was Dick Madison, a slightly built man with olive skin, black hair, shiny white teeth, prominent nose, and a bone crushing handshake.

Madison grunted at Smith, but Farzaneh gave her a big grin, and asked about the skiing conditions. Before she could launch into an enthusiastic description, Madison made a comment about how much he hated snow. The rest of the drive back to Trafalgar, Winters filled them in.

He told Smith to drop them at the hotel, where Gavin, Townshend, and Lopez were working, and sent her back to the station to get on with her shift.

He was still carrying the photograph. He'd considered leaving it in the house, hiding it under his socks, like he'd hidden the dirty magazines he and his friends passed around when they were kids, but found himself stuffing it into his shirt pocket instead.

He'd worked late, and got home after Eliza had gone to bed. That wasn't unusual, but for the first time in their marriage he slept in the spare room. Up before the sun, he left the house while Eliza was still sleeping. He showered in the locker room at the station and got an egg sandwich for breakfast from Big Eddie's Coffee Emporium.

He still had no idea what he was going to say to her.

Once again the police settled comfortably into the conference room. Instead of coffee and sandwiches, they were given coffee and bagels with small pots of jam and cream cheese on the side. Winters wondered if he'd be expected to pay for all this. No way in hell would the Chief authorize it.

Gavin and Townshend had nothing new to report. They'd finished fingerprinting the room and were ready to start digging up the bathroom. Farzaneh would give them a hand and Townshend would move into the adjoining room, Mrs. Steiner's room. An initial look showed nothing out of the ordinary, but she'd see what she could find. It was possible the killer had visited Mrs. Steiner first.

It was also possible that half of Trafalgar had visited Mrs. Steiner's room.

Winters discussed what he'd discovered so far, which was precious little. When found, the body was in full rigor, and the coroner roughly estimated the time of death to be about ten to thirteen hours before the discovery of the body. He could be fairly precise largely because the temperature of the hotel was consistent and measurable. The time coincided with the report, vague as the witness had been, of the sound of a gunshot around nine in the evening. The autopsy was scheduled for late that afternoon, and Madison said he'd attend.

The meeting began to break up.

Farzaneh and Lopez would carry on interviewing staff and hotel guests while Winters would go back to the phones and computers and dig into Steiner's past.

"But first," Madison said, "let's have a look at the scene."

Winters' phone rang. It was the station.

"Great," he said, scribbling a note. He hung up. "The room service waiter called in. He's home."

"Let's go then," Madison said, putting down his mug.

Winters was nominally in charge of the investigation, and it was understood that Madison and Farzaneh would defer to his local knowledge. But that was a formality, and they all knew the Mountie's decisions would carry the day.

◇◇◇

Ronnie Berkowitz lived just around the corner from Happy Tobaccy, the store that sold legal drug paraphernalia and hemp products and was owned by people very active in the campaign to legalize marijuana. That they also sold, on occasion, marijuana itself, was well known to the police. Every time he drove by, Winters itched to barge in. Someday, maybe, the store owners would cross the invisible line the Chief had drawn.

A group of young people were standing outside the store, but no one appeared to be smoking anything illegal. A girl, holding a dirty faced toddler by the hand, recognized the GIS van and said something to her companions. They watched the police drive by. One man gave them the finger, and then pretended he was lifting his hand to rub his forehead.

"Don't know why you let them get away with flaunting that place in your face," Madison grumbled.

Winters made no comment.

They pulled up in front of a typical Lower Town house. Old, badly maintained, divided into four apartments, an unkempt front yard. The melting snow had revealed a season's worth of dog dirt. Berkowitz's door was down a level from the street, the entrance dark and gloomy. A tall dead stalk, remains of a plant of indeterminate variety, was stuck in a cracked terra cotta pot. They didn't have to knock, the door was open. Berkowitz was a good six feet four at least and probably didn't tip the scales at much more than a hundred and fifty pounds. He sported a strange beard, about a half inch long, which covered only the tip of his chin.

"Come on in," he said in a deep booming voice. "This is cool. I just got home and Harry said the police were looking for me." He laughed. "So I burned my stash and gave you a call. What's up?"

Stash or not, Berkowitz didn't sound like a man who was worried about police attention.

The door opened directly into the kitchen. The appliances were ancient, the floor covered in green linoleum, the countertop stained and chipped. The sink was piled high with dishes and boxes of cereal and pasta were haphazardly stacked inside door-less cupboards. Cartons of empty beer bottles leaned against the far wall. Typical transient lodgings.

"Take a seat," Berkowitz said, gesturing to the two vinyl-topped chairs pulled up to the Formica table. Winters remembered when he was a child, family meals and homework around a table and chairs exactly the same.

"You're a waiter at the Hudson House?" he asked, declining to sit. Madison moved a mug so he could lean against the counter.

"Room service waiter. Part time."

"Worked there for long?"

"Since last May. I finished school, thought I'd get a summer job before going back for my masters. Decided I liked it here, liked the women anyway, and stayed."

"You delivered a tray to room 214 night before last, is that correct?"

"I figured that's what you wanted to talk to me about. I heard the guy in that room was killed. Shot, right?"

"Do you remember the time?"

"Eight-thirty, round about. They'll have a record of when he placed the order on file, and we weren't busy that night so I would have gone up soon as it was ready."

"Did you go into the room, or leave the food outside?"

"I went in. He opened the door and asked me to lay the stuff out on the table. He told me to open the bottle of champagne, which I did, then I left. He gave me a pretty pink bill." Fifty bucks, a generous tip.

"Can you describe the man?"

Berkowitz described Steiner perfectly.

"Was he alone?"

"No."

Winters took a breath. "Who else was in the room, please?"

"A woman. I figured that was why the big tip. He was trying to impress her. She didn't look impressed. Don't think she even noticed."

"Can you describe her?"

"Sure can. She was well worth describing. Beautiful really. Tall, about five foot nine or ten, and quite slim, although hard to say for sure 'cause she had her coat on."

"She was wearing a coat?"

"Yes, and holding a bag over her shoulder. She didn't look like she was planning to stay. The coat was still wet, so she hadn't been there long either. It was raining that night, I remember 'cause I'd been outside for a fag. I got the impression she wasn't too happy. She wasn't smiling and didn't say anything at all when I put out the food and opened the champagne. It was the good stuff, too. In fact, she turned her back on it."

"Age?" Madison asked.

"Older chick. Older than me, I mean. Forty maybe. Not young anyway. Brown hair with dark blond highlights, about here," he waved his hand under his chin. "She had these green eyes, gorgeous big green eyes, strong cheekbones, and a little pointed chin."

"You really did notice her," Madison said.

"Like I said, she was worth a second look."

John Winters was aware of his heart pounding in his chest.

"Can you describe her coat?" Madison asked.

"Looked expensive. Light brown, camel colored, with a dark brown belt. Her bag had a Burberry check."

"What's that?"

"Burberry's a company. They make high-end bags and stuff with a pattern of brown, cream and red. I know that 'cause my dad gave my mom a scarf for Christmas one year and she was over the moon."

"This woman was the only person in the room, aside from Steiner?"

"Yes."

"Did she say anything?"

"Not while I was there. She just looked irritated at the interruption."

From the bottom of a deep well, Winters was aware he was being addressed. "Sorry, what?"

Madison gave him a look. "I said, could this woman be the wife?"

"The wife? Oh, Steiner's wife. No. Nor the assistant. They're both in their twenties."

"Mr. Berkowitz, I'm going to ask you to work with a police artist and come up with a sketch of this woman. I'll let you know when."

"Happy to help."

The police took their leave.

"I'll drop you back at the hotel," Winters said, once they were standing on the sidewalk. "I have something I have to do."

"What?"

"I'll fill you in later. I have to go."

His mind was racing, but he couldn't think straight. He needed to dump Madison, who was looking at him as if he'd lost his mind, and think.

He didn't need a police artist to draw a sketch of the mysterious woman with the Burberry bag. He could see her face every time he closed his eyes.

Eliza.

Chapter Seven

Molly Smith's phone rang approximately every fifteen minutes. Always Adam. She wanted to switch it off, but was afraid to in case her mom needed her.

She'd been about to ask Adam to come for a coffee and tell him about Charlie Bassing's vaguely threatening behavior toward her, but she'd changed her mind. If Adam would punch out Dave Evans, in the station, in front of everyone, over a few words, what might he do to Bassing? Bad enough if Adam went around and slugged him, but if he was in uniform, armed? It didn't bear thinking about.

She couldn't stop thinking about it. She'd wanted to say something to Winters on the way to the airport, but he was bothered about this murder and fighting with his wife, so Smith didn't think it was a good time.

"Five-one?"

"Five-one here."

"911 call at 285 Elm Street. Report of a B&E."

She took the next corner and forgot about Adam Tocek and Charles Bassing.

The house was a nice one, warm wood and glass, with a view of the river and the mountains beyond. A man walked over to the car when she pulled up. "That was quick," he said as she got out.

She smiled. "What seems to be the problem, sir?"

"We just got home from vacation. Two weeks in Mexico. Someone's been in the house. Stolen things. Looks like they came in the basement window. It's broken."

"Was much taken?"

"Computer stuff for sure. I called you right away. My wife's checking upstairs."

The home was as beautiful inside as out, modern and minimalist in shades of white accented by touches of striking Chinese red. The wood floor was the color of the petals of daisies at dusk and shone with a rich gloss, and Smith wanted to drop to her knees and run her hands over it. Instead she allowed the man to lead the way through the living room to a small study which overlooked the gardens and what on a sunny day would be the view to the glacier. A large wooden desk was against the windows. Cords and wires crisscrossed the desk, leading to nothing. A thick twisted rope, a dog toy, well chewed, lay on the carpet beside the office chair.

"I had a laptop, modem, printer, video monitor. Also my iPod and electronic book reader." A thin sheen of dust outlined where the items had been.

"You didn't take your book reader with you on holiday?" she asked, before realizing that was none of her business.

"I use it on short flights and taxi rides," he said. "On the beach I prefer a nice thick paperback."

"Do you take a lot of short flights?"

"I go back and forth to Vancouver several times a month."

They turned at the whisper of stocking feet on smooth wood. A woman came in, holding a wooden box inlaid with small drawers. She shook it. The rattling of the drawers was the only sound. "Empty."

"Your jewelry box?" Smith asked, redundantly.

"Yes."

"If you could start making a list of what's missing, please." She spoke into her radio. "I need a detective here."

"Ten-Four," Denton said.

Where on earth he was going to get someone, with the town's entire complement of two detectives working flat out on a murder, was not Smith's concern.

"Did you have anyone looking after the house while you were away?"

"Judy, next door." The man sighed. "At least the plants got watered."

"Can you show me that basement window? I've got a camera in the car and I'd like to take some pictures, if you don't mind. Then I'll go over and speak to Judy, if she's home. They'll be sending a detective around, but I can't say when he'll get here. It would be helpful if you could have that list ready for him. Try not to touch door handles, window frames that sort of thing until he's been."

The man showed her to the door with an attempt at a smile. The woman didn't move, just stared into the depths of her jewelry box.

Smith got the camera, took pictures of empty spaces, in both the computer room and the master bedroom. She finished as the doorbell rang. It was Judy from next door who'd seen the police car and hoped everything was all right. She was appropriately shocked to hear of the robbery, but claimed she hadn't noticed anything amiss when she'd been in the house two days ago.

As Judy had nothing more to add, Smith said her good-byes and went to her car, where she sat, typing her report into the computer. She was mildly disappointed at not hearing any more from Winters about coming to the interview with Mrs. Steiner. But, as she hadn't, she'd drop into the hospital, say hi to her dad.

Chapter Eight

John Winters stood in the doorway to Eliza's office for a few moments, watching her. She was not a vain woman, and didn't display pictures of herself taken in her glory days. The room was painted in a neutral color, chosen to show off her small, but very good, collection of West Coast Native art. A shallow pottery bowl, decorated with a stylistic view of Stanley Park and Lions Gate Bridge in Vancouver, holding paper clips and scraps of note paper, was on her desk, beside a small photo of him in a simple wooden frame. She'd taken it last year when they'd been house hunting in the mountains. He thought the picture made him look old and grumpy, but for some unknown reason Eliza liked it. The CD player was on, playing a Bruce Springsteen track. She loved Springsteen. He could hear the click of computer keys, and smell the vanilla scent of the hand cream she always used. Her hair, her *chin length brown hair with dark blond highlights,* was stuffed into an elastic band, and she was dressed in the pink and black yoga wear she wore to pad around the house.

He didn't make a sound, just watched her, but her radar sensed him and she turned.

"Goodness, John, what are you doing standing there?"

"Have you heard the news today?"

"Only the business news. I'm worried about the tar sands controversy and am considering getting rid of some oil company stocks. What is it? What's happened?"

"Read the paper?"

She stood up. The chair slid sideways. "I glanced at the *Globe* headlines, but didn't see anything significant. Please, John, you're scaring me. What's happened?"

"Murder in Trafalgar might not make the big papers. Unless it's a high-profile kinda guy."

She extended one well manicured hand. He stepped back.

"Or a high profile suspect."

"What are you saying? You're talking gibberish."

He looked at his wife of twenty-five years. The woman he'd adored every minute since the first time he set eyes on her. Her face was worried, concerned at his behavior, her green eyes bewildered. She didn't look guilty, or if she were hiding something.

But she was hiding something.

Strands of hair hung lose from the ponytail, making her look about sixteen. Like the girl in the picture.

He pulled it out of his pocket and handed it to her.

She didn't touch the picture, she didn't need to. All the blood drained from her face.

She looked at him. "John, I…"

"Would you like to know how I happen to have this in my possession?"

"No."

"Tough. I'm going to tell you anyway. I came across it in the performance of my duties."

She stumbled backwards, and dropped into the chair. His cell phone rang. He ignored it. He pushed the button on the CD player and Bruce shut up mid-note.

"That picture was taken a long, long time ago, John. It isn't me. It isn't the me I am now."

"It's enough of you that if it got handed around the station, I'd be a laughing stock."

"I'm sorry, John. So sorry." She started to cry. "I didn't know what to do. I wanted it back, but I wasn't going to get into a brawl over it."

"Do you want to know why I have it?" Just holding the photograph made his fingers feel dirty. He stuffed it back into his pocket.

"I assume he gave it to you." The sound of her sobs and ragged breathing grated on his nerves like shards of glass. "He can be very spiteful when he doesn't get what he wants."

"He!" Winters shouted. A black cloud descended over his eyes, blood throbbed in his temples. "Whoever the hell *he* is, I don't know. Ron Gavin gave it to me. He removed it from a crime scene because he's my friend. And I didn't give it back, damn it. That's a criminal offense."

Tears ran down her face. She wiped her nose on the sleeve of the pretty pink and black top. "It was a long time ago, John."

"No, Eliza, it wasn't very long ago at all. It was Monday in fact. Monday night when you were alone with some man in his hotel room quaffing Champagne."

She looked up. "How do you know that?" Her eyes were very red.

"You don't deny it, I note."

"Don't come over all cop on me."

"Hell, Eliza, all cop is what I am." He waved the picture at her. "Speaking of which, do you want to know why Ron Gavin was in the position to find this...thing."

She took a single deep breath and stood up. "No, I do not. Not while you're being so aggressive." She walked toward the door. His arm shot out and he grabbed her. He jerked her around so she faced him. The ponytail bounced. She stared up at him. Her face was wet with tears but her neck was straight and there was a flash of defiance in the depths of her eyes.

God help him, he wanted to hit her.

"Let go of me, John."

He griped her tighter.

Her eyes widened with shock, the defiance faded, and for the first time ever, she was afraid of him. Good. He wanted her afraid. He wanted her hurt. He clenched the fist of his other hand.

His phone rang.

"Are you going to answer that?"

"No."

The red cloud lifted, and he realized how close he'd come to crossing the line. With a shudder, he dropped his arm and released her.

She stepped away. "I'm going upstairs until you calm down so we can discuss this reasonably."

"How well do you know Rudolph Steiner?"

"I used to know him. It was he who took that picture."

"Did you know him in the biblical sense, Eliza?"

"I wasn't a virgin when we married, John. As I recall, neither were you."

"Did you kill him?"

"Of course I didn't kill him. What kind of a question is that?"

"Someone killed him. Someone who was in his hotel room at around, oh, eight-thirty Monday night."

She put her hands to her face. Tears were drying in streaks down her cheeks. "Rudy's dead? But why are you…John, you can't possibly think I'm responsible."

What on earth am I doing? All his anger fled as he realized that he was practically accusing his wife, the woman he loved beyond reason, of murder. He stepped back and lifted his hands. "Oh, Eliza."

They looked at each other for a long time. Finally she spoke. "What do you want me to do?"

"You need to come in, to the station. Speak to the detective from IHIT. I'm sorry."

"Rudy was alive when I left him, I swear."

"You'll have to make a statement to that effect."

"I'll get my purse," she said. He watched her walk away. Her head was down and her steps heavy. She wiped at her eyes.

He remembered how angry she became when she realized they weren't going to make the flight to Vancouver. Had she known what had been found in room 214 at the Hudson House Hotel? Had she been wanting to get out of the country before it was discovered?

He loved her so much; he'd always loved her. Did he believe her?

What kind of a damn question was that?

The phone again. This time he flipped it open and barked hello. Madison.

Winters didn't give the Mountie a chance to speak. "I've found the woman the room service guy identified. Meet me at the station. Fifteen minutes." He put his phone away and followed Eliza.

Chapter Nine

Barb poked at the number on her computer screen with the tip of her pencil. She'd made an error somewhere, and the detectives' expenses weren't balancing. It had been hard to concentrate. Tension was high in the station, and all day people had been coming and going through the Chief's office. It was none of her business what went on inside his office when the door was shut, unless he chose to tell her, but sometimes she couldn't help pricking her ears up a bit higher than normal. Fortunately, he'd been at a meeting with the mayor when Adam and Dave had that fight in the lunch room. She hoped no one would tell him about it. The Chief regarded his officers with almost as much proprietary interest as he did his children, and he'd be upset to think there was dissention in the ranks.

When the Chief Constable was upset, Barb was upset. She herself regarded the Chief with almost as much proprietary interest as she did her husband. She'd worked here for almost thirty years; several Chief Constables had passed through her office. She considered it to be part of her job to train him, always a him so far, as to how she did things. Paul Keller had proved easy to train.

She looked up to see John Winters standing in the doorway. He looked like hell, his face was pale and drawn and he had bags under his eyes Barb had never seen before. His wife was with him, and she looked even worse. Her eyes were red, her hair tied back in a stubby pony tail with strands sticking out all over. She was dressed in black stretch pants with a pink stripe on the leg, a pink and black top with mismatched red wool sweater, and her bare feet were stuffed into unlaced running shoes.

Barb started to stand. She'd met Eliza Winters at the annual pot luck last summer, and had thought the sergeant's wife was charming and elegant. Now, the woman looked as old and worn as if she'd spent the night in the drunk tank. "What on earth?"

"I need to see the Chief," Winters said. "Now. No matter what he's doing."

A man stood behind them. Barb didn't know him, but she knew the IHIT team were in town. She punched the intercom to her boss' office.

Winters didn't wait for the go ahead. He threw open the Chief's door and pulled, pulled! his wife in behind him. The unknown man followed, dark and scowling. He slammed the door.

Barb heard the Chief shout, just once, "What?"

She went to the hallway and looked out. The staff were standing in the corridor, open-mouthed, shifting from one foot to another.

"What's going on?" Barb asked.

"They've arrested Sergeant Winters' wife."

Barb echoed the Chief Constable. "What?"

The by-law officer said, "For the murder."

"You can't be serious."

"I am."

"She hasn't been arrested," Jim Denton said. "Brought in for questioning."

"That's bad enough."

"Who's been arrested?" Dave Evans came out of the constables' office. He took a swig from the can in his hand.

"Mrs. Winters."

Evans almost sprayed them with pop.

"Who's that man with them?"

"IHIT. Sergeant Madison."

A man knocked at the glass wall to get attention. He said he was here to request a record check. No one rushed to serve him.

The door to the Chief's office flew open, and the staff scattered in all directions. John Winters came out, face like a thundercloud. He put his head down and stomped toward his office. Mrs. Winters was next, followed by the RCMP sergeant. He grabbed her arm, none too gently, and steered her toward an interview room. Barb noticed that he did not take her to the nice room, where they questioned victims and witnesses.

"That's Mrs. Winters?" the by-law officer said in surprise. "I heard she was a model. Must have been a long time ago."

◇◇◇

The person in charge of maintenance for the Hudson House Hotel agreed to come into work a few minutes early to talk to Detective Lopez. His name was Dennis Jones and he was a beefy man with the bulbous red nose of a serious drinker and the prominent, round belly of a serious eater. He was dressed in overalls, spattered with paint and oil, covering a gray T-shirt that had probably once been white. His hair was thin, badly cut and greasy, and his nails didn't look as if he washed his hands all too often. Small black eyes in a pudding face darted around the room: a man used to checking a place out before settling down.

"Heard some guy got his number punched, eh." Jones pulled a chair up to the conference room table and started the conversation. "Guess that's why you want to talk to me. Shoot." He laughed heartily and, Lopez thought, too forcefully.

Lopez took his own seat, reminding himself that just because someone was not comfortable being questioned by the police didn't necessarily mean he had something to hide.

"Your manager tells me you were on the second floor Monday evening?"

"Yup. Lamp needed replacing. I figured it was the bulb at first, but nope, the bulb was still good. It was the lamp was broken. So I replaced it."

"Room number?" Lopez asked, although he knew it. It was recorded on the hotel log.

"Second floor. West end, third door from the fire escape. Don't remember the number."

"Not a problem. Time?"

"Round about five-thirty. I remember that 'cause it was the last job before my dinner break."

"Did you see anyone in the hallway when you were there?"

"No." the man answered, very quickly.

"Are you sure?"

Another bark of a laugh. "I figured you'd ask that question, Detective. I'm way ahead of you." The room wasn't warm, but Jones pulled a handkerchief out of the pocket in the bib of his overalls and wiped his forehead. "Was thinking about it last night, see. No, I didn't see anyone. Place was quiet as a tomb." He laughed again.

"How long were you upstairs, on the second floor?"

"Two minutes maybe. Checked the bulb. Went downstairs for a replacement lamp. Another two minutes to swap them."

"Did you take the elevator?"

"You don't understand about the hierarchy in a place like this, do you? Of course I didn't take the elevator. That wouldn't be right, would it? Can't let the fancy pants guests rub shoulders with the person who pulls their condoms out of the toilet or changes their lamps." A vein throbbed in the fleshy neck, and his fists were tightly clenched. "A hotel works invisibly, you know."

The bitterness in Jones' voice came across loud and clear. Irrelevant, Lopez thought, unless the man had finally snapped and murdered a demanding guest.

"Thank you, Mr. Jones. That's all I wanted to know." He handed over his card, and Jones took it with calloused fingers. "If you remember anything, give me a call at that number."

◇◇◇

John Winters punched the keys to unlock his computer with almost enough force to break them. To no one's surprise, he was off the murder case. He was lucky he hadn't been shown the door altogether, at least for the time being. The Chief, after getting over his initial shock, ordered Winters to stay absolutely clear of any involvement in the investigation into the murder of Rudolph Steiner. He wasn't to so much as talk about the case with anyone. If the subject came up in his hearing, he was to leave the room immediately. The Chief also suggested, avoiding looking at his lead detective's face, that for the time being Winters vacate the family home.

Eliza had sat in the chair in front of the Chief's desk, curled up into herself, mentally and physically. She hadn't said a word. It hadn't been necessary for Keller to ask her if this was true—her face was confession enough. Winters had been told to go back to his office and see what else needed his attention, and Madison took Eliza to be questioned.

Winters was still carrying the dammed picture. The opportunity to produce it hadn't presented itself, and he hadn't made one.

The top item in his inbox was a report of a break and enter on Elm Street. It had come in less than an hour ago. Constable Smith asking for a detective to go around and take prints. He called her.

"Molly, I'm looking at the report on the B&E on Elm. Are you finished there?"

"Yes, I took some pictures of where the missing stuff had been, and the basement window, which was broken. They told me it hadn't been broken when they last looked, so that was probably where the perp got access. There's a tall fence around their yard and that window's not visible from the street. I spoke to the neighbor, who saw nothing, heard nothing. I thought it wouldn't hurt to get prints so I called for forensics. I guess they're pretty busy, eh?"

"I'm going to take it."

"You?"

"Yes, me. Do you have a problem with that?"

"Of course not. I just…"

"Meet me there in five." Winters hung up without bothering to ask if she was in the middle of something else.

He stopped at the equipment room before leaving. Everyone he passed avoided looking at him. The door to interview room two was closed, and he could hear nothing coming from inside. Barb rounded the corner. "Oh, John," she said, with a strained sort of cheerfulness. "I was about to put the kettle on. Would you like to join me in a cup of tea?"

"No. That is, no thank you. On my way out. A call. Back soon."

He thought he heard a wave of excited chatter as the door slammed behind him, but that might only have been his imagination.

He arrived at the house on Elm Street before Smith. Winters knocked on the front door, and a man answered. "Wow," he said when Winters showed his ID. "You people sure are quick. My friends in the big cities will be green with envy. My wife's still working on the list your officer asked her to prepare. It doesn't look like they've taken much. Just the good stuff, small and portable, electronics, jewelry. I'm Fred by the way. Fred Webster." He held out his hand.

Winters shifted his case to his left hand and shook. "John Winters. Any damage, Mr. Webster?"

"No. They were neat and tidy about it."

The patrol car pulled up and Smith joined them. The man showed them into the house, and a woman came down the wide staircase. She held up a piece of paper. "I think this is all," she said, handing it to Winters.

"Thank you." He glanced at it. The handwriting was shaky, nerves probably, but he could make it out. As the man had said, there wasn't much. Just the good stuff. A group of photographs accompanied the note.

"Pictures of the jewelry," Webster said. "For the insurance."

"That's very helpful. Do you have copies, can I take these?"

"They're all yours. We can print off more." His face fell. "Oh, now all I need is a printer. And a computer." He turned to his wife. "Darlene, when did you last do a backup?"

"Day before we left," she said. "I've checked and the CDs are still here."

Winters spoke to Smith. "I'm going to do the whole house. Windows, doors, counter tops, tables. Every surface."

"What?"

"While I'm doing that, I want you going up and down the street and ask if anyone saw anything."

"But…"

"You spoke to the woman who was minding the house?"

"Yes."

"If anyone saw anyone come to this house other than her, I want to know about it."

Smith shot him a look, but she was wise enough not to argue in the presence of the homeowners.

Winters ignored her. "It was probably done at night, so you'll have to come back again when people are home from work. Do it tonight, before they start to forget. I'll authorize the overtime."

"I'd like to lie down," Mrs. Webster said. "Is that all right?"

"Is there a spare room you can use?"

"Yes, we have a guest room."

"Was anything taken from there?"

"I don't think so."

"Give me a few minutes. I have a couple of questions, and I'll do that room first, then you can lie down."

The woman nodded. Winters wasn't qualified in forensics, but he did have a SOCO course under his belt that allowed him to take fingerprints. In a department the size of Trafalgar, officers needed to be able to multi-task.

"Report to me when you're finished," he ordered Smith. He turned back to Mrs. Webster. "Why don't we sit down." She headed toward the back of the house and he followed. He heard the front door shut, perhaps with more force than necessary, as Smith left.

Time to stop fooling around. He'd had enough of whoever was doing this. There'd been a series of B&Es just like this one over the past six weeks. Nice houses, nice neighborhoods, family away on vacation. It was always the same—straight to the electronics and jewelry. No muss, no fuss. No random destruction.

One house had nothing taken. The owner lived alone except for an elderly dog, she had her laptop computer and accessories with her, owned no electronics other than an out-of-date radio and CD player, and no jewelry worth stealing. Drawers had been opened, clothing moved aside in the search for something that might have been hidden, and that was it. Other than the disarray and a broken lock on the back door, she might not have known someone had been in the house.

After going to the bother of breaking in, if they couldn't find anything of value thieves often trashed the place. Just to be mean.

This bunch didn't even leave footprints. They'd had a lot of snow over the winter and when it started to warm up all that snow made a lot of mud. Winters could see a set of footprints in the entrance hall. He'd need to get someone around to make a cast of the prints, but they were almost certainly from Molly Smith's boots. The homeowners were in stocking feet, their shoes neatly lined up at the door.

All of which indicated to John Winters that he was looking for a highly professional set of thieves. In and out. Grab the good stuff and get the hell out. Most of the houses that had been burgled had a neighbor bringing in the mail and watering the plants. In every case the watchful neighbor hadn't seen or heard a thing.

They'd done the usual fingerprinting for these sorts of cases— door frames, window sills, the surfaces the stolen objects had been resting on. And found nothing except the homeowners' and random prints matching nothing on file. Smith obviously thought it was a waste of time to fingerprint the whole house.

It was his time to waste.

◇◇◇

Meredith Morgenstern rolled her eyes behind the woman's back. What a freakin' waste of time. Anyone who knew anything about this killing wasn't talking and everyone who didn't know a single thing, but wanted the attention, wouldn't shut up.

The third-assistant-sub-cook, or whatever she was called, thought Meredith would be interested to know she'd seen Mrs.

Steiner leaving the hotel the morning of her husband's death. As no one had suggested Mrs. Steiner kept herself in purdah, that was hardly a revelation.

This had the potential to be a major story. Rudolph Steiner had been a big-time fashion photographer in his day. That lately he probably couldn't get anyone to take his calls wouldn't matter when news of his death got out. Nothing revived celebrity like headlines screaming brutal murder.

Before anyone else came sniffing after the story, Meredith was determined to have the details. IHIT had been called in. That was good—it meant the case would be out from under the thumb of the Trafalgar City Police and Sergeant John Winters. Winters absolutely hated her. She was just a reporter trying to do her job, but Winters had really taken against her.

Her attempts to interview Mrs. Steiner had failed. The hotel receptionist, nose in the air, said they had instructions not to put any calls through, and she certainly wasn't going to tell Meredith what room the woman had been moved to. She'd decided to find out where the IHIT guys were staying and maybe run into them in the bar later. Her cell phone rang.

"Hi, Meredith, it's Emily. Emily Wilson? How's things?"

Meredith knew Emily, vaguely, friend of a friend. "Sorry, but I can't talk right now, I'm really busy. You heard about this murder at the Hudson House? I'm working the story."

"I figured you would be, that's why I'm calling."

Meredith couldn't imagine what Emily might know about this. The girl worked in town, a clerk at Rosemary's Campfire Kitchen.

"Gotta run. I'll call you later, Emily." She was about to hang up, try to get back upstairs and see what was happening. If the police wouldn't talk to her, perhaps she could at least get a shot of the forensic investigators in their white suits. The public loved that sort of stuff. Before she disconnected, Meredith remembered one interesting thing about Emily Wilson. "I have to see someone but…uh…they can wait a minute."

"I heard something I thought you might like to know. Something the paper might like to know, I mean."

"Go on."

"Dave popped in to say hi." The interesting thing about Emily Wilson was that her boyfriend was Dave Evans. Constable Dave Evans. Evans was cute and Meredith had occasionally looked his way, thinking it wouldn't be a bad idea to have an inside source on the police department. Evans had ignored her overtures, which she put down to his fear of Sergeant Winters.

"Go on," Meredith said.

"Do you pay for information?"

"We're a small local paper, Emily. We don't have money for that sort of thing." She wanted to reach down the phone line and grab Emily by the throat.

"Rosemary's gone to the bank. When she gets back I can go on my break. Buy me a coffee at Eddies?"

"Look Emily, like I said, I'm busy. Can you tell me what it's about?"

"I bet you have an expense account, Meredith. I'd like to go to Flavours for dinner one night. Dave won't take me there because he says it doesn't look right if people think the police are making too much money."

Spit it the hell out! "I might be able to talk Joe into coming up with something if it's worthwhile."

"Okay. Dave says John Winters' wife has been arrested for the murder. Winters has been demoted, taken off the case. He left the station in a temper, and they're questioning her now."

"Big Eddie's in five minutes. Flavours as soon as I'm free." Never mind Joe or the paper, for a scoop like this Meredith would treat Emily herself.

Chapter Ten

For the rest of the afternoon, the mood at the police station was funereal, to say the least. Barb stayed at her desk, and no one came in for a casual chat or to ask if there was something tasty in the bottom drawer. She could hear people going about their business, but no one laughed, and voices were kept low. Ray Lopez came in, at a run, his hair windblown and his jacket askew, wanting to see the Chief. He'd said no disturbances, Barb told the detective. Lopez looked as if he might argue, but turned and left, every inch of his body showing his displeasure.

John Winters had been in Trafalgar for little more than a year, and he hadn't gone out of his way to make friends; Barb practically had to order him to attend last summer's pot luck. But he usually had a pleasant word for everyone and went about his work with quiet efficiency. As far as Barb knew, everyone in the department liked and respected him.

Madison spent almost an hour in the interview room with Mrs. Winters, before escorting her to the front door. Barb looked up as they went by. Eliza's head was down, her hair covering her face. Madison's face was set into a dark scowl.

He was back immediately, and went in to see the Chief.

The expense sheets were still on Barb's computer, still out of balance. Quitting time, and she hadn't accomplished anything all afternoon.

The Chief's door opened and Madison came out. He left without so much as a glance at her. Paul Keller stood in the doorway. His lips were drawn into a tight line, and he was rubbing the fingers of his right hand together, as if hoping a cigarette would magically appear. His uniform shirt, usually a pristine white, ironed to a knife-edge, was rumbled. He let out a puff of air. As always, the scent of tobacco hung over the Chief like a storm cloud over the mountains.

"Do you have to leave on time?" he asked.

"No."

"Come in then. Have a seat. Shut the door, will you, Barb. This is not for anyone else's ears."

In all her years Barb had never breathed a word of department business outside the station or the Chief's confidences outside his office. She wasn't going to start now. She sat down. The chair was still warm from the last visitor.

"This is a nasty, nasty business." Keller reached into the bar fridge he kept behind his desk and pulled out a can of coke. "Want one?"

"No thanks."

He popped the top, and took a long pull before dropping into his chair. "I guess everyone knows John Winters' wife was brought in for questioning?"

"Yes."

"Let's hope we can keep a lid on that. We're not keeping her; she's been allowed to go home. The yellow stripes," meaning the Mounties, "are close to arresting her."

"Oh, dear," Barb said. "That's not good."

"No kidding. If it happens, we will not be able to keep a lid on it."

"What's the reasoning?"

"Mrs. Winters admits she was in the man's hotel room last night around eight-thirty. She says she was only there for a short while, and when she left Steiner was alive."

"And…"

"Madison thinks she's lying. She was vague about why she visited Steiner in his room, why she only stayed a short while, why she didn't even take off her coat and have a glass of Champagne.

He's out there now, trying to find someone who saw her leave the hotel later than she claims."

"Did she know this guy?"

"Apparently she was engaged to him when she met John. She broke it off with Steiner and married John. She says she's only seen him a few times since, in passing at parties and the like."

Keller finished his drink, and gave the can a shake, as if he couldn't believe it was all gone.

"Until this week?" Barb prompted.

"He contacted her. Told her he was going to be in town and wanted to get together and invited her up to his room."

"Nothing wrong with that."

"We've been told he doesn't like to eat in restaurants if he doesn't have to. The room-service waiter says Eliza, Mrs. Winters, looked tense and angry, not as if she were there to talk about the old days and have a friendly drink."

"What does she say?"

"Very little. She says he wanted to renew their professional relationship, to take photographs of her for an art magazine. She told him no and he got hostile and rude. Then the waiter arrived. She left immediately after."

"But," Barb said.

"But, Madison doesn't believe her. If she didn't want Steiner to photograph her, why didn't she just send him an e-mail and say so? He can't think of a reason Eliza Winters would meet with a man she hasn't seen in years and kill him, but he's determined to keep looking.

"Steiner was almost certainly killed by someone he knew, someone he'd let come up behind him while he was leaning over the toilet."

"He was being sick?"

"Looks that way, yes. Although the physical evidence, shall we say, isn't there."

"Did Mrs. Winters say he looked ill?"

"She says he appeared to be poor health in general, but not immediately sick, when she left."

"If it came on fast, and he had to run for the bathroom, he might not have cared who was sneaking up on him. That sorta thing takes all your attention."

Keller cracked a small smile. "Good point. But right now Madison has his sights on Eliza Winters. I haven't met him before, and I don't know that I care for him. Too single minded for my liking. I looked up his record. He was promoted last month. This is his first big investigation, and he'll want a nice quick, clean arrest. I can only hope he's not the sort to go in for grandstanding."

Keller was intensely loyal to his staff, and he'd stand by John Winters come hell or high water. But, Barb knew, if Mrs. Winters was charged, it was unlikely John could continue working here.

"It was eight o'clock in the evening in a busy hotel. Which is good, lots of potential witnesses. And bad, too many people going about their own business confuses everything. Madison's going to try to find someone who can say what time Mrs. Winters left, and if anyone else was seen on that floor around the time in question."

"Without a motive…"

"Motive's not necessary to bring charges, Barb. Not even to get a conviction. But it helps, and you can be sure Madison's going to be taking a good look into Eliza's history."

Barb shuddered.

"Not many of us have snowy white pasts," Keller said. "Don't know I'd want someone trying to dig up the dirt on me."

Barb didn't even try to make a joke.

"I hope she wasn't in the States recently," Keller said.

"Why?"

"The gun. She denies having ever owned one. It could have been bought in any back alley in Canada, of course, but I don't imagine a woman such as Mrs. Winters would know where to go looking for one. They're a lot easier to find across the border."

Barb said nothing. The border with Washington State was only an hour or so away, closer as the crow flies. Spokane was closer to Trafalgar than to any comparable-sized Canadian city; people went there all the time, for shopping, to see shows or concerts, for a Sunday drive.

Silence stretched through the office. Traffic hummed outside the window, and a man shouted a greeting, and a woman laughed. Barb studied the collection of pictures on the wall behind the Chief's desk. Official poses, shaking hands with various dignitaries. Personal photos, of his family and his numerous fishing successes, cluttered the battered wooden desk.

"If she did buy a gun…" Barb began.

"Then it was premeditated."

◇◇◇

Elm Street had been reclaimed from what had once been a bustling industrial waterfront in the days when Trafalgar was a thriving center of industry. It was now a street of modern, expensive homes with spacious lots, well-maintained gardens, and great views over the water. People who lived on Elm were the kind of families with professional jobs, double incomes, and two well-scrubbed children with names like Ashleigh and Riley who had near-perfect attendance at the local public school. They were unlikely to be found at home in the middle of a Wednesday afternoon. People who lived on Elm spent their evenings ferrying Ashleigh and Riley to hockey practice and piano lessons, supervising homework, eating meals made with organic food (in season and when available) prepared in the upgraded kitchen, watching the latest popular TV series on DVD after the kids were in bed, and heading for their own beds after Peter Mansbridge or Wendy Mesley read the CBC National News. It was highly unlikely anyone who lived on Elm Street peered out their windows watching for suspicious activity on the street.

Questioning the neighbors this afternoon had been a waste of time, as Molly Smith could have told anyone. Now she was supposed to come back in the evening and pound on doors again? She had planned to see a movie with Adam tonight. Cancelling that wouldn't be a problem—she was in no mood to have a conversation about proper professional conduct around one another's co-workers.

Everyone would be working hard with this murder case going on.

Come to think of it, why was Winters so fired up about this B&E when there was a murder to be investigated? Sure IHIT had taken over, but there were only two of them and you'd think they'd need all the help they could get.

She turned the corner into Monroe Street, and into the parking lot behind the station. She'd have time to go to the hospital and visit her dad, have something to eat, and get back to Elm Street when people were settling down in front of the TV after dinner. If she learned anything of interest, she'd eat her hat.

Phone. Adam again. She backed into a parking space before answering. "Hi."

"Geeze, Molly, I've been calling you all day."

"I've been busy."

"Look, about what happened earlier."

"Yes?"

"I guess you're pissed, right?"

"What makes you think that? Why would I care that I am the object of pity amongst my colleagues? And those are the ones who like me. The ones who don't like me assume I need a big strong man to take care of me."

"I'm sorry that happened, but I doubt anyone's thinking much about you this afternoon, Molly."

"Why?"

"You haven't heard?"

"Heard what?"

"Not over the phone. Are we still on for tonight?"

"No, we're not. I got pulled for extra duty. I have to be back at eight. Winters is suddenly in a sweat over a B&E."

"I guess he would be."

Dawn Solway waved to Smith before letting herself in the back door.

"Adam. I have to go. I need to pop into the hospital soon as I get off."

"We can't leave it like this, Molly. I'll pick up a pizza and come around to your place before you go back to work." He hung up without waiting for her to refuse.

◇◇◇

Andy was sitting up in bed complaining about the food when his daughter walked into his room. His color was bad, skim-milk blue, and his hair was lank and greasy. A pot of miniature roses sat on the window ledge beside a teddy bear with a cheerful red bow around its neck and several get well cards. His roommate's bed was empty, and neatly made. Molly decided not to ask where he'd gone.

She leaned across the meal tray to give her father a kiss. "That doesn't look so bad," she said, eyeing the slice of poached chicken, dab of rice, and string beans on his tray.

"Well it is. Chicken must have died of old age. Which is what's going to happen to me if I stay here any longer." He shifted uncomfortably and his face twisted in pain.

"Any news?"

"Surgery's tomorrow," Lucky said, coming out of the bathroom. "First thing in the morning. The tests showed negative for a stroke, so that's a relief. There's a lot of bruising from landing badly on those skis, but none of that seems to be serious."

"I'll be here. I can take the day off, although we're pretty busy, and I have to go back to work tonight. You heard about the killing at the Hudson?"

Lucky shrugged. "The nurses were talking about it." Molly wrapped her mother in a hug, realizing how worried Lucky must be. Normally she wanted to know every detail of what was happening in town.

They chatted while Andy poked at his food. She debated telling her parents about that scene between Adam and Dave Evans, but one look at her mother decided her against it. Lucky's normally cheerful face was drawn into lines of strain and the usual sparkle in her eyes was nowhere to be seen.

"Your brother should be here around midnight," Lucky said. "Perhaps a bit later."

"Why so late?"

"He had to attend a meeting this morning, then he couldn't get a flight, so he's driving."

"Are the kids coming?" Smith said, thinking it would do her mom good to have the grandchildren, Ben and Roberta, rushing around the house, filling it with noise. Besides, Smith hadn't seen them for more than a year.

"He didn't want to take them out of school, and Judy's busy with a big project."

"Dad's busy with a big project right about now, too."

Lucky gave her a look.

"Yeah, okay. Whatever."

"Is the cafeteria still open?" Andy asked.

"I think so."

"Get me a bag of chips will you, Lucky. A large bag." He pushed at the plate in front of him. "Not enough food there to feed a kitten. And don't tell me it's bad for my heart. I'm not having that hospital muck for my last meal."

Lucky burst into tears.

Molly put her arms around her mother and pulled her close. Over Lucky's shoulder, she looked at Andy. His blue eyes, the same shade as hers, overflowed with sorrow. He looked so helpless, pale and frightened, wearing a worn hospital nightgown, his skinny legs outlined by the bed sheets. Frightened as much, Molly realized, for his wife as for himself. He let out a deep breath and their eyes met. She nodded, just a bit, and the ghost of a smile crossed his face.

Lucky freed herself from her daughter, and dug in the pocket of her too-big, not very well made, craft-sale sweater. Andy looked toward the window. Molly handed Lucky the box of tissues from the side table.

"Let's give Dad some down time. Come on, Mom, I'll walk you to your car. The chips," she said to her father, "Can wait until tomorrow. I'll bring one of those party-sized bags to celebrate a successful operation."

"Sausage rolls would be nice, too. And maybe some of those frozen pizza roll ups."

"Done." She kissed her father's paper-thin cheek. It was rough with bristles. He smelled slightly sour, of disinfectant and medication and fear.

He stretched his arm out and Lucky took his hand.

"You are my life," he said, and Smith turned away at such a naked sign of intimacy.

"Try not to worry, eh, Mom?" she said as they crossed the parking lot to Lucky's car. "Dad's a tough old buzzard."

"That he is. How's Adam?"

Smith took a breath. "Great. He's great. We're great."

"It makes me happy to see you happy." Lucky stroked her daughter's arm. "Ask him to come and visit. Your dad likes him, you know."

"Dad would like anyone who might make an honest woman of me."

"Everything else going okay?"

"Great, Mom. Life's just great." Smith tried to keep her voice light, playful. Her mother could usually read her like a book, but tonight Lucky's mind was elsewhere.

"I'm happy for you," she repeated.

Smith barely made it home before Adam was knocking at the door. Balancing a large, flat cardboard box, he followed her upstairs to her apartment over the bakery. The odor of fresh pizza mingled with the smell of the day's baking, and Smith briefly wondered if that's what heaven smells like.

"I don't have long, Adam," she said, as he placed the box on the coffee table. Underneath the heavy stubble on his jaw, the skin was turning purple from the punch he'd received from Evans. Not wanting to start thinking about that again, she went into the kitchen and ripped sections off a roll of paper towel. As she reached up into the cupboard for two plates, she heard the floorboards creak under his weight. His arms slipped around her waist and his hands moved upwards, feeling for her breasts. Still holding the plates, she wriggled free and turned around. He took the dishes from her and put them on the counter.

"Let's have dessert first." He bent down and aimed a kiss at her. She pushed him away. "I thought we were going to talk."

"Molly, I'm sorry. I really am. Evans is such a jerk, and what he said about you…"

"I heard, Adam. Everyone in the goddamned station heard. He made some stupid crack about our sex life, way outa line, but it would have ended there if you'd walked away. You're the one who made it into a big deal."

"It was a lot more than a joke about sex, Molly. I couldn't stand there and let him insult you like that, and that smirking bastard McMillan taking it all in."

She threw up her hands and walked out of the kitchen. "Insult me. That's what it was about, isn't it. He *insulted* me. Are you defending my *honor*? I don't have any goddamned honor to be defended." She turned and faced him, her anger boiling up inside her.

He looked like a little boy, a six-foot four, two-hundred and twenty pound little boy, trying to explain why he'd been in a fight in the school yard.

"Do you think I don't know what Dave Evans thinks of me? Do you think he doesn't know what I think of him? But we go out on the streets every day, and we do our jobs, and we watch each other's back. Because we're cops first and being cops is the only thing that matters. Now you've gone and made it *personal*."

"Evans made it personal."

They'd met at a riot. Not the most romantic of settings. She'd been scared out of her wits, but she'd done her job, and Constable Adam Tocek had done his job and the incident had ended well. She was afraid of what might happen in the same circumstances now. Would Adam be able to take control of the situation, move the officers into position, talk calmly to the crowd, as he'd done that day? Or would he be distracted, concerned about her, too busy checking she was all right? Thus putting them both, and everyone around them, in danger.

Plenty of police were married to other officers. They seemed to be able to work together okay. Maybe it needed more time. It was still so new, and…

Sensing her resistance fading, he took a step toward her. "I love you, Molly."

…and he was so much in love with her.

"Please, Adam," she said, knowing her voice sounded small and weak. "Don't try to protect me anymore."

He kissed her again, a long deep kiss that went all the way down to her toes, and this time she kissed him back.

◇◇◇

Molly Smith headed out the door of her apartment, grabbing a slice of cold pepperoni pizza from the unopened box to munch on the way to the station.

Adam was dozing, but he'd be gone soon after her. He couldn't leave his dog, Norman, at home alone all night.

She ran down the stairs, feeling warm and happy and loved.

But nothing, she knew, had been resolved.

Chapter Eleven

The IHIT team had taken over interview room two. Every time John Winters had to pass it he felt himself getting angrier. On his way back from the Websters' house, his kit bulging with fingerprint samples, he'd stopped at the drug store to pick up deodorant, a toothbrush and toothpaste, and an electric razor. He kept telling himself that Eliza had nothing to do with the death of Steiner. But he couldn't stop wondering, as well as wondering what she'd been doing in the man's hotel room that night. Whatever it was, she hadn't said anything to her husband about it, not when she got home nor the next morning when they were getting ready to leave for San Francisco. She'd been edgy and nervous, he remembered, as she'd been for most of the week. He'd put it down to restlessness—she hadn't had a decent job offer for months—and winter blues.

He trusted her, he loved her, he believed in her.

But he just didn't want to face her tonight.

He worked alone in the small forensic office, developing the prints and scanning them into the computer for uploading into the national database. If anyone with a record had been in that house, he'd find them.

Once that was done, he spent some time at his desk, typing up notes about the thefts, reading his old notes, trying to find similarities. No matter where he looked, he was coming up blank. The homes and homeowners appeared to have nothing in common. They didn't know each other, except in that casual way that everyone in a small town seems to know almost everyone else. They had not advertised in the paper for someone to mind their homes in their absence, and had all used a different neighbor, if they used one at all, to check on the house. Some of them took the *Gazette*, some did not; some had cancelled delivery for the time they were away, some had not. They weren't even geographically close, scattered all over town. They took their dogs to different kennels, and their children went to a variety of schools and played on a variety of sports teams. Not all of the homeowners even had children. A few went to church regularly, but to different churches, and most of the victims didn't have a church at all.

He looked up to see Molly Smith standing in the doorway. Behind her, all was quiet and the lights were dim. Everyone gone home, IHIT either at the scene or finished for the day.

He waved toward a chair. "What did you find out?"

"Nothing." He suspected she held herself back from adding, "as I could have told you."

She shifted her equipment belt and plopped down. "I did hear a lot of variations on what is this town coming to. People have read about the break-ins in the paper and aren't happy. And, let me tell you, that killing hasn't helped any. What's happening with that one anyway?"

He looked at her. Her hat was in her lap, and she rubbed at the short blond hair on the top of her head, and her pretty face showed simple curiosity. Apparently she hadn't heard about Eliza. The police department grapevine wasn't as efficient as he'd thought. Then again, she was no doubt avoiding listening in on anyone's conversation, knowing that after that fight in the lunch room, she herself could be the topic *du jour*. He felt a twist in his gut. News of Eliza being brought in for questioning would have pushed a simple fist fight right off the radar.

"I want a full report of what you heard, anyway," he said, ignoring her question. "Have it on my desk before lunch.

Tomorrow night, go up to Station Street, do the section where last week's break-in happened. Same questions."

"Tomorrow's not good, John. I'm off."

"I told you, I'll authorize the overtime. You don't keep bankers' hours, Molly."

Her blue eyes opened in surprise. "My father is having an operation tomorrow. I'll take the day off I've been given, thanks." She stood up. "I'll do the report before I leave."

"You do that." He hesitated before turning back to his computer. "Give your dad my best wishes." She nodded, and then her footsteps echoed in the quiet hallway.

He took off his reading glasses and rubbed his eyes. His hand reached for the phone, hesitated, and returned to the keyboard. He couldn't face talking to Eliza. Not yet.

He put his glasses back on and continued typing.

◇◇◇

That was such a waste of time, she might indulge herself and spend the overtime money on something completely frivolous. A day at the spa maybe, or some new clothes. It wasn't fun, interrupting people when they were relaxing at home, watching fake police solve cases in an hour including commercials, who then took the opportunity to give her an earful about the state of policing in Trafalgar. If Winters demanded she march around to every house in town, she might make enough to be able to treat Adam to a weekend of spring skiing in Whistler.

Adam. She felt herself smiling at the thought of him. He'd said that he loved her. Sure he was trying to get her to forget she was mad at him and into the sack, but she knew he meant it. She hadn't said the words back though.

She'd recently come to the difficult decision that it was time to leave Trafalgar; if her career was to go anywhere she needed better policing experience than she would get in this small, generally peaceful town. She'd stayed in touch with a woman she'd met at police college, who was now working in Toronto. Last week her friend phoned, telling Smith it was a good time to apply. She'd started updating her resume, but it remained in her computer, unsent.

Did she want to leave Adam? They'd tell each other she'd visit Trafalgar regularly and they could have a long-distance relationship, but everyone knew those things rarely worked out. She could suggest he move to Toronto too, but the RCMP didn't have many officers in Ontario, and she knew that Adam loved the Mounties.

It was difficult sometimes to be a police officer in Trafalgar, where her mothers' friends passed her on the street, dressed in full uniform, body amour, radio, gun, baton, and said, "hello, dear." Where the newspaper reporter still hated her because of some slight when they were sixteen years old that neither of them remembered. If she were to get ahead in this career Molly Smith knew she needed big-city experience. But she also knew she was falling in love with Adam Tocek, and it would be very difficult to leave him.

It was late and even *Feuilles de Menthe*, the restaurant next door to her apartment, was dark and quiet. There was no traffic on the street and everything was still. Spring was coming, although taking its time, and the night air had a crisp, sharp bite. She yawned, remembering she had to be at the hospital in a few hours. There was no welcoming lamp over the back door that led to the stairs up to her place and the street light across the alley didn't reach the entrance. It was wrapped in night's gloom.

Something was on the door, darker than the shadows. Smith froze in her tracks, and her hand rose to her mouth.

A rat. Impaled onto the door by a knife.

She whirled around, pulling out her flashlight and switching it on. She played the beam of light around the alley, probing the shadows. No one was watching her and there was no sign of anyone hiding and her radar wasn't twitching. Only when she was confident she was alone and unobserved, did she bend over and rest her hands on her trembling knees. Her stomach churned, and she took one deep breath and then another. Finally, she straightened up and pointed the flashlight at her door. The rat's black eyes were dark pools in an ugly face; the long naked tail didn't move. It was, thank heavens, dead. Blood glistened in the bright white light. Still wet.

It would be morning soon, and people would cut down the alley to get to work and school. She couldn't leave the hideous thing here. She knew she should call this in, get the knife fingerprinted. John Winters was still at his desk, she'd seen the light in his office when she left after finishing the report. He was acting so damned prickly, she was reluctant to call him out. The forensics people were so busy they'd not be happy at being woken up to investigate the murder of an alley rat.

Particularly as there wasn't much of a mystery about the identity of the rodent-killer.

Charlie Bassing. Guaranteed.

Smith slipped her hands into a pair of latex gloves and grabbed the handle of the knife. She braced herself and pulled. It came away from the door so easily she toppled backwards. She stumbled to keep her footing, and the rat dropped to the ground.

She studied the knife under the beam of her flashlight. It was a kitchen knife, the blade about six inches long, the handle showing signs of wear. A knife of the sort anyone could buy anywhere to slice onions and chicken breasts. Blood, deep red, almost black, glistened in the light. A few drops fell to the ground. She shuddered and again felt her stomach move.

She kicked the dead rat into the bushes, then played the beam of the flashlight around the alley, lighting up the dark corners. All was quiet. He could be hiding, just out of the range of her light, watching her, but she didn't sense him. Just in case, she lifted the knife and held it up, into the light, trying to look tougher than she felt. She spat on the ground.

She turned and unlocked her door and went up stairs to get a wet rag to clean the door and a plastic bag for the knife.

Chapter Twelve

The hill was steep and Barb Kowalski was overweight and approaching retirement age, but she ran all the way. She arrived at the police station boiling hot, dripping sweat, gasping for breath. Her fingers shook as she punched in the access code to open the door. "Paul in yet?" she shouted to Jim Denton, settling himself down with coffee in a mug that said "World's Greatest Granddad".

"Yes. You're early. What's the matter now?"

Barb didn't answer. As Jim said, she was early and the office staff hadn't arrived yet. The Chief's door was open; he was snapping the tab off the day's first can of pop.

He stared at her. "What on earth?"

She waved the newspaper. "Have you seen this?"

"No."

She handed it to him. It was today's *Gazette,* delivered to Barb's house in time for breakfast as every morning. She'd taken one look at the headline, abandoned her bowl of home-made granola, and her startled husband, and ran all the way to the office, trying to read while she went.

Keller turned pale. He looked up at Barb. "I do not want to read this," he said, in a low flat voice. But he read.

Most of the front page was taken up by a picture of Eliza Winters, snapped last summer at a party at the site of the proposed Grizzly Resort outside of town. A small picture was inset next to the bigger one, taken at the height of her modeling career. In that one she was young, and so incredibly glamorous as to be almost unworldly. Barb dropped into the visitor's chair while the Chief read. The former supermodel, now semi-retired and living in Trafalgar, the article said, was being questioned by police in regards to the brutal murder of her former lover, the internationally renowned photographer Rudolph Steiner. The article described Steiner as a many-times-married playboy, and failed to mention that he and Mrs. Winters had been lovers more than twenty-five years ago.

It was sparse on details of the killing and the police investigation and heavy on innuendo and gossip. As the Chief read, exclaiming in anger every couple of sentences, Barb knew he was hoping to get to the end without finding a mention of Eliza's husband. But it was there, sure enough, in the last paragraph. Sergeant John Winters, of the Trafalgar City Police, had been relieved of his duties due to the potential conflict of interest.

Keller threw the can of pop into the trash. It wasn't empty, and he missed, and brown liquid splashed up the walls. "Is John in yet?"

"I don't know."

"Find out. If he's here, bring him to see me. Someone," he said, pronouncing each word with careful deliberation, "in this department has spoken to that bloody Morgenstern woman. When I find out who it is, and I will find out, his, or her, career is finished. Soon as they're open, call our lawyer. I want a meet ASAP."

Barb scurried out of her boss' office.

She found John Winters at his desk. He was wearing the same clothes he had on yesterday, and his eyes were red and his face drawn. "Haven't you gone home?" she said.

He grinned, without much mirth, and rubbed the face of his watch with the pad of his thumb. "Home's a bit awkward right now. I slept on the couch in the interview room. Very comfortable, I might move in permanently. What's up?"

"Have you read the *Gazette* today?"

"No. I was about go out and get something for breakfast."

"Chief would like to see you first."

◇◇◇

Ray Lopez was scraping up the last bit of oatmeal when his cell phone rang. Madeleine leaned across the table and plucked the sports section of yesterday's *Globe and Mail* out from under his elbow. "You won't be needing this any more," she said.

It was the station, telling him that Mrs. Steiner would be available at eight-thirty for an interview.

The small clock over the kitchen door said "Kootenay Time" and all the numbers were jumbled. But the hands were true and it was not quite seven-thirty. He made a grab for the newspaper. "Plenty of time."

Madeline grinned and placed her elbow firmly on the paper. "Not a chance, buddy. I've got it now."

He arrived at the hotel a few minutes before eight-thirty and took the elevator to the third floor. A man answered his knock. He was well dressed, too well dressed, and put Lopez in mind of a courtroom.

"Detective Lopez, I assume," he said. "I am Larry Iverson, Mrs. Steiner's attorney. Can I see some identification, please?"

Lopez produced it, it was examined and Iverson stepped back to allow the detective into the room.

Josie Steiner sat at a table by the window, with a glass of clear liquid at her elbow. She was ready to head for the exercise room in black workout clothes and running shoes. Her hair was tied back in a simple ponytail and her face was scrubbed clean. She looked, he thought, her age and a lot better for it.

"Thank you for agreeing to see me, Mrs. Steiner," he said.

"Mrs. Steiner is of course most anxious to see the killer of her husband brought to justice," Iverson said, indicating that Lopez could sit. The room was part of a suite, no beds but sofa and chairs arranged around a TV and coffee table. A desk stood by the window, and from the third floor they had an uninterrupted view looking out over town and across the river.

"We apologize for the delay," Iverson continued as Lopez sat down. "But Mrs. Steiner has not felt well enough to be interrogated."

Hardly an interrogation, Lopez thought, but he let it go. "Thank you."

"Now," Iverson said, taking his own seat beside the woman, "What would you like to know?"

"You mentioned you last saw your husband at around six-thirty on Monday night. Is that correct?"

"Yes." Josie spoke for the first time. Her voice was very low.

"The habits of Mr. and Mrs. Steiner may seem unusual to you, Detective," Iverson said, "but Mr. Steiner was unwell in recent months, as well as being a man of strict routine. He was a very private person, and Mrs. Steiner respected that. It was one of the reasons their marriage was so strong." Even the lawyer looked like he couldn't quite swallow that one.

"That's correct," Josie said.

"You didn't go back to your husband's room after six-thirty?"

"I did not."

"What did you do for the rest of the evening?"

"I rested in my room."

"Was anyone with you?"

"Certainly not."

"Ms. Barton, perhaps."

"I had little to do with Diane at any time. She was Rudy's assistant, not mine." Her tone was so huffy, Lopez guessed Josie had tried to get Barton running errands for her and had been strongly rebuffed.

"That didn't answer the question."

"She answered it perfectly, Detective. Mrs. Steiner was in her room for the rest of the evening. Alone. Can we continue?"

"What did you do for dinner?"

"Nothing."

"Nothing?"

"I rarely eat dinner," she said. "And never alone."

Lopez remembered her telling Winters she didn't eat break-fast. What on earth did the woman live on? He studied her face. Her eyes were a bit red and puffy, natural considering her husband had just died, but her nose wasn't running and her pupils were a normal size. No obvious evidence of drugs.

"What did you do?"

She nodded toward a pile of magazines tossed on the floor. "I read, I watched T.V. I turned out the light and went to sleep about ten."

"Did you go for a walk?"

"No."

"Your husband's room was right next door," Lopez said. "Did you hear anything…unusual?"

"No." She grabbed a tissue out of a box on the table and held it to her eyes. When it came away, he could see that she was crying. "I like the TV to be on loud," she said. "Perhaps Rudy called out to me when…when it happened. And I did not hear."

Iverson got to his feet. "Mrs. Steiner would like to go to the gym now, Detective. She finds that the exercise offers her some small degree of comfort."

Lopez knew when he was dismissed.

His next stop was the hotel office. He asked Peter Wagner to check room service records.

In the eight days the Steiners had been in residence, fourteen bottles of wine, some of them costing as much as two hundred dollars each, had been delivered to Mrs. Steiner's room. Instructions were always to leave the order outside the door, and in the morning the empties were picked up by the chambermaid.

By the looks of it, Josie Steiner lived on alcohol. By nine o'clock on any given night she could be counted on not to notice much.

◇◇◇

The Smith family was shown into the waiting room beside the OR. They'd been allowed to have a few minutes with Andy before he was taken away. His color was better this morning, Molly thought. Lucky, on the other hand, looked simply dreadful. It was unlikely she'd had much sleep. Sam had arrived with their mother. He gave his baby sister a deep hug, and she was glad he'd come.

Lucky dug into her purse for her reading glasses and a thick paperback. She sat in the chair, turning the pages, staring into space. Smith had also brought something to read, but the words couldn't keep her attention.

"I'm going downstairs to get a coffee," Sam said suddenly. "Mom? Moon?"

"Coffee would be nice," Lucky said. Smith shook her head.

Images of dead rats returning to life had plagued her dreams. Line after line of them goose-stepping in formation like black-booted, stiff-armed Nazi soldiers on parade. She'd woken before the alarm, feeling thick-headed and groggy and mildly sick to her stomach. She stood under the shower for a long time, and by the time she was toweling her hair dry, had decided to call Sergeant Winters after Andy's op. Charlie Bassing had beaten up Christa Thompson because she was too kindhearted to think he was anything more than an annoyance. Molly Smith, of all people, had better not make the same mistake. Winters would know what do to. Before leaving, she opened a file on her home computer, and sent a copy to her e-mail at work. Time to start recording what was going on.

She heard the sound of an ambulance coming up the hill. Then a police siren, followed by another ambulance.

Sam, who had never forgiven his parents for naming him Samwise after the *Lord of the Rings* character, came back with two coffees and a bag of muffins. A thin newspaper was tucked under his arm. "Big happenings at the police department, Moon," he said, handing her the paper. "Won't they be missing you?"

"It'll be tough but they'll get by." She took the paper. "Oh. My. God."

Lucky and Sam looked at her. "What?"

"This is awful. Just awful. Meredith again, of course. She needs to be taken out and shot."

"What? What's happened?" Lucky repeated. Smith ignored her and read.

So that was the sergeant's wife. Smith had never met her, but had seen her around town without knowing who she was. She was pretty hard to miss. Even though she must be almost fifty Eliza Winters looked a lot younger, still attractive, and usually dressed in comfortable, casual clothes that said this woman had no shortage of money or taste. No wonder Winters had been so edgy yesterday. The paper said he'd been relieved of duties. That wasn't true, he'd been hard at work when Smith left last night, but as a matter of procedure he would have been taken off the homicide. No wonder he was so intent on the B&E—it wasn't as if he had a murder case to be involved in. Or a pleasant home to return to at the end of a hard day.

Lucky jumped to her feet and Smith stopped reading. The doctor was standing there, in green scrubs, his surgical mask pulled down around his neck.

"Already!" Lucky cried. "You can't be finished already. What's happened?" Her children each took one of her arms.

"We've had to delay the procedure, Mrs. Smith," the doctor said. "I'm very sorry. There was a major vehicle accident on the highway, involving a van taking children on a school trip. There are several life-threatening injuries and we need the OR and every resource we have. I know this must be upsetting, but it can't be helped."

"When?" Lucky said.

"I'll let you know when we can re-schedule Mr. Smith. They'll be taking him back to his room shortly."

They stared at his back as he walked away.

Lucky moaned.

◇◇◇

Meredith was highly pleased with herself. Her story was a sensation, and she was hopeful the bigger papers would spot it. She'd had to fight hard to get it printed. Joe Gessling was as timid as ever. He wouldn't let her say that Mrs. Winters had been arrested, just as well as that turned out not to be true. She couldn't say Mrs. Winters was a suspect, only that she was being questioned. Meredith had wanted the headline to mention that the woman was married to the TCP's head detective. Something like: "Did

Top Cop's Model Wife Murder Lover?" But Joe said they weren't a tabloid, and he wasn't going to go anywhere near implying the police were attempting a cover-up.

Still, despite all the changes, she was pleased with the piece. She could only wish she were a fly on the wall at the station this morning. The Chief Constable would be in such a fit, he'd start smoking without benefit of a cigarette. If they tried to get her to give up her source, she'd fight them all the way to the Supreme Court.

That would be nice.

She stopped daydreaming about being the nationally famous defender of press freedom as a patrol car pulled up in front of the hotel. Sergeant Madison got out, and Meredith approached him.

"Meredith Morgenstern, *Trafalgar Gazette*," she said with a bright smile. "Do you expect to be making an arrest shortly, Sergeant?"

"I'll be arresting you, if you don't get out of my way," he snarled.

"Just doing my job. Will Eliza Winters be assisting you further?"

"You know I'm not going to say anything about that."

"What are you going to say? The people of this town are naturally interested in the progress of your investigation."

"Chief Constable Keller will speak to the press when, and if, we have anything to say." Madison brushed her aside and went into the hotel. Dave Evans sat behind the wheel of the patrol car. She saw him staring at her, his face set into a deep scowl. She tossed him a friendly wave. He threw the car into gear and sped away as if he were in a high speed chase.

It would appear she wouldn't be getting any more scoops from the dishy Constable Evans. Meredith turned around. A man and a woman watched her from the hotel steps.

The woman was Josie Steiner, the widow, the man much older. His gray suit, red tie shot with matching gray thread, and white shirt ironed with too much starch were perfect. Too perfect for the casual town of Trafalgar where wearing socks with shoes was considered formal. Meredith checked her professional smile was in place and approached them.

"Mrs. Steiner," she said, "My condolences on your loss."

"Thank you. Everyone has been so kind. You're with the newspaper?"

"Meredith Morgenstern, *Trafalgar Daily Gazette*."

The man held out his hand. He was shorter than her, and she should see the top of his round bald head, surrounded by a fringe of gray hair. "I'm Larry Iverson, Mrs. Steiner's attorney." Meredith shook.

"Would you care to join us for a coffee?" Josie said. "Maybe you can help us make sure my husband's killer is brought to justice."

Meredith accepted quickly, suspecting Iverson was about to object.

"She wasn't his lover, that old bag," Josie said, apropos of absolutely nothing. "She must be like, what, forty?"

"Do you mean Eliza Winters?"

"You said in the paper she killed him, but she'll get off because she's married to that detective. I spoke to him yesterday. If I'd known he was involved I would have walked out."

"That's not what anyone is saying, Josie," Iverson said with a heavy sigh. He sounded as if he was tired of repeating himself. "Please don't make wild accusations."

"I'd love to hear all about your husband. I've admired his photography for a long time," said Meredith, who had never heard of the guy until the day before yesterday. She'd been wondering how she could convince Mrs. Steiner to give her an interview, and here it was presented to her on a plate. Her luck was turning.

Josie dabbed dry eyes with a tissue. "He will be greatly missed."

Chapter Thirteen

"What are you doing here?" Jim Denton said. "I've got you down as having the day off. Is your dad's operation over already?"

"It never happened," Smith said. "He got bumped for the kids from that crash up on the highway."

"Bad one," the dispatcher said.

"I couldn't stand sitting around listening to Mom trying not to cry. I'll need to take another day when they try again on Dad so told Al I'd come in."

"I'm sure he's happy to have you. Everyone's busy driving IHIT around." He lowered his voice. "You heard about the Sarge?"

"Read this morning's paper. How'd the Chief take it?"

"About as well as could be expected. The Coke delivery truck backed up to the doors earlier. Seriously, Molly, this is bad. He's on the warpath. Someone leaked that story, and I wouldn't want to be in his shoes when the boss finds out who it was." Denton shook his head and answered the phone.

Staff-Sergeant Peterson ordered Smith to go around to the hotel and help IHIT out. By which she figured he meant run errands for them. She didn't mind. She never minded peeking over the detectives' shoulders. Right now she was happy being a constable third class, breaking up fights, keeping an eye on the drunks, helping old ladies cross the street. One day, one day, she might like to be a detective. Which reminded her that she still hadn't decided what to do about Toronto. She'd never make detective if she spent her whole career in Trafalgar. She briefly considered joining the RCMP and getting a posting with Adam, but dismissed the idea. It probably wouldn't work out too well if she were in the same department as her over-protective boyfriend.

She took a car and drove to the hotel. She stopped at a red light and watched a laughing couple cross the street, arms around each other. She realized that she hadn't even asked Adam if he wanted to move. Jobs for dog guys probably weren't all that easy to find.

Ray Lopez gave her a weak smile as she put her head into what had been Steiner's room. He looked as if he hadn't slept in days.

"Al told me to ask if you need anything," she said.

"Double double and a chocolate glazed," a man said. He was wearing the white SOCO outfit, kneeling on the floor under the window, examining the sill. He looked up, and his face almost visibly lit up when he saw that she was young and attractive. He jumped to his feet and crossed the room, peeling off gloves. "Hi. I'm Kevin Farzaneh. We met at the airport, but we didn't get a chance to talk."

"Molly Smith."

"I'll come with you to get those coffees, Molly." Kevin was about her age, tall and lean and good-looking. His dark brown eyes twinkled with charm and mischief. He didn't have a single hair on his head.

"That can wait." Madison walked through the door. "I want this room finished today. The hotel needs the floor back."

"Sure, Sarge. Come get me when you're ready to go for lunch, will you, Molly." Farzaneh gave Smith a wink and went back to his work.

Sergeant Madison wasn't a very friendly guy. She might have been the doorman for all the attention he paid her.

"Did you speak to her?" he barked at Lopez.

"Yes."

"Out in the hall." He noticed Smith. "You. Get out of here if you don't have anything to contribute. You're distracting Kevin."

"I wish," Farzaneh shouted.

She felt her face burning and hurried into the hall. Where she stood, because no one had told her what to do now.

"So?" Madison asked Lopez. The detective opened his note book.

"Her story seems straight. She wasn't supposed to be working this floor, but asked one of the other maids if she'd switch. They didn't tell the head of housekeeping about it, who said it's unusual for maids to switch floors. So we wondered if she had a reason to want to be near Steiner. And she was the one who found the body."

"You're telling me what I already know. Get to the point."

"I like to refresh my memory," Lopez said. His words were clipped, as if he'd taken a pair of scissors to the ends of each one. That was not, Smith knew, a good sign. Lopez was usually pretty easy going, but when he blew he had a temper to match his red hair.

"She, Rachel Lewis the chambermaid, wants to be a model."

"She sure doesn't look like one," Madison said.

"Nevertheless, she does. That checks out. She has a bunch of photographs, what she calls her portfolio, taken by a professional last year. She showed me the pictures, and I called the photographer's studio and confirmed. She says when she heard Steiner was staying here, she figured if she could get close to him she'd show him her portfolio and he'd make her a star."

"Well that isn't going to happen is it?"

"Not now. She was lurking—my word not hers—around the hallway for days and spoke to him Monday morning, probably on this very spot, and asked if he'd like to see her pictures. He said he would, and she brought them in on Tuesday, when she found him. She'd been planning to leave the pictures on the bed, with a note. She was at home alone, so she says, the night before, when he was killed. No alibi, but no reason to sneak back and off him."

"Maybe he laughed at her for wanting to be a model, and she took offense."

Smith said nothing. If every woman shot a man who insulted her looks, the world would be a less-populated place.

"Maybe," Lopez replied. "But unlikely."

"Did you check her?"

"She has no record of any sort."

"Okay. We'll look elsewhere. Speaking of which, you," he turned to Smith, "do you know where Winters lives?"

"Me?" she blinked. "Yes. Yes, I do."

"You can take me there. I'm going to speak to the wife again." Madison looked at Lopez. "Do you have a problem with that, Detective?"

"Yes, actually, now that you've asked. I know Mrs. Winters, not well, but I've met her a few times. I do not believe she snuck up behind some guy and shot him in the head. Didn't happen."

"When I want your opinion, I'll ask for it. You, do you have a personal opinion about Mrs. Winters?"

"I've never met her," Smith said.

"Then you can drive me. You'll wait in the car, though. This department appears to have a problem with confidentiality."

He walked away. Smith and Lopez exchanged looks before she hurried to catch up with the Mountie, who was pounding at the elevator button as if the number of hits would determine the speed at which it would arrive.

He said not a word in the car. When they pulled up at the Winters home, he ordered Smith, once again, to remain in the vehicle, and stalked up to the front door. There wasn't a car in the driveway, but the double garage doors were closed, so that meant nothing.

Getting no answer at the door, Madison walked around the house. Smith knew where Winters lived only because her mother, who knew everything that went on in the Mid-Kootenays, had told her. The house had been built to blend seamlessly into the forest setting. It was all wood and stone, aged perfectly, with lots of tall windows, and evidence of a gigantic fireplace. The property was high up a winding mountain road, the last home before the mountain got steeper and civilization was defeated. The view, Smith thought, must be spectacular; you could probably see the river from up here. The property was large, dotted with outbuildings. Lawns led from the house to the woods, and no other homes interrupted their privacy. Scattered piles of dirty snow still lined the driveway and walkways, and the flowerbeds were bare, with only a few thin dead stalks sticking up out of the mud. A cluster of purple and white crocuses, the first brave flowers of spring, huddled against one wall. Their faces were partially closed on the cloudy day. A spacious deck ran off French doors at the left side of the house. Orange tarps protected stacked outdoor furniture from winter storms. A large gas barbeque, judging by the shape, was covered, but placed close to the door, ready for action.

It was a beautiful home, probably well beyond the pay of a police sergeant. Rumor said Mrs. Winters had pots of money.

The front door opened. The woman herself peered out, looking over a pair of reading glasses pulled down her nose. She saw Smith watching. Smith half-lifted her hand to wave, but put it back on the steering wheel. Should she go in search of Madison, tell him Mrs. Winters had answered the door?

But he was back. He climbed the front steps, spoke to Mrs. Winters. She stepped aside to let him in. She looked at the patrol car, once again, and shut the door.

Madison wasn't inside for long. He let himself out, and Smith didn't see Eliza Winters again.

They drove down the twisting road, back to the highway that followed the river and over the big black bridge into town. "To the hotel?" she asked.

"You're a local, Smith." She was surprised he knew anything about her, including her name.

"Born and raised."

"Do you know what Sherlock Holmes said about the countryside?"

"No."

"'The lowest and vilest alleys in London do not present a more dreadful record of sin than does the smiling and beautiful countryside.' *The Adventure of the Copper Beeches.*"

"The great detective never came to Trafalgar, sir. I think he'd find it peaceful here. Most of the time."

"I'm not interested in what happens here most of the time. Drop me back at the hotel. I have an appointment to see the grieving widow."

She pulled up to the hotel entrance. Madison made no move to get out of the car. The silence lay between them, long and uncomfortable. Peter Wagner, the hotel manager, stood on the steps talking to guests. He didn't look pleased to see the patrol car parked out front. A reminder of what had happened in his hotel only days ago. "Friends with Sergeant Winters, are you?" Madison said at last.

"Me? Heavens no."

"I heard you were close."

"You did?"

"His wife denies killing Steiner. She would, wouldn't she? She says he was alive when she left his room that night. She also says he wanted to photograph her and was rude when she told him no. I can't help wondering if photograph is a euphemism for something else."

Smith had no idea why he was telling her this.

"My first wife," Madison said bluntly, "was a slut. We lived in a small town in Saskatchewan. She screwed half my colleagues before I realized what was going on. Until I came to my senses and divorced her, I might have done some damage to any guy I found with her." He opened the door and went into the hotel.

Smith sat in the car, stunned. *What the hell?* What was there about talking to Mrs. Winters that made Madison think about Sherlock Holmes and sin? Was he warning Smith to stay clear of Winters? He couldn't seriously be suspecting John Winters of the killing. Could he?

That last statement sounded as if he were dismissing her. She checked her watch. What with the upset stomach in the night, then the worry about her dad, she hadn't eaten all day. She'd stop for a quick sandwich before going back to the station.

The Sunshine Grill was the closest place to the hotel. Smith parked the patrol car in a no-parking space and went in. The place was full, all the tables taken. A row of strollers lined the walls and babies bounced on parents' laps and toddlers ran around the room, dodging people ferrying food and drink to tables. Although there was a long line in front of the cash, no one was in much of a hurry. The woman making the lattes and cappuccinos, who looked about to give birth any minute, chatted to a man with a beard almost to his chest and a tattoo, in full color, of a Canadian flag on the back of his bald head. The boy taking orders described, in great detail, the provenance of the ingredients in each of the cookies to an elderly woman in twin-set and pearls who kept asking him to repeat himself.

Smith took a place in line and studied the chalk board displaying the menu. She was debating between the smoked salmon bagel and the curried chicken wrap when her sixth-sense prickled. She turned her head to see Meredith Morgenstern at a table in the back corner. The reporter was with an older man, dressed in a very good suit, and a skinny young woman. The woman wore a crisp white blouse, with several buttons undone, and tailored jeans. Her legs were crossed and a shoe with a heel like a knife blade dangled from her toes.

Smith and Meredith had been in high school together. They'd hated each other back then. Now that one was a cop and the other was, in Smith's opinion, an interfering journalist of the sleazy sort, their relationship hadn't improved.

She'd find a place with a better class of clientele.

"Molly, hold on a minute," Meredith called.

Smith bolted for the street. The last thing she needed was to be seen talking to Meredith Morgenstern. As Denton had said, the Chief was on the warpath, and his quarry was Meredith's informant.

"Wait up." The reporter skirted tables and brushed past chairs. People gave her questioning looks and stepped aside to let her by. A young boy pulled his cup of hot chocolate, precariously topped with a mountain of whipped cream, out of the way with barely enough time to avoid disaster.

Smith stopped. She could hardly run down the street, pursued by loud-voiced journalist. She'd look ridiculous.

"What do you want Meredith? You must know you're *persona non grata* for the police today."

"Can I quote you on that, Moonlight?"

"No." *Not another word,* Smith told herself. *Don't say another word.*

"I'm wondering if you can make a comment for the press? I couldn't help but notice you driving Sergeant Madison earlier. What's the status of his investigation?"

Meredith's table companions had joined her. The man held out his hand. Smith instinctively took it.

"Larry Iverson. Pleased to meet you, Constable."

The skinny woman dismissed Smith with a glance.

"I have nothing to say, Ms. Morgenstern."

"I was telling Larry and Mrs. Steiner what old friends we are. Sorry to hear about your dad."

Mrs. Steiner. Smith eyed the woman with new interest. So this was the widow. She didn't look too broken up, but then again you can't judge by appearances. Iverson must be her father.

"The department will make a statement to the press at the appropriate time, Ms. Morgenstern. My condolences on your loss, Mrs. Steiner."

"Thank you."

"Nice meeting you, Constable," Iverson said.

Meredith didn't follow when Smith walked away.

She was unlocking the door of the patrol car when a woman ran past. Tall and thin with an overlarge nose and hair cut boyishly short, she wore loose jeans, a baggy jacket, and well-used running shoes. Her sharp features were set into tight lines, and her eyes formed narrowed slits. "What the hell are you playing at?" she yelled when she reached the group on the sidewalk.

She stabbed one finger into Mrs. Steiner's abundant chest. "I'm talking to you, you fucking bitch."

Meredith's ears almost visibly stood up, like a dog when he heard a sound on the wind.

Mr. Iverson said, "Now see here, young lady."

"You're next, buddy," she said. "Those pictures are mine, and I want them back."

"Diane," Mrs. Steiner said, with an expression as if she'd stepped into a steaming pile of dog poo, "Larry will explain the situation."

"There is no situation." The woman poked again, hard enough to make Mrs. Steiner totter on her ridiculous heels.

"That's enough." Smith walked over. "I suggest you go somewhere and talk this over in private."

"I assume," Iverson ignored the police officer, "you are Diane Barton, Mr. Steiner's assistant."

"I was a damn sight more than an assistant and I want my pictures."

People stood in the café doorway watching. Across the street, a dog finished peeing against a lamp post, but his owner made no move to continue on his way.

"Miss," Smith said. "You're creating a scene. I'm asking you to move along."

"I don't give a flying fuck what you're asking me to do. In fact, you can arrest her. She's stolen my property."

"Okay, let's go to the station and sort this out."

"That's hardly necessary," Iverson said. "Miss Barton, you must realize it will take time for the family to go through Mr. Steiner's possessions. The police gave Mrs. Steiner his papers and his cameras back yesterday. In light of his tragic death, his photographs may have some considerable value and…"

"My photographs. That decrepit old man hasn't taken a picture worth five cents in years. She's going to pretend they're his and sell them." Spittle flew, propelled by the woman's rage.

Smith touched her arm. "I'm going to have to ask you to come with me, Miss."

"Will you mind your own business," Barton yelled. Turning, she shoved Smith in the chest, hard. Taken by surprise, the policewoman stumbled backwards.

"I don't think…" Iverson began.

Barton punched Mrs. Steiner in the face. Quicker than she looked, Mrs. Steiner pulled her head to one side, and instead of breaking her nose, the blow glanced off her cheek. With a scream so piercing she sounded like the banshee of Irish legend Smith's Grandmother Casey had told her about, Steiner flew at her attacker. Her blood-red nails were as sharp as knives. She went for Barton's eyes. Barton lifted her arm and blocked the hand, but Steiner's other hand slipped in to scrape down her opponent's right cheek. Blood spurted, and Barton screamed.

"Break it up." Smith pushed the button to activate the radio at her shoulder and shouted for assistance. The crowd was growing, fast. Someone yelled that he had twenty dollars on the tall one. Smith threw herself between the two women. They continued the fight around her. Barton swung at Steiner's face, blood flowed from the woman's nose, and she was back again, red nails outstretched and moving like claws on an attacking grizzly bear. They were both howling abuse, at each other and at the policewoman. Smith hooked her foot around the back of Barton's knee and pulled. The woman went down, knocking into the one leg Smith was using to hold herself up. She crashed to the pavement, landing hard on her butt. Shock raced up her spine into her head, and stars danced in front of her eyes. She could hear a siren, very far away.

"Who hoo," a man shouted. "Now they've gone and done it. Forty dollars on the bitch with the nails."

"My money's on the cop. Shoot 'er, Molly."

"I've called 911," someone a bit more helpful said.

With her opponent on the ground, Steiner moved in. Her feet moved as fast as a dancer's, her heels were high and the toes of her shoes sharpened to a point. She managed to plant one good kick in her enemy's ribs before Smith's head cleared. She grabbed a flailing foot and twisted and brought Steiner down. The woman looked at her. Her face was ugly with hate, and bloodlust moved behind her eyes. Mascara ran down her cheeks in a river of black, her nose was bleeding, and her carefully tousled hair was just tousled. She swung her right hand, and pain streaked across Smith's face. She launched herself back to her feet and pulled the baton off her belt. With a practiced flick of the wrist, it extended.

Red and blue lights washed the sidewalk and the sound of sirens was everywhere. Steiner and Barton were on the ground, rolling together like lovers. Larry Iverson hopped from one foot to the other, his mouth open in shock.

"Break it up," a man's voice said. Dave Evans grabbed the woman on top, Steiner, by her hair and dragged her away. She swore as she landed on her feet, and swung toward Evans, but he caught her hand. "Don't even think about it." He flipped her around, pulled her wrists together, and snapped handcuffs on.

Sergeant Winters looked at Smith. "Okay?"

"I'll live," she said. She stood over Barton, and waved her baton. "Is this over?" Barton wiped the back of her hand across her mouth and nodded. "Good. Get up," Smith ordered. When the woman was standing, Smith cuffed her.

There must have been a hundred people watching. A sizeable crowd for an April afternoon in Trafalgar. Meredith was holding a camera up. She must, Smith thought with a spurt of anger, have gotten some good shots. Meredith saw the policewoman watching her, smirked, pointed the camera directly at Molly Smith and pressed her finger. Smith turned away.

Evans' car was half on the sidewalk, lights flashing. Winters had come in the nondescript blue GIS van, now parked in the middle of the road. Drivers leaned out of their cars, gawking.

"You can remove the cuffs, Constable," Iverson said to Evans. His suit was still perfectly clean, his cuffs and tie straight. "I am this lady's lawyer. I can assure you she won't cause any trouble." His voice was tight with anger, and, judging by the look he gave his client, she was in for a stern talking to.

"I don't think so," Evans said.

"Constable Smith," Winters said. "Where's your vehicle?"

She pointed.

"Come back for it later. Go with Constable Evans and take these *ladies* to the office."

"Yes, sir," Evans said.

"I'll come with you," Iverson said.

"You can follow, if you must," Winters said.

"My client…"

"Is under arrest for assaulting a police officer."

"Hey, I didn't hit her." Mrs. Steiner tried to play insulted innocence, but she couldn't pull it off. "She just got in the way."

"Tell it to the judge," Evans said.

"Interfering bitch," Steiner said.

"Don't say another word, Josie," Iverson warned her.

Smith and Evans stuffed the two women in the back of the car. Smith was afraid they'd start kicking each other, but they sat down and said nothing. Mrs. Steiner tried to give Evans a flirtatious smile, but it didn't look too good with the blood and mucus all over her face.

Winters waded into the multitude to take details for later statements if necessary. Most of the spectators gathered around, happy to contribute, a few slipped away.

Charlie Bassing stood on the steps of the hairdresser next door to the café. He was laughing, and made the thumbs up gesture at Smith. He came down the steps and swaggered away.

Over the roof of the car, Evans studied her face.

"What?" she said.

"Hope your tetanus shots are up to date."

Chapter Fourteen

Molly Smith eyed herself in the mirror, and didn't like what she saw. The cut across her cheek wasn't too deep, but it had bled, and Smith had been told to take care of it while Evans processed the two women. Those fingernails should be registered as lethal weapons. As she'd pulled Steiner out of the car, she'd noticed with a small tinge of satisfaction that half the woman's nails had broken off.

Better put some anti-bacterial on the cut. No telling where those fingernails had been. The thought made her stomach move, and she leaned over the sink. She breathed carefully, paying attention as each breath moved in and out, and when she felt stronger she lifted her head, and turned the water on to scrub off the dried muck. Her rear hurt where she'd ignominiously landed on it.

She and Adam planned on going to the hospital tonight to visit Andy. Her father and Adam seemed to like each other and got on well. Lucky, who had not been pleased when her daughter joined the police, wasn't too enthusiastic at having a cop as a potential son-in-law, but Lucky's earlier attempt at matchmaking had gone so disastrously wrong she accepted Adam with warmth.

Smith hated to think what Adam and her dad would have to say about her face. She touched the wound, now clean. She could plaster the make-up on, but that was so out of character they'd immediately know she was trying to hide something.

She could only hope Meredith didn't put a picture of Molly Smith, flat on her butt on the sidewalk, face covered with blood, all over the front page of the paper. If so, they'd be putting Lucky into a bed beside Andy's.

Larry Iverson was at the front desk, demanding to see his client. Jim Denton nodded and typed at his computer. John Winters came through the doors, having taken down names and numbers of people to talk to later about the incident.

"You'll have to wait until Mrs. Steiner has been processed. I'd suggest you come back in half an hour."

"To whom am I speaking?" Iverson asked.

"Sergeant John Winters."

Iverson introduced himself and said, "You have no reason to hold her, Sergeant Winters. Mrs. Steiner has suffered an enormous shock at the *murder* of her husband and…" His eyes narrowed as the penny dropped. "Winters. Oh, yes. Your wife is a suspect in that case, I believe. This is outrageous. I demand Mrs. Steiner be released immediately. Clearly, you're not going to be impartial in any matter regarding the wife of your wife's…*friend.*"

Winters walked away. He passed Smith, his face set into angry lines.

Iverson pulled out his Blackberry. "I have some calls to make," he told Denton. "I'll be back shortly."

"I've no doubt about that," Denton said to Smith. He studied her face. "Doesn't look too bad."

"I'm going to have a long soak in a tub of steaming bleach. God, what a couple of harridans."

"I can hear the lawyer now—grief does that to a woman."

"Being a mean bitch does that to a woman," Smith said. "I'm going downstairs, see if Dave needs a hand. They're probably trying to get his pants off even as we speak."

◇◇◇

John Winters logged onto his computer. His eyes felt like sandpaper and his head was stuffed with cotton wool. Despite what he'd told Barb, the couch in the interview room was not at all comfortable. He intended to keep both Steiner and Barton in jail until they could get to court. One of them had hit Molly

Smith, and assaulting a police officer was not a charge Winters took lightly. Never mind causing a major disturbance in the center of town and requiring three officers to subdue them.

But the ink was scarcely dry on their fingers before the Chief Constable came running down the stairs to the cells. Iverson had wasted no time in telling him that Mrs. Steiner, the *grieving widow,* had been arrested two days after her husband's murder. How would that look? he asked. Winters couldn't care less how it looked. Iverson had, with more subtlety than his foul-mouthed client, threatened to go to the papers to point out that one of the arresting officers was personally involved in her late husband's case.

And that, the Chief Constable agreed, would not look good.

Therefore Josie Steiner was released into her lawyer's care with orders not to leave town and to appear in court when demanded to do so.

They could hardly hold Barton, faced with lesser charges, having released the woman with money and a good lawyer. Perhaps it was time to retire, Winters thought, rubbing the back of his neck. He and Eliza could…Eliza. He couldn't ignore her forever. His initial anger, his pure white wrath, at her involvement with Steiner had ebbed. Now he just wanted to go home and find out what the hell was going on.

But he couldn't do that.

Keller had suggested he take some vacation; Winters reminded him they had a spate of high-profile B&Es going on, and department resources were strained with the Steiner investigation. Keller agreed, reluctantly.

"We can't afford any more suggestions that this department isn't completely impartial in the way we enforce the law," he said.

Winters assured him he'd run a mile if he saw Josie Steiner coming his way.

He touched his chest. The picture was still in his pocket. Madison hadn't said anything about it, which meant Eliza hadn't told him. Why? Because it didn't matter? Or because it was so incriminating it mattered a lot?

Winters had only seen Steiner either curled up over a toilet with the back of his head missing or lying on the coroner's stretcher before the sheet was placed over his face. Not the most flattering of circumstances, but the man didn't look like he'd have much appeal to Eliza. Unhealthily thin, flabby flesh indicating he'd lost a lot of weight too fast, balding, bulbous red nose. Why would she have been in his hotel room for a *tête-à-tête* over *Moët et Chandon* and a cheese plate?

Was he threatening to blackmail her over the picture? Did she think she had to give in because if her husband saw that picture he'd react…exactly the way he *did* react?

Or, did she decide not to give in to the blackmailer's demands and sort the problem out another way?

Impossible. Calm, rational, level-headed Eliza coming up behind a man and blowing his brains out? Impossible.

If he loved Eliza and believed in her love for him, he had to trust her enough to let her tell him what had happened between her and the dead man.

He wanted to go home. To curl up in bed with the woman he loved and forget all about Rudy Steiner and Dick Madison.

But as long as Madison remained in town, Eliza under suspicion, that was not going to happen. He wondered if it was time Eliza found herself a lawyer.

His e-mail program beeped. Incoming. Doctor Shirley Lee, the pathologist.

The results of the Steiner autopsy.

No one had thought to tell Dr. Lee Winters had been ordered to stay away from anything to do with the case. Dr. Lee was all business, all the time, and would be unlikely to ask Madison and Lopez, who'd attended the autopsy, where he was. Madison, for whom the term taciturn had been invented, might not have mentioned it, and Lopez, in a rage over the insult to his boss, wouldn't have.

As always, Dr. Lee had copied Winters with her results.

He opened the file and skimmed the report.

The subject, an underweight Caucasian male in his mid-fifties, had died of a single gunshot wound to the head. Time of death...blah, blah, blah...description of injury...blah, blah, blah...last meal...blah, blah, blah...Existing conditions... Winters went back and read that part again.

The shooter had merely hastened Rudolph Steiner toward his appointment with death. He had a brain tumor, a sizable one, inoperable. Three months to live—tops—was Doctor Lee's opinion.

Winters leaned back in his chair. On the window sill, Lopez's carefully tended African violets stood in a neat green and purple row, the only touch of color in the view. Gray clouds hung low over the mountains, hiding the glacier. One window in the office building across the street was open, trying to let in an early touch of spring air. Lace curtains fluttered in the breeze.

Steiner had to have known he wasn't long for this world. What did people do when they knew they were dying? Theoretically, they tried to make amends, to make up to people they'd fallen out with. Was that why Steiner had contacted Eliza after all these years?

What else did dying people do? They made or adjusted their will. Perhaps someone didn't want Steiner to change his will. Mrs. Steiner? No need to wonder if she was capable of violence. The evidence was written on Molly Smith's face.

He'd get a warrant to take a peek at Steiner's will.

No, he reminded himself. He wouldn't do anything. If he even suggested Madison open the will, he'd be accused of interfering.

He'd have to trust that the IHIT team could do their jobs.

His phone rang, and he answered.

"John, what on earth is going on over there?"

"Hi, Rose. I'm well, how are you?"

"This call isn't about me. Eliza. There's a story going around saying Eliza's involved in a homicide investigation."

"Sadly true," he said. "She knew the guy, that's all. The story in the paper is wildly exaggerated."

Inspector Rose Benoit had been Winters' partner when he first made detective. She was still with the Vancouver Police

Department, but had an office job now, investigating serious fraud cases. Her solve rate was impressive, and she seemed to be thriving behind a desk, buried in numbers. Winters and Eliza had dinner with Rose and her husband, Claude, whenever they got a chance. Claude was a well-known, and highly controversial, sculptor, a match ridiculed almost as much as cop and model. Perhaps that was why they'd stayed friends.

"That's good then," she said. "The idea's preposterous. Do you have a leak in your department?"

"A bad one. Heads are going to roll. Providing they catch whoever it is."

"That's not the least of your problems. I hear you've arrested a lady by the name of Josephine Steiner for assaulting a police officer."

"How the hell do you know that, Rose? The revolving door is hitting her on the ass right about now."

"I have a flag set for anything to do with her maiden name."

"Which is?"

"Marais."

"Oh, I thought you were going to say something that means something."

"It means something to me. Guy Marais runs a well con-nected organization. Very well connected to our friends in New York, if you take my meaning. He's been moving into the lower mainland over the last year, slowly but surely. All low key stuff, money laundering, extortion, a bit of protection. His daughter, his only daughter, Josephine, aged twenty-one, wanted to be a model but no matter how much pressure her father could bring to bear she was thwarted in that ambition. So she did the next best thing and married a glamorous fashion photographer who goes by the made-up name of Rudolph Steiner."

"Not so glamorous any more. I've seen his autopsy photos. Which I'm not supposed to have access to, so keep that under your hat."

"Kept."

"Have you heard of a lawyer name of Larry Iverson?"

Benoit whistled. "Ooh, yeah."

"Probably not because he can be counted on to side with the police and defend the downtrodden, eh?"

"Iverson is Marais' west coast lawyer."

"He's in Trafalgar, running interference for the daughter."

"Understandable. Marais is not going to be happy that his dear Josephine is caught up in the police spotlight. Not happy at all."

"She turned that spotlight directly on herself by getting involved in a punch up in the street in broad daylight and assaulting an officer."

"She's the apple of her daddy's eye. He has four sons, all involved in the family business, but like the old-fashioned crime families, he keeps his females out of it. He might feel the need to come to your town to check up on her. I'll keep you posted, John."

"Unofficially."

"Right. Can I call Eliza, say hi? Is she at home?"

"I don't know, Rose. I haven't spoken to her since this broke."

"That," she said, "is probably a mistake. I'll get Claude to phone her." She hung up.

◇◇◇

Sergeant Madison was not happy. He stormed into the constables' office as Smith prepared to go home.

"You," he said. "Could have told me."

"Told you what?"

"That Mrs. Steiner had been arrested."

"I'm sorry, sir," she said. "I didn't think you needed to know."

"I told you I had an appointment with her."

"I apologize, sir, but I was rather busy."

"Learn to multi-task," he snapped, "if you want to get anywhere in this job."

She bit her tongue and pushed her chair away from the desk.

"You said you've never met Mrs. Winters," he said. "Is that correct?"

"If I said it, then it is correct."

"Don't get smart with me, Constable."

"Suiry, sir."

"What's your impression of Sergeant Winters and his marriage?"

"What kind of a question is that? I have no impression of Sergeant Winters' marriage whatsoever. I've never been inside his house, never met his wife, never seen his holiday snapshots. I don't even know if he has a cat."

She might not have spoken.

"Would you suggest his marriage is a happy one?"

"I wouldn't suggest it is or it isn't. I don't know. Why are you asking me these questions?"

"In a long-time marriage, I've found, if one party is playing away from home, the other usually is as well."

She stared at him as understanding dawned. She stood up, and spoke before thinking. "Just because your wife screwed around on you, doesn't mean everyone else's wife is doing the same. Don't try to drag me into your nasty insinuations."

"Am I making insinuations, Constable?"

"Fuck you, buddy." She grabbed her jacket off the rack. The sleeve stuck on the hook and she struggled to get it off, anger making her clumsy. Finally it came free and she half-ran out the door. When she looked back over her shoulder, she suspected Madison was smiling.

Chapter Fifteen

Ray Lopez was not a happy man. This had to be the worst case he'd ever worked on. Not only was his boss' wife a suspect, and his boss removed from the case, but the IHIT Sergeant was a single-minded idiot. Madison seemed to have settled on Eliza Winters as the killer, and all he cared about now was gathering evidence to support his assumption.

Some people, Lopez thought, watched too many movies. No way could the gentle, soft-spoken Eliza kill someone.

He looked at the list of names in front of him. Almost finished interviewing the hotel employees. To his disappointment, no one had noticed anyone on the second floor at the time in question. No one but the room service waiter, that is. Other than the one man who thought that, maybe, he heard a noise that might have been a gunshot over the sound of his TV, no one heard anything either.

But someone had been on the second floor—someone had shoved Steiner's face into the toilet and shot out the back of his head. Someone, Lopez suspected, who'd taken care not to be observed.

He glanced at his watch. Almost seven. His second daughter, Amanda, went to the University of British Columbia in Vancouver. She was home for a couple of days before heading to Europe for three weeks, and then starting her summer job planting seedlings in the northern forests of Ontario. Lopez had met her boyfriend once and hadn't liked the sullen young man one bit. He wasn't happy Amanda was going to Europe with this guy, or that the reason she wanted to spend the summer in Ontario was because her boyfriend had gotten them the jobs. Amanda was smart and had big plans for her future. He didn't want to see that messed up by some lazy lowlife who kept all his brains in his pants. He needed to spend some time with her, find out how serious she was about this guy, and remind her, without appearing to do so, that she had the whole world ahead of her. She left tomorrow, and he'd been so tied up with this case he scarcely had time to say "hi". One more call to make, and he'd be able to get off home. Take Amanda out for a drink and a nice father-daughter chat.

Winters had the GIS van, but Lopez didn't bother to call for a ride as his destination wasn't far from the hotel. He set off at a trot toward town. The police radio had been busy with the bust-up between Josie Steiner and Diane Barton. Both women taken into the station, charged, released. He wouldn't say he was surprised. If Lopez had to lay bets on the cause of Rudy Steiner's demise, his money would go on the widow. She was about the same age as Amanda, and a nastier piece of work he'd rarely come across. It was raining and he ducked under storefront awnings and dodged puddles as he made his way down the street.

Trafalgar Thai was busy on a Thursday night, and a cluster of people were standing inside the door, shaking off rain and waiting for tables. Lopez excused himself and pushed his way to the front. The phone beside the cash register rang as he reached the desk, and a pretty young woman dressed in black skirt and white blouse snatched it up. She lifted one finger to the detective, telling him to wait. She pulled a pencil out from the knot of hair in the back of her head, and began to write. It was a take-out order, a long one, with much discussion about what went with what and how many people each dish would feed. Lopez adjusted the collar of his jacket to get the wet part away from his neck, shifted on tired feet, and studied the room. The scent of hot food and potent spices mingled with wet wool and tramped-in mud. He stepped aside to allow a large group, Mom, Dad, Grandma, about ten kids, leave.

"Wanting a table, Mr. Lopez?" The waitress asked. "Be about fifteen minutes."

"Not tonight, thanks, Lynne," he said. The girl was a friend of his third daughter, Marlene. "I need a couple of minutes of your time."

She pushed back a lock of hair, and exhaled. "We're really busy."

"Won't take long. Were you working Monday night?"

"Yes."

"Then I'd like to speak to you."

"Okay. Let me seat these people first." She picked up menus, put on a smile, and told the cluster of people standing in the doorway their table was ready. She was back a minute later, wiping her hands on the sides of her skirt. "Do you want Mr. Chen too?"

"Yes, please."

She led the way into the back, sticking her head into the kitchen as she passed. A man joined them, carried along on a wave of spicy steam and cooks' chatter. He was small with black hair slicked back and nicely dressed in a black suit, white shirt, and grey tie. "Police?" He looked alarmed.

Lopez gave what he thought was a reassuring smile. They went into an alcove beside the kitchen. The room was piled high with all the detritus of running a food business, leaving barely enough space for the three people to stand.

"Monday night," Lopez said. "Around eight-thirty. I'm wondering if you noticed a woman. She would have been alone, ordered shrimp rolls, pad Thai, couple of beer." Mr. Chen looked blank.

"Woman," Lynne said as she mimed someone eating. Her boss smiled and nodded energetically. Lopez doubted he was nodding because he recognized the feeble description.

"She was in her early twenties. Five-eight, hundred and thirty pounds, round about. Short dark hair, little or no makeup. Probably wearing glasses. Jeans and a blue sweater. Oh, and a silver ring on every finger."

Lynne thought for a few minutes. "I can't be sure, Mr. Lopez. We get so many people in here, they're all a blur, but not a lot of women on their own. Maybe. Yeah, maybe, I saw her. She sat in the window booth, I think. Okay, it's coming back. She had a lot of beer. I think she had two before the pad Thai was even served, and then a couple more. She took her time over her meal and was here for a while. Can't be sure it was Monday though."

"Pad Thai," Mr. Chen said with a smile. "Good."

"Very good," Lopez, who got a take-out lunch from the restaurant at least twice a week, agreed.

"Were you working Saturday and Sunday also?" he asked Lynne.

"No. I was in Kelowna with the swim team on the weekend."

"Can you estimate the time she was here?"

Lynne thought. "It's coming back. I light the candles on the tables soon as it starts getting dark out. She had her face buried in her beer and glared at me when I leaned across her. So eight, eight-thirty, would be about right. I'm pretty sure it's the woman you're describing, I noticed all the rings."

He thanked them for their time, and Mr. Chen escorted him to the door. "Killing," he said over a handshake, "bad."

Bad, Lopez thought. Very bad, indeed. Diane Burton had told them she'd eaten at the Trafalgar Thai Monday night after eight. Which would have been at the same time her boss was in his hotel room, ordering Champagne for Eliza Winters and being murdered. Burton had paid in cash, and didn't keep the receipt. She got a per diem from Rudy when they traveled, she'd explained, so didn't need to account for her meals.

He walked up the hill, back to the station, to get a ride home. Still time to take Amanda out for a drink and some father-daughter time. Lynne's identification of Diane hadn't been positive, but it was close, and she wasn't sure it was Monday night. Again, close enough. She hadn't been working on the weekend, so couldn't have seen the photographer's assistant then. Tuesday and Wednesday evenings, they knew where Diane Barton had been. So Monday it was, as she'd said. And darn close to the time her boss was being killed.

◇◇◇

Meredith looked up from her computer at a shout from Joe Gessling's corner. His father, the previous editor of the paper, believed in keeping an eye on everything, and he'd ripped down all the internal walls long ago. Joe, wanting to appear too important to have a desk out on the floor like everyone else, had arranged the bookcases around his desk in an attempt to give himself some privacy.

He came out, not looking happy. "Are you crazy?" Everyone in the office turned to stare.

He marched toward Meredith's desk. She'd filed her story on the fight outside the Grill and was preparing to head out again. She hoped to resume her interrupted conversation with Josie Steiner. No doubt Steiner would be more than happy to spread muck on Diane Barton. Not noticing that she was spreading it on herself as well.

"You've gone too far this time, Meredith," Gessling said.

She batted her eyes. "Gee, Joe. What do you mean?"

The staff weren't even pretending not to listen.

"I went out on a limb with that story of yours about Mrs. Winters because your source seemed good. Although I'm damned glad I didn't let you say Winters had been fired. Now this piece, it's downright inflammatory."

"I told it like it was, Joe, that's what good reporters do." She made a point of opening her desk drawer and taking out her purse. "Night, all," she said, standing up.

"This isn't a news story, Meredith. It's a personal vendetta against Constable Smith."

"Okay," Meredith said, knowing she had to give some ground. "Drop the picture. I think it adds a touch of human interest to the story, but if you're afraid of offending the Chief Constable…"

Gessling's eyes began to bulge. "I'm not afraid of offending anyone. I'm pulling this whole story. It's not news."

"Not news! Are you nuts? Two women close to a man murdered in our town get into a street brawl and you think that's not news? You wouldn't know news if it rose up and bit you on the ass."

The arts editor laughed out loud and the receptionist smothered a giggle. Gessling shot them a furious glare and they quickly returned their attention to their computers.

"The Chamber of Commerce meets tomorrow morning, and in the afternoon Mrs. Atkins is giving a talk at the library about her new book. I want a full story on each of those events."

"You are kidding, right? You want me to drop the story of the year for a businessmen's snooze-fest and the launch party for a self-published book about an old broad's years teaching in local schools?"

"Yes," he said. "That's precisely what I want. Not another word about the Steiner people until the police have made an arrest and certainly not any inflammatory pictures of one of their officers."

She was aware that although the staff might be staring at their computer screens, no one was hitting a single key. She looked at Gessling. He was a weedy little guy, all Adam's apple and knobby elbows, but for the first time she saw some fire behind his eyes.

"No," she said. "I will not give up on this story."

"Then you're fired," he said. He walked back to his desk behind the bookcases.

Meredith lifted her head high and picked up her purse. "I will be back tomorrow for my things," she said, as she headed out the door.

A wave of conversation followed her.

◇◇◇

John Winters pulled up in front of a cheap motel on the outskirts of town, the smell of Chinese food drifting out from a Styrofoam container resting on the seat beside him. This time of year the parking lot was mostly empty. The Vacancy sign was on, the 'V' burned out.

He should have gone someplace where no one would know him, but that would put him too far out of town. He still had to work, and even though he wasn't supposed to have any involvement with the Steiner case, he intended to be close by if something broke. He rubbed his head, picked up his food, and got the small bag containing the few toiletries he'd bought earlier out of the back seat.

The man behind the desk looked up when the door opened. He was reading a magazine and stuffed it quickly out of sight, but not before Winters caught a glimpse of pale flesh and breasts like balloons. He shot to his feet, eyes narrowed in apprehension. Winters suppressed a sigh. He'd arrested the man a few months ago for flashing a couple of schoolgirls. The girls, rather than fainting or screaming like panicked maidens, had laughed and pointed and used their cell phones to first take a picture of the offence and then to call 911. The pervert was well known to the police and quite recognizable in the pictures.

"Do you have a room for a couple of nights?" Winters asked, placing his supper on the counter.

The man, emitting the sour smell of teeth unbrushed and clothes unwashed, grinned. "We're almost full up," he said, drawing the words out, "but I guess I can find one of our finest rooms just for you, Sergeant."

Winters filled out the form, took his room key, and turned around to see a newspaper box with the front page of the Gazette prominently displayed.

Chapter Sixteen

"Earth to Moonlight."

She cradled her cup of coffee. "Don't call me that."

"It's cute."

"So is a litter of mongrel puppies, but they don't make good cops either."

"You're more than a cop, you know."

"No, I'm not. I'm a constable third class and I'm a woman, so if I ever want to be more than a constable third class, I've got to be all the job, all the time."

He shot her a look. "You're wrong, Molly."

"What would you know about it?"

"Lighten up, will you. I thought it would be nice to have breakfast together before going to visit your dad. I don't know what's eating you, but keep up with this mood, I can tell you Andy would prefer you don't bother."

She rubbed the back of her neck and her face twisted.

"Sore?"

"Yeah, I must have slept crooked."

"You need someone to watch your back when you sleep."

Molly Smith cracked a smile at that. Her neck hurt, but she'd been pleased to look in the bathroom mirror this morning and see that the cut on her face was almost invisible. The waiter arrived and put plates piled high with food in front of them. "More coffee?"

Adam pointed to his cup. "Please."

"Moon?"

The smile disappeared. "No."

"You'll always be Moonlight to people in this town," he said, reaching for the jam. "Don't fight it."

She took a breath and thought about telling Adam her thoughts about getting other jobs, moving away. But this wasn't the time, or the place.

"I don't have to like it," she said. She placed her hand in the middle of the table. He took it, and they looked at each other. His dark brown eyes were warm with love, and the bruise on his jaw was fading. All around them the clatter of the busy restaurant carried on. The woman at the next table complained that she'd said no onions, someone shouted for more coffee, the glass in the front window rattled as a group of laughing boys on the street tapped to get their friends' attention.

"Excuse me?"

Smith looked up. A man with a belly like a nine-months pregnant woman was trying to get by. She sucked her own stomach in and pulled her chair closer to the table. The man squeezed past.

"I am sorry, Adam," she said, picking up her fork. "I'm worried about my dad, and my mom, who's taking this so hard. Things at work aren't exactly a laugh-a-minute what with..." Conscious of the crowded restaurant, she lowered her voice. "You know."

He leaned back to allow the waiter to fill his cup, and when he looked at her again, she was chewing on scrambled egg hash. He sighed and cut a slice of bacon. She almost told him about Charlie Bassing, watching her yesterday at that fight between the women, but something held her back.

He talked about a course next week. Some further training for Norman at the RCMP dog service center in Alberta. "I was going to suggest you come," he said, "get away for a couple of days, maybe stop in Banff for a night on the way back, but not with your dad's op still up in the air."

After that they chatted about nothing much at all, and by the time breakfast was finished, her mood had lightened considerably. "I'm sorry I was so snappy," she said once they were on the street. "I shouldn't be taking things out on you."

"That's what I'm here for," he said.

She smiled. "No, it's not." She stood on tip toes and kissed him on the mouth. He laughed and put an arm around her and pulled her close.

"I have to go into work this evening," she said, breaking away. He took her hand and they began to walk toward his truck. "Winters wants me asking more questions about the B&Es. He's got a real bee in his bonnet about it."

"Keeps his mind busy, I'd guess," Adam said. "Do you think his wife did it?"

"I don't know her, but really, I can't imagine Sergeant Winters being married to a homicidal manic, can you?"

"No."

It was early, but the sun was already warm. There was nothing quite as wonderful as spring sunshine after a long, hard winter. It bathed the town in a joyful yellow glow, had people merrily tossing off heavy winter clothes, dried up the mud, made everyone happy. Outside the craft co-op, someone had planted a tub of cheerful purple and yellow pansies. Their faces were turned to the sun, in exactly the same way as those of the people walking past. Smith had chosen to wear beige capris and sports sandals today. Jumping the season, but it felt great to be out of coats and boots.

She thought for a few moments, and chose her words with care. "That Madison, I'm worried about him. He's looking for something to point to Mrs. Winters' guilt. Or, perhaps even better…" she needed to tell Adam that Madison had hinted that she, Molly Smith, was inappropriately involved with the Sergeant. The idea was ridiculous, but she'd better warn Adam in case whispers started.

"Officer Smith, I'm glad I ran into you." It was Diane Barton.

Smith let go of Adam's hand. She wasn't about to be friendly with Barton. First thing this morning, she ran down the street to buy a paper. Nothing about the fight outside the Sunshine Grill, she'd been pleased to see.

"If you have something to say, Ms. Barton, please go to the station and make a report."

"No need," Barton said. "I'd like to apologize. That was so unlike me yesterday. I've never been in a fight in my life."

Adam moved away, giving the women some space.

"Can I buy you a coffee?"

"No." Smith kept walking. She could feel the comforting bulk of Adam behind her, keeping pace.

"Okay, but I want to explain." Barton walked slowly, limping slightly, probably from the kick to the side Steiner had given her. Instinctively, out of politeness, Smith slowed to match the woman's pace. Two deep scratches ran in parallel lines down Barton's right cheek, beginning close to the eye.

Smith could see Adam's truck in the next block. The light turned red and she stopped. "One minute."

"Thanks," Barton gave her a smile, probably trying to look friendly, but it didn't reach her eyes where traces of yesterday's dark anger still lingered. "It's nice of you to give me some of your time. Is that your boyfriend?" She smiled at Adam and gave him a wiggle of her fingers in a wave. Sunlight bounced off the silver rings on every digit. Adam didn't return the wave, nor the smile. "Nice catch. He's a cutie. I'm really sorry about what happened. I didn't want you to be involved, you know, it was her, that insufferable bitch." Barton's voice began to rise as the smile died.

"Your minute is almost up."

She almost visibly took control of herself. "Sorry. I'm, I mean I was, Rudy's assistant. I'm a good photographer myself, a lot better than him, truth be told. As well as helping Rudy by scouting locations and carrying his equipment and all that, I've been taking shots myself. Some of them are good, really good, and I think I can sell them, maybe start getting noticed. I printed them out and showed them to Rudy Monday night. He wasn't at all interested in helping me with my career, he never gave a second's thought to anyone but himself, but he had a good eye and he knew what was marketable."

"I'm sorry, Ms. Barton, but if you know something about the death of Mr. Steiner you should be talking to the detectives, not to me."

"I don't know anything about that. I want my photos back. I left them in his room on Monday night. He said he had some ideas. They were scooped up with all his stuff by the police. And given to her. She's going to say he took them, and sell them. His pictures will be worth a lot more money now he's dead. And they'll be worth even more if they're good—and they are good because I took them. His stuff was pure crap."

Knowing she shouldn't be involved, Smith couldn't help asking, "Surely you use a digital camera? Print another copy."

The light changed and she crossed the street. Barton limped along behind.

"It'll be my word against hers. She has money and serious connections. She gets those pictures published and even if I take her to court and win it'll be too late to do anything with them."

Smith couldn't imagine Josie Steiner having connections to anything but the latest gossip blog. "Take my advice. Stay out of her way. You're not helping your case being up on charges."

"Easier said than done," Barton said. "They owe me money, my pay, my expenses."

"Get a lawyer."

"How am I going to pay for a lawyer?" Her voice began to rise. "Tell me that. I don't…"

"Good-bye, Ms. Barton."

Barton's glasses were streaked and the cut on her face was red and angry. She looked as if she were going to continue arguing; instead she said, "Thanks for nothing," and walked away, her steps hard and determined, but still leaning to one side.

Smith grimaced to Adam and shrugged her shoulders. They got into the truck and went to the hospital.

Sam hadn't met Adam yet. Molly introduced them and they shook hands beside Andy's bed. The window sill was full of flowers. Lucky had snatched the tables next to the empty beds and used them to hold potted plants and get well cards. Smith flicked through the cards while Adam and Sam made getting-to-know-you chat. All the cards were from Lucky's friends. Like many men his age, Andy didn't really have any friends of his own.

He looked better, she thought; the pain medication must be working. He had more color in his face and his cheeks had lost some of that god-awful gauntness. His thin gray hair was freshly washed and combed. Sun streamed through the window, and the spring light made everyone look good.

"Any word about the operation?"

Lucky was smiling at Adam. *Hearing wedding bells?* Smith wondered. She was pleased he hadn't tried to intervene in that strange conversation with Diane Barton. He had stood aside and let her get on with it.

"Monday, they're saying," Lucky answered. "Let's hope. Those poor children from the accident put everything behind and some more serious cases got moved ahead of your dad. It looks as if all the kids are going to be okay, so we can be grateful for that."

"If I don't get out of here soon," Andy said, "they'll be transferring me to the mental hospital."

◇◇◇

Ray Lopez concentrated hard on keeping his professional face in line. Not to please the good citizenry, but to stop from slugging the RCMP Sergeant.

Madison had told him he was running a weapons check on John Winters.

"Waste of time," Lopez said.

"We'll see," Madison replied.

Lopez blew out a lungful of air. They'd almost finished on the second floor. Steiner, his wife, and his assistant's rooms had been gone over with, literally, a fine-tooth comb. Other than Steiner's bathroom, they'd found plenty of nothing.

It was reasonably conclusive that Steiner had been killed in his bathroom, shot in the back of the head as he crouched over the toilet. There had been no indications of a fight, no defensive wounds, no signs of restraint on the body.

Lopez had read the autopsy report. Steiner didn't have long to live: all the killer had to do was wait a couple of months and save himself a heck of a lot of mess and bother.

Did the killer not know that, or did he have reason to want the death to be hurried up?

Lopez reminded himself the proper phrase was *he or she*.

Winters had told him, very unofficially as he wasn't supposed to know anything, Mrs. Steiner was a mob-daughter. Lopez phoned Rose Benoit, got the official version, and told Madison. Who hadn't appeared to be particularly interested. Benoit also told Lopez that one of Marais' lieutenants had been spotted in the Vancouver airport, waiting for a flight to Castlegar, the airport nearest Trafalgar. She doubted he was en route to a hiking vacation in the mountains.

Lopez thought about the mob angle. Was it possible Guy Marais had decided to hasten his son-in-law's death? It was definitely possible, but did he have reason to do so? The initial peek into Steiner's financial situation didn't look promising. Unless he had hidden money, and it was early days yet, the guy didn't have much. Which didn't stop him living as though he did. Luxury condo in False Creek, a matching pair of BMW convertibles for running around the city. Mrs. Steiner was well known in the antique and high-end decorating shops for having a lavish budget although not much taste.

The mortgage on the condo was almost the worth of the property itself and both cars were financed to the max. The man's line of credit was more than Detective Lopez's annual salary. Not much of an inheritance.

"Waste of time," he repeated.

Madison glared at him, but did not respond. They walked into the police station. It was the end of the working day on Friday. Most of the nine-to-five staff had gone and the night shift had yet to rev up. The office was quiet.

Madison had his regular end-of-the-day meeting with the Chief. Lopez, notably, had not been invited.

He went to the GIS office he shared with John Winters and tossed his jacket on the hook by the door. He was relieved that Winters wasn't in. Then he felt guilty for being relieved. This had to be darn tough on the man. Lopez studied the row of African violets on the window sill. He took his watering can down the hall to the lunch room, filled it, and came back to give the plants a drink. He checked each one out, nipped a few dying flowers off, removed a leaf browning around the edges. Satisfied with the condition of his small garden, at last he sat down to the computer to write up a report on the day's findings.

Madison had been asking some strange questions about Molly Smith and John Winters. Questions like how often Winters asked the young constable, the *pretty* young constable to assist him, and whether they'd ever been seen together *outside* of working hours.

Lopez growled. They were cops, they didn't have working hours.

If Adam Tocek got wind of Madison's insinuations, there really would be a punch up.

He wondered if he should have a word with the Chief. Mention that Madison seemed fixated on Eliza and John Winters to a point that he, Lopez, thought was distracting from the investigation.

No. Not yet. Wait and see a while longer.

He worked at his desk, continuing to run background checks on the list of people in the hotel at the time in question, the hotel staff, the other second floor guests.

He sat up straighter as he finally hit on something of interest.

Dennis Jones, the hotel maintenance man, had a series of drunk and disorderlies, four months in jail for his second charge of driving under the influence, six months for a bar fight that resulted in injuries. An all around nasty, but small time, guy, who, after his last stint in jail, decided to leave Nova Scotia and grace the town of Trafalgar with his presence.

Maybe the man had changed—he hadn't been in any trouble in Trafalgar. More likely he just hadn't been here long enough.

Lopez's index finger moved toward to the mouse button, about to consign Dennis Jones to the files, when he saw something that made him hesitate. Jones had been born in Sydney, Nova Scotia. Where had he seen that name recently?

He opened another file, and sat back with a low whistle. Rudolph Steiner, nee Albert Jones, born in Sydney, Nova Scotia. He checked the two men's birth dates. Three years apart. Jones was a common name, but Sydney…he quickly googled it…was a small place. About twice the size of Trafalgar. Still, entirely possible there were several Jones families living there at the same time.

He picked up the phone.

Chapter Seventeen

Molly Smith was also wearing her professional face. At seven o'clock she was back in uniform and doing the rounds on Station Street where last week's break-in had occurred. More houses, more questions, more people who hadn't seen a thing. Winters had been in the office when she checked in. His shirt was badly rumpled and his mustache not as neatly trimmed as usual. He barked at her and told her he wanted every person on that street questioned.

There was no news about the murder investigation. Not that she'd heard, anyway. She probably wouldn't hear until something broke. She didn't see Madison, and was glad about that.

In an affluent neighborhood, most people were happy to be helpful to the police. Some had nothing to contribute, but wanted to be seen as helpful, nonetheless. There were always a handful who thought giving her a lecture on how the evils of the parole system, or the leniency of judges, even the removal of "the strap" from schools, had caused an increase in crime. She smiled, thanked them for their time, and moved on.

A harried young mother, vaguely familiar, came to the door directly across from the house which had been burgled. Two toddlers, twins by the look of them, well-scrubbed and pajama-clad, tugged at the bottom of her stained and faded T-shirt while a baby fidgeted in her arms. A small brown dog circled her ankles, overcome by excitement at having a visitor, barking his greetings. Its intelligent brown eyes were rimmed in black as if drawn with eyeliner. Women spent hours to get that look.

"What?" the woman at the door said, sounding as irritable as she looked.

"Sorry to bother you ma'am," Smith said, "I'm investigating a problem that occurred on this street last week—Friday night—and I'm wondering if you noticed anything unusual, say after dark."

The woman gave her a weak smile. "I don't have time to notice an earthquake open up a crack in the middle of the street. Anyway, I was on nights last week. Too bad they had to postpone your dad's op. Waiting is always the worst part." Now Smith recognized the woman, she was a nurse at the hospital, coming on duty about the time visitors were leaving.

"I understand," Smith said.

"My husband would have been here. Jason," she nodded down to the left, to the red headed boy, cheeks full of freckles, making faces at his twin by pulling his lips apart and sticking out his tongue, "had a cold and was up most of the night."

"Is your husband at home?"

"Yes," said a voice, "I am. Jeremy, I'd strongly advise you not to hit your brother. Here," he said to his wife, "give him to me." He took the baby, and the older boys ran in circles behind their mother.

Jeremy, or maybe it was Jason, reached toward Smith's gun. "I'm gonna grab this and shoot you," he said.

She swiveled her hip out of range. "You can't. It's got a secret lock on the holster."

"Oh," he said, disappointed. "Does it work?"

"No."

"They work on TV."

"Don't believe everything you see on TV."

"Why not?"

"Why not, indeed," the woman said, "I'll take these guys out of your hair. Come on boys, one cookie and then time for bed." They dashed off, more interested in food than Smith's equipment. The dog followed, probably in hopes of cookie crumbs falling to the floor.

"Keeps us from getting bored," the man said, and Smith laughed.

"I'm Frank Spencer, and I'd shake hands but they're kinda busy." He shifted the baby and wiped a trickle of drool off his face. "You're wanting to know something about the previous Friday night?"

"April 7th. I'm wondering if you saw anything unusual, particularly late at night. Your wife said you were up."

"I haven't had a proper night's sleep in three years," he said. "Can't remember why I thought having kids would be a good idea."

In the background, one of the twins began yelling that he wanted another cookie.

"Yes, sir," said Molly Smith, deciding never to have children.

"I was up with Jason, who was pretty sick, as Marianna told you, most every night that week, but I wasn't looking out the window. I'm sorry, Constable."

She handed him her card. "If you think of anything?"

"Sure, I'll let you know. I'm guessing you're investigating the robbery across the street, right. My neighbor was telling me about it."

"Thank you for your time," she said.

She heard the door close, shutting out the sound of the baby starting to cry, as she walked down the steps, heading for the next house. *What a complete waste of time.* She might have more luck if it were summer, people gathering in backyards having parties, barbeques. A lot of these gentrified old houses had front porches decorated with swings and wicker furniture, and residents sat out on warm nights.

Not in early spring, when the night air still brought snow down from the mountains, and rain fell sharp and cold. People in Trafalgar didn't sit in their windows at night, binoculars at the ready, spying on the neighbors. About her only hope would be to find a late night dog walker. Someone who'd seen a figure clad all in black, scaling a wall with a black face mask, a long rope and a sack bulging with loot tossed over his shoulder.

Bloody John Winters. Why was she the one trudging around the streets because his wife had found herself in a compromising position?

She rang the next doorbell.

◇◇◇

Smith had left the patrol car at the end of Station Street. It was after nine o'clock when she walked toward it. A piece of paper had been slipped under the windshield wiper. Without much interest, she pulled it out. It was dark and the streetlight was weak. She shone her flashlight onto the paper.

Someone had sketched a happy face in yellow crayon. The thing you saw everywhere: round circle with two dots for eyes and a wide smile. The artist had added something extra.

A red dot was drawn in the center of the forehead and smaller red dots dripped down the face to run off the edge of the page.

Chapter Eighteen

Ray Lopez kissed the most beautiful woman in the world. Overcome by emotion he kissed her again.

She laughed. "That's enough, Dad. I'm going to Ontario, not the ends of the earth."

All of his daughters were beautiful, in Lopez's opinion. The most beautiful was the one standing in front of him at any given moment.

Alone of their four daughters, Amanda resembled her father. But on her, he thought, it was beautiful, not geeky. Vibrant red hair, scattering of freckles across pale cheeks, eyes the color of the open ocean on a sun-drenched summer's day.

"Ontario or the moon, take care, eh?"

His wife, Madeleine, smiled. "When have you ever known a nineteen-year-old to take care?"

"There's always a first time." He slammed the trunk of the car shut while Amanda climbed into the passenger seat. Madeleine gave him a light kiss and joined her daughter.

As the family car waited at the top of the driveway to turn into the street, Amanda twisted around and gave her father a smile and a thumbs up.

He grinned and went to work feeling good.

Dennis Jones hadn't been at home last night when Lopez called. He'd checked with the hotel and was told the maintenance man would be at work today, even though it was a Saturday. Like crime, stopped toilets didn't pause for the weekend.

The assistant manager was a young woman, small and pseudo-cheerful in the way you knew she was being friendly only because it was her job to be so. Her name badge said Maria Fernanda Sanchez—Spain. Presumably Spain because that was where she was from. She greeted him with the lightest of accents. When he introduced himself, Detective Lopez, she gave him a genuine smile and switched to rapid-fire Spanish. Sorry to disappoint her, he had to confess he couldn't speak a single word of that language. It was embarrassing sometimes. Particularly on the phone, people assumed he spoke Spanish. He knew nothing about his natural family, except that they had to have come from Ireland somewhere along the line with that coloring, and didn't particularly care to. The Lopezes were Mom and Dad, Grandma and Grandpa. Even they, dark-eyed, dark-haired, dark-skinned, had been in Canada long enough that Mexico was nothing other than a place to go for a holiday.

"Sorry," he said to Ms. Sanchez with a shrug, "We'll have to speak English."

"That's okay," she said, fake smile returning. He wondered if she was lonely in this foreign country, missing the liquid flow of her own language. "How may I help you?"

"I'm looking for your maintenance man, Mr. Jones. He's at work today, I understand."

"That's correct."

"Will you take me to him, please."

She carried a radio on her belt. She pulled it out and asked Mr. Jones to reply.

They took the back stairs down to the basement. The corridor was long and gloomy, lit by forty-watt bulbs. No need to waste electricity. Lopez was always interested in what public places looked like behind the scenes. As with people, they often dropped their façade of respectability the moment appearances no longer mattered.

They found Jones in a storage room, standing on a ladder, attaching a screw to a shelf. The shelf had presumably fallen, bottles of ketchup were stacked haphazardly on the floor and a couple had rolled against the wall. The room was lined with shelves, piled high with kitchen supplies: bags of sugar and flour, tins of coconut milk, bottles of oil and vinegar. It smelled of dust and stale spices. One wall was taken up by a white freezer large enough to walk in.

"Yeah?" was Jones' greeting. The bib of his overalls was heavily stained, the knees frayed. Thick deposits of dirt were trapped under his ragged fingernails and torn cuticles.

"Couple of minutes of your time, Mr. Jones," Lopez said.

"I'm busy." He looked down and nodded at Ms. Sanchez. "She runs a tight ship."

Lopez spoke to the assistant manager. "Thank you. I'll find my way out."

She hesitated and, with a glare at Jones, left.

Jones returned his attention to the shelf.

"If you can leave that for a couple of minutes, Mr. Jones."

The man hesitated long enough to make his point and slowly descended the ladder. His face was dark and hostile, and he held the screwdriver clenched in his hand, like a weapon.

"I'm only wanting a chat," Lopez said. "It'll take a lot longer if we go down to the station, but if that's what you'd prefer."

Jones dropped the screwdriver and it rang against the bare concrete floor. The shelf teetered against the unattached screw, but stayed in place.

"Tell me about your brother," Lopez said.

"He's dead."

"I know. I was at the autopsy."

Jones shrugged. The straps of his overalls moved. He was wearing a short-sleeved black T-shirt. Multi-hued tattoos covered his arms.

Lopez sighed inwardly. He'd get the answers to his questions, eventually, but it was going to take a lot of teeth pulling.

"You didn't tell me Mr. Steiner was your brother."

"You didn't ask."

"I'm asking now."

"He was my brother in that we had the same parents and were kids together, but that was it. The last time I saw him was at our mother's funeral, twenty some years ago. Flashing his money around, big car, high-maintenance wife—not the same woman he brought here. He'd changed his name, too fancy for a proper working man's name like Jones, I guess. Rudolph," the man snorted. "I always expected him to show his true colors one day and show up with a pretty boy on his arm. What kind of a man calls himself Rudolph? He went to the church, said hi to Dad and me. Could hardly bear to shake our hands. He carried around a bottle of that stuff you spray your hands with. You see it more these days, like at hospitals, but that was a first for me. It was a real insult, I can tell you. Man shakes your hand and then has to wash himself." Jones' face was set into dark lines and storm clouds moved behind his eyes. He clenched and unclenched his fists and his shoulders looked as if he were getting ready to punch someone. No need to be a detective to see that there was a powerful animosity between these brothers, probably dating from long before their mother's funeral. "Mom was active in her church and the ladies put on a nice spread after the service. Al, damned if I'll call him *Rudolph*, came to the reception. Stood there for a few minutes, with his hands behind his back, saying hi to folks who'd known him when he was a kid. He left when I wasn't looking. Didn't say good-bye. The sexy wife, never did get her name, stood in a corner with her nose stuck in the air the whole time. Dad said he was surprised Al'd even bothered to show up. He didn't come five years later when it was Dad's funeral. I thought he might, though, if only to spit on the grave. I kept looking around the church wondering if he was going pop up with his bottle of hand washer."

"Your mother's funeral wasn't the last time you saw him," Lopez asked, "was it?"

"Last time until the other day."

"Did you know he was coming here?"

"He didn't even send a card to Dad's funeral. We didn't exactly keep in touch, is what I'm trying to tell you, Detective. So no,

I didn't get a nice letter saying he'd be in town and why didn't we get together with the wives and down a few beers and toss steaks on the Q after work."

A long, complicated answer, Lopez thought, to a simple question.

"When did you first see him?"

"When they were checking in. I was heading for the bathrooms in the restaurant, plugged toilet, water all over the floor. The ladies who come here for a nice lunch don't like to get their feet wet when they're having a shit. He was with two women, two young women, and I thought, lucky guy, wonder if he needs some company. Then he turned around, and I knew it was him right away. He looked like hell, but it was Al."

"How do you mean, he looked like hell?"

"He's my younger brother." Jones shivered and some of the lifelong anger faded from the set of his shoulders. "But I hope I've aged better than that. He looked like he was a hundred and ten. Tell you the truth, Detective, he looked like our father the day he died. Fuckin' scary." If suddenly aware he was being sentimental, Jones cracked a joke. "Guess doing two women at once'll do that to a guy. Not that I'd know."

"You think Mr. Steiner was having a sexual relationship with his assistant?"

"Nah. Just imagining." He winked. "I don't know who Al was screwing. None of my business."

"You recognized Mr. Steiner as your brother when he was checking in. Then what happened?"

"Nothing."

"Nothing?"

"Not a damned thing. He looked right through me and went to the elevator, his harem trailing along behind. He recognized me though. I could see it in his eyes, the prick, too high-and-mighty to acknowledge his brother 'cause he wears working man's clothes."

"Did you see him again?"

"Next thing I knew the cops were all over the place, and the boss was having a fit. He's a heart attack waiting to happen, I can tell you. Someone told me a man had been murdered on the second floor. Didn't even know it was my own beloved brother until I overheard his name mentioned. His fake name that is. He couldn't even die under the name Jones. No loss to me. Look that's all I know, okay. I have to get back to work. That ball-breaking wop'll be on my case fast enough." He realized what he'd said and panic flashed across his ugly face. "No offense eh, Mr. uh...Lopez."

"Why didn't you come forward with this information? Tell us Mr. Steiner was your brother."

"Didn't think it mattered."

"This is a murder investigation, Mr. Jones, we'll decide what matters."

"I'm guessing you've seen my record. I've got a good job here, trying to stay out of trouble, but I don't go out of my way to come to the notice of the cops."

Lopez refrained from mentioning that by not telling the police of his relationship with the dead man, he'd brought a lot more attention onto himself.

"The day your brother was killed, where were you around eight, nine o'clock?"

"I've told you all this."

"Tell me again."

"I was on afternoons. There's always some shit to be done around this place. You've no idea how fuckin' fussy some people can be. Expect someone to drop everything and come up to their room in the middle of the night because the window is squeaking."

"You were fixing a window?"

"No, that's just an example. I don't know what I was doing at that time, but I was here because I work here, get it? I've got a steady job, an apartment, and you're giving me grief because I was actually at work and not in a bar, knockin' some heads together." He punched his right fist into his left hand, as if illustrating what he'd like to do to Lopez's head. "Fuckin' cops, you're never happy."

"I'm hardly giving you grief, Mr. Jones. I'm asking a simple question."

Jones took a deep breath, visibly making the effort to get himself under control. Probably learned some anger-management techniques in jail. "And I gave you a simple answer. I was working, so I was in the hotel. I don't remember doing exactly what, but I keep a log and hand it in at the end of every shift. They'll have it in the office. I told you I had a lamp to fix on the second floor, but that was earlier."

"Did you go into your brother's room at any time?"

Another breath. "I've been in most every room in this place at one time or another."

"Were you in Mr. Steiner's room while he was staying there? It's only been a week, surely you can remember that."

"No." He looked Lopez in the eye.

Liar.

"If you leave town, let us know where you can be contacted." Lopez handed the man his card. "Thank you for your time."

Jones' right eye twitched as he dropped the card in the pocket of his overalls.

Lopez took the stairs to the main floor. He'd have to go back to everyone he'd questioned earlier and ask a new question. Did anyone see the maintenance man on the second floor around the time Steiner died?

Jones said he didn't care about his brother one way or the other, but his body language and expressions and weak attempts at jokes told Lopez a different story. Hard not to be jealous of a younger brother who'd done okay in the world, money, prestige, glamour, trophy wife, when you were a washed up ex-con plunging out toilets and hanging shelves.

Whether it was instinct or the ability to tell a lie when he heard one, Lopez knew Jones had been in his brother's hotel room. Maybe nothing more serious than having a peek around, see what his long-lost brother had been up to for all these years.

But maybe more, much more, than that. Did Jones ask Steiner for money? Did he ask only for acknowledgement? Or did he let loose with the resentment of a lifetime and settle the score once and for all?

If the forensic tests came up with a match to Jones in Steiner's bathroom it would be worthless. As the guy said, he had good reason to go into every room, every nook and cranny, in this hotel as and when he needed.

◇◇◇

Meredith Morgenstern sipped her white wine. It was crisp and clear and reminded her of summer, sitting out on a sun-filled deck overlooking the blue waters of Kootenay Lake. It was perhaps the best wine she'd ever tasted. Her budget didn't normally run to this sort of thing.

Josie Steiner had ordered and the bottle sat in an ice-filled bucket at the side of the table. She'd almost finished her first glass.

"I'm not entirely sure why you've invited me to lunch, Mrs. Steiner. The paper is, of course, interested in the story of Mr. Steiner's brutal murder. The citizens of Trafalgar are shocked that this could happen in our town. We covered your husband's death quite extensively and will continue to do so when the murderer is caught and brought to trial." Meredith had decided that, for the time being, she wouldn't mention she was no longer employed by the *Trafalgar Gazette*. If Gessling didn't want this story, she would try to do something with it on her own, sell it freelance perhaps.

She didn't have much time. She had nothing in the way of savings, her credit card was at the max, and she wasn't eligible for employment insurance because she'd been fired. She had to make some money fast, or she'd be forced to go to her parents for a handout just to pay the rent.

Josie yanked the bottle out of the cooler and poured herself a healthy shot. She was looking rather nice today, Meredith thought. Her dress was dark blue, hemline cut to the knee and all but the top button done up. Her shoes were flat pumps, her make-up had been applied with a light hand, the overwhelming perfume was gone, and simple silver hoops in her ears were her only jewelry. Meredith suspected the outfit was new; Iverson had probably sent Mrs. Steiner to the store to buy something appropriate for the new widow to wear in public.

"If you're worried about that," Meredith coughed, "other business, *The Gazette* isn't interested." She stopped talking to allow the waitress to put her Asian chicken salad on the table. Mrs. Steiner had ordered a bowl of clear vegetable soup.

"Rudy was famous," Josie said, "I would have expected there would be more coverage of his death in the national news." By which Meredith assumed she meant she'd rather deal with a bigger paper, but had to settle for Meredith Morgenstern and the *Trafalgar Daily Gazette*. She wasn't offended—she'd rather deal with the major media too.

"He deserves a nice, big splash," Josie said. "A feature story. Perhaps you could print some of the pictures he took of famous people. He photographed Naomi Campbell for Vogue. Of course that was before I met him. It would be nice if some of those people could say how much they liked working with him, don't you think?"

Meredith chewed chicken and thought. "The *Gazette* editor isn't likely to be interested in something like that. Rudy wasn't local."

"He died here, isn't that local enough?"

"Unfortunately not. I could put something together, though. Those magazines you mentioned, they might want to run a piece, sort of a memorial."

Josie Steiner grinned. "A tribute to Rudy. They'd like that. Then once it gets out, no doubt the TV stations would consider doing a documentary. I called, well, I called a couple of places, but they weren't interested in talking to me. They don't know me, so I thought of you. You're a journalist, you'd do a good job. Do you have a photographer you work with?"

"Yes, I do." Meredith didn't mention her photographer was a kid working part time while he went to college. She also didn't mention that one didn't normally take pictures for a memorial article. The person Mrs. Steiner had in mind was clearly intended to photograph the widow. Meredith had no interest in generating publicity for Josie Steiner, but at the moment she didn't have anything better to do.

The waitress returned. "Can I freshen your drinks?" she said.

Meredith shook her head, but Josie held hers up for more. She hadn't touched her soup. "Where's Mr. Iverson, your lawyer?"

"At the police station, wasting time on that other nonsense." Meaning her arrest on the charge of assaulting a police officer. "He…uh…he isn't too keen on my idea for this story," Josie said. "So I'd prefer you don't mention it if you're talking to him."

"Why?"

"He thinks we should downplay Rudy's death, because… well, because he was murdered. Larry works for my father, you see, not for Rudy and me. My father doesn't like publicity. I'd appreciate it if you keep this between us." The look she gave Meredith was almost pleading.

Josie appeared to be upset more because the media wasn't taking calls from the Widow Steiner than her husband's death. That didn't bother Meredith; lots of people didn't care for their spouses. Had Josie realized that her husband, instead of being her introduction to the glamorous world of fashion and photography, was an anchor around her ambitions? Easy enough to leave the guy, but then she would have been back where, presumably, she'd started, namely nowhere. Had Josie decided she needed a nice burst of publicity to get the limelight focused on her?

And if so, how far had she gone to get that limelight?

Meredith sipped at her own wine. That might be a story worth pursuing.

◇◇◇

Lucky Smith splashed water onto her face. Mustn't let Andy or the kids know she'd been crying. She straightened up, slapped on a smile, and studied herself in the mirror. She looked exactly like a woman who'd been crying and was trying to hide it. She splashed more water.

Two more days until Andy's operation. She didn't know how she was going to survive. *If something went wrong.* More water as she reminded herself that this was the twenty-first century and a modern hospital. People had operations all the time, and lived for many years after.

She cracked a smile.

Not good, but it would have to do.

When Lucky came out of the washroom, Samwise and Moonlight were coming down the hall. She carried a cardboard tray with four coffee cups and he swung a paper bag bulging with treats. Sam said something and they laughed together, and Lucky was pleased to see her children being friends. From this distance, Samwise looked so much like Andy when they'd first met. Lean with long arms that swung at his side as he walked and long, long legs, which gave him a loping gait. His cheekbones were prominent in a thin face, and the nose turned slightly to the left. The young Andy had worn his blond hair down to his shoulders and a Fu Manchu mustache; Samwise's hair was black and cut very short and his face cleanly shaven. His eyes were brown, like those of Andy's mother.

It was Moonlight who had inherited her father's blue eyes and blond hair the consistency of cornsilk.

Moonlight saw their mother watching and grinned. She lifted the coffee tray in greeting and said something to her brother. Samwise winked at Lucky. The years fell away and it was Andy Smith tossing her a wicked wink from across a crowded lecture hall.

Lucky burst into tears and ran back into the washroom.

Chapter Nineteen

When Molly Smith arrived on Saturday afternoon for her regular shift, she found a message waiting for her. Frank Spencer had called. She couldn't remember who he was at first, and then it came to her: the homeowner on Station Street, up at night with a sick toddler. She called him back, but got an answering machine. She left a brief message before heading onto the streets. She was on the beat tonight, and it would be her job to walk up and down Front Street and into side streets and alleys, keeping the peace. Later, when the bars started filling up, she'd pop in regularly, show the flag.

The early part of this shift could be darn boring. She knew the contents of every shop window in town, and could set her watch by the time the retired guys from the electrical union gathered on the bench in front of city hall. April was quiet in Trafalgar. The resort at Blue Sky closed the first week of April, and skiers and snowboarders headed out of town in a stampede. The summer tourists were yet to arrive, and nights were still too cold for locals to spend much time outside.

Two young people were sitting outside Crazies, a coffee shop at the east end of Front Street near the tourist center. The girl was dressed all in black, her hair shaven to the scalp, except for a patch, dyed brilliant purple, running across the left side of her head. A row of rings ran up both of her ears. She was thin, dressed in faded black tights and a black T-shirt. Her fingernails were painted with black polish, badly chipped. His clothes were ill-fitting, patched many times, and his hair hung in lank strands around his face. The boy had multiple piercings through his lips. Smith shuddered. *How utterly repulsive.*

No crime in looking repulsive, but they were sitting on the curb, holding coffee cups, their feet sticking out into the street. If a car came by hugging the curb they'd know it.

Smith stopped beside the boy. "You'd better move or you'll get run over."

He turned his head and looked at her boots. His eyes moved up, following the blue stripe at the side of her pant leg. When he eventually reached her face she could see that his eyes were clear, the pupils normal sized. "Fuck off, cop," he said in place of a greeting. "It's still a free country, and I'll sit where I want."

"Not my feet going be mashed into pulp when a truck pulls up, but no one wants to clean up the mess. Please, get out of the road."

He sipped his coffee and turned his attention back to the opposite sidewalk. The girl hadn't reacted at all.

"Miss," Smith said. "Will you move your feet off the roadway, please."

People came out of the coffee shop, some stopped to watch.

"You're new to the area," she said. "A couple of things you need to be aware of. This is a small town, the police keep a good eye out, and we're always around. I walk down this street a lot, so you can be certain of seeing me again, many times. It would not be a good idea to make my acquaintance first time by making me haul your asses off to jail."

"What is this, a fuckin' police state? We're just sitting here, not bothering anyone. You can't arrest us for that."

"You are creating an obstruction," Smith said, "and I will arrest you for that if you don't take my advice and move."

Without a sound, the girl rose to her feet like a stream of water flowing back into the tap. "Not a problem," she said. "We've places to be. Come on, Lloyd."

The boy hesitated. Smith guessed he didn't want to be seen as backing down in the face of authority. "Five seconds," she said, "and I'm calling this in."

"Don't be a jackass," the girl said.

He took it slow. He lumbered upright, keeping his feet firmly placed in the street. A SUV swerved around him. He smirked and stepped back onto the sidewalk.

"Very sensible," Smith said, turning to the young woman. "What's your name?"

"None of your business," he said.

"I'm Constable Smith. As I said, you'll be seeing me around a lot, if you decide to stay."

"Margaret. That's Lloyd."

"Margaret and Lloyd. Stay out of trouble."

She walked on, thinking *that went well*. Potential troublemakers and she'd brought them into line with a couple of well placed words. Hopefully, her mention of the constant police presence would encourage Margaret and Lloyd, particularly Lloyd, to take up residence elsewhere. She pulled her notebook out of her pocket and made a quick note, reminding herself to write up an informal report on the incident when she got to a computer, to let everyone know Lloyd might be looking to make trouble.

The rest of the afternoon passed peacefully. She gave visitors directions, swooped up a toddler who made a dash for freedom—and the traffic—when his mother's attention wandered, helped an old lady pick up some coins that spilled when she fumbled in her wallet for change for the newspaper box. Mostly she accepted greetings for her dad.

She really would like to have a job that didn't involve giving updates on her father's medical condition.

She walked on, thinking about how badly shaken she'd been finding that note stuffed under the windshield wiper of her patrol car. Back at the station, she'd made an entry in her record of Charlie-incidents, put the note into a plastic evidence bag, labeled the bag with date and time, and slipped it into her locker. So far he'd done nothing that couldn't be called a juvenile prank, and she didn't have proof Charlie was responsible. Anyone could have killed the rat, or left the drawing.

She knew it was Charlie, and she knew he wanted her to know it.

She hadn't slept well, tossing and turning and trying to decide if she should tell Staff Sergeant Peterson, her boss. Peterson was a good guy, although bit straight-laced, but he could be pretty old school, and Smith wondered, sometimes, if he didn't entirely approve of women on the job. She knew a large part of the reason Dawn Solway hadn't come out of the closet was because she suspected Peterson was a homophobe. Smith had thought Dawn was finding prejudice where it didn't exist, but now she thought about some of the off-hand comments Peterson had made, and wondered. Would he tell her to stop acting like a nervous girl and get some balls before crumpling up the bleeding smiley-face and toss it in the garbage?

As she slept she made up her mind to keep quiet for now about Charlie. She could not chance Peterson, or anyone else, thinking she was over-reacting.

She peeked through the window of Mid-Kootenay Adventure Vacations. Her brother Sam was inside, behind the counter, reading a magazine. He looked up when the bell over the door tinkled.

"Not busy?" she asked.

"Flower had to take the afternoon off, so I'm minding the place. Good thing it's the off season, with Dad laid up and Mom spending all her time at the hospital. I'm glad you're here, got a minute?"

"What's up?" Her radio crackled and she held up a hand while she listened. MVA in Upper Town. Not her call.

"We need to talk to Mom, find out what kind of insurance they have on this place."

"Insurance? Why?"

"In case…well, I mean, you know, in case one of them…dies. Neither of them can run the business on their own, at least not at first, in case it's…sudden."

"Geeze, Sam. I don't want to talk about this."

"Of course you don't, neither do I. You're a cop, Molly, of all people you should know people die." He looked her up and down. "It doesn't suit you, that uniform. It makes you look hard. Tough."

"It's supposed to."

"That's not who you are, not what you're like."

"I doubt you know much about what I'm like."

"How serious are you and this Adam guy? You're not just looking for a replacement for Graham, I hope."

"I thought we were talking about our parents' insurance?" Sam was several years older than she, and when they'd been growing up, he'd always acted the possessive big brother. It hadn't taken him long to slip back into that role. Far from making a replacement for Graham, Molly's late fiancé, she'd resisted Adam's attentions for a long time, afraid it would be a betrayal of Graham, and today she bristled at Sam's assumptions.

"I want you to be okay, Moon. Judy thinks becoming a cop is your way of getting revenge on the people who let Graham die. She…"

"She doesn't know a goddamned thing about anything."

"I don't want to see you making a mistake with your life, that's all."

"Are you and Mom some kind of a tag team? She finally stops ragging me about my career choice and now you're stepping in. Screw you, Sam. Sorry I dropped in. Go back to your magazine."

She began to turn around. He held up his hands in supplication. "Calm down. I'm sorry. I was out of line. Forgive me?"

"If I must," she said, having forgiven him already.

"Even though you look like a storm trooper in that outfit, you're still my baby sister. Remember the time you went as a cop on Halloween? I wonder if that was some sort of premonition."

"That was your idea, not mine. I wanted to be a princess. Dad was away and Mom made you take me around." She laughed, the memory warm in her belly. "You didn't want to, but made the best of it by dressing as a convict in striped pajamas and chains, and making me be the cop."

He smiled at her, a quick flash of white teeth before the smile faded and he was back in lawyer mode. "About the insurance. We need to find out what kind of pension arrangements they've made. If the store fails because they can't keep it going, do they have enough to live on? I suggest a family meeting tomorrow. Before the surgery. Are you working?"

"I'm off, but I doubt Mom's going to agree to us sitting around Dad's hospital bed talking about how much money she's going to have if he dies."

"Most people are afraid to face their mortality. It's our responsibility to make sure Mom and Dad know what their options are."

"Five-one, five-one?"

"Five-one here."

"911 call from Rosemary's on Front Street. Woman left without paying. Are you nearby?"

"Next door. I'll be right there." She turned to her brother. "Gotta go. Storm trooper assistance required. If I'm lucky, I'll find someone to dress in striped pajamas."

Rosemary's Campfire Kitchen was a catering business, specializing in hearty outdoor fare vacationers could prepare quickly over a campfire. The small store with attached kitchen was located next to Mid-Kootenay Adventure Vacations, and both businesses benefited from the proximity. In the off-season, Rosemary concentrated on preparing take-home meals and office lunches. She also stocked a variety of snacks and wilderness food such as nuts and trail mix and granola bars.

As Smith walked into the store, she radioed "10-15." *On the scene and all is okay.*

"That was quick," Rosemary said.

"I was next door."

"Sorry about your dad, Molly. I've been meaning to take a casserole over for Lucky. Why don't you take it when you leave?"

Smith groaned to herself. Walk out bearing a fragrant meal and some do-gooder would accuse her of taking a bribe. "Thank you, but no, I'm here on business. You called 911?"

Rosemary tugged at her long gray ponytail. She was in her fifties, but Smith knew she biked a good ten kilometers or more to work every day, most of it up the mountainside on the way home. She wore shorts and her legs showed the result of all that exercise. "It's that girl again. I probably shouldn't have called you, but I've really had enough."

"Enough of what? What girl?"

Rosemary began arranging bags of nuts and chocolate. The bags didn't need straightening, but it kept her hands busy. "She has a somewhat loosy-goosy approach to the concept of paying for one's purchases. She doesn't mean to actually steal. I shouldn't have called, I'm sorry, Molly. Forget about it." She thrust a bag of trail mix at the constable. "Here, take this for your trouble."

"Rosemary, I don't need to be paid off, and it wasn't any trouble. Look, why don't you just tell me what happened, and we can decide if you want to take it further?"

Not the first time she'd been called by someone who immediately wanted to retract the complaint. Often there was another call, far more serious, not long after.

Rosemary blew out her cheeks. "Okay. It's hard enough running a small business, I'm sure you know that, without people making it harder. It's been a really bad day. I guess that's why I got so mad. But you don't want to hear about my bad day.

"Do you know a girl named Amy? I'm afraid I don't know her last name. She works at the Doggie Daycare place sometimes. She's, well, mildly mentally handicapped."

"I know her. She has a son and lives with her brother, Mike." Smith knew Amy quite well. Amy, being what they called moderately-functioning, had gone to the same high school as Smith. Molly had occasionally provided extra assistance for her. Amy still visited the Woman's Support Center, where Lucky volunteered, for help with her year-old son, Robbie. Smith had heard Amy now had a part-time job walking dogs for a new business that catered to busy, or lazy, pet owners. It was probably a good job for her. Amy was a kind, gentle young woman.

"She comes in here sometimes. Now she's making some money, she likes to buy things for Mike. She says he likes the nuts." Rosemary nodded toward the display. "It's kind of her to think of her brother."

"But..." Smith encouraged.

"She doesn't always pay. Emily chased her down the street last week and Amy was surprised when Emily asked her for money. She said she planned to come back when she got paid. I've known her to come in, even a couple of days later, and give me what she owes. She knows she makes money, and she knows she needs money to buy things. It's just that she doesn't seem to realize I need the money at the same time she takes the goods.

"I know what she's like, so I keep an eye on her when she's here. Today, I answered the phone when Amy came in. It was my daughter, with some...some really bad news. We didn't talk for long but it shook me up." Rosemary's chest moved and her eyes filled with tears. She pulled a tissue out of the pocket of her shorts and wiped her eyes. "Sorry. When I could pay attention to my store again, I realized Amy was gone, a big bag of trail mix and a twelve-serving container of chili were also gone, and there was no money beside the register. I'd had enough, and so I called 911."

"You did the right thing, Rosemary."

"I don't want her arrested, Molly. That would be awful. She can't go to jail, that poor thing!"

"Calm down," Smith said with a smile. "Someone needs to have a talk with her, and probably Mike as well."

"You're not social workers."

"No, but we understand about mentally handicapped people. I know where Mike works, and I'll go around now and tell him what's happening. Then we'll have a talk with Amy and tell her what she did was wrong, and she has to come back and pay you what she owes."

"It's not the money..."

Smith lifted one hand. "I hear you, but Amy needs to pay up, Rosemary. This can't go on. One day she'll take something valuable, like a piece of jewelry, and the store owner won't be quite as sympathetic as you. I've an idea, I'll get my mom to talk to Amy and Mike and maybe she can help. It would be nice to get Mom's mind on someone else's troubles for a while."

"Thanks, Molly."

"What time do you close?"

"Ten minutes ago."

"Can Amy come by tomorrow?"

"Tomorrow's Sunday. I don't open on Sundays in the off season. Monday would be fine."

Molly left, hearing the lock in the door turn behind her. She'd love a bag of that trail mix, but when she went to pay, Rosemary would insist on not taking the money, and then it would be graft and corruption.

She went to the Bishop and the Nun, where Mike, Amy's brother, worked as a bouncer. Mike was a good guy and he did his best to look after Amy and Robbie, but he was a young man and it was a hard responsibility.

◇◇◇

Eliza hadn't seen John since they'd gone to the police station. He hadn't come home, not even to get his shaving kit and a change of clothes. Did he really think she'd killed Rudy? If he believed her capable of that, could she remain married to him?

She took a container of yogurt out of the fridge and looked at it. Her stomach turned and she put it back. She'd had to call Barney, her agent, this morning and cancel the meeting she was supposed to be attending in Vancouver on Monday. It was the first meeting with an ad agency that had a campaign for a new company selling workout wear specifically aimed at boomer women. Cancelling the meeting, Barney said, would in effect be telling the agency to look elsewhere for their model.

"I don't know when I'll be able to get to the coast," Eliza said. "Go ahead and tell them I'm not interested."

Barney sputtered, and argued, and then asked, "Is something the matter, sweetie? I can come down and see you, if you'd like." They had been good friends for a long time.

"Everything's fine," Eliza said. "I'm making some decisions about my future, that's all. I'll let you know soon." Barney read nothing in the newspapers other than business and fashion and art gallery openings. If the piece about Eliza from the *Gazette* had been picked up by the Vancouver papers, Barney would have missed it. Eliza didn't want to tell her that the workout wear people might not want her anywhere near their campaign.

She headed upstairs, might as well have a bath and try to relax. She could worry in the bath as well as she could pacing the house. The staircase was wide and it made a ninety degree turn at the landing, where a large stained-glass window was set into the wall. Movement caught her eye and she glanced outside. It was early enough that the sun hadn't quite set, and long shadows reached across the lawn from the forest edging the property. A car was pulling into their driveway. It was an RCMP patrol car, and Dick Madison sat in the passenger seat.

Chapter Twenty

"Yeah," John Winters barked into the phone.

"Sergeant Winters? It's Corporal Farzaneh here. Are you good to talk?"

He was sitting on the bed in his room eating another take out meal without tasting it while watching a hockey game on the old TV. The game was no more distracting than the food. He'd be more than happy to talk shop with Farzaneh. Anything would be better than watching a stupid hockey game and avoiding thinking about his wife's tear-stained face. He'd thought about phoning her, talking to her, telling her he loved her and was on her side. But somehow he ended up switching on the TV and turning the sound up too loud.

"What's up?"

"I saw something of interest just now, and figured you should know about it. It's your town after all, and probably not related to the Steiner case."

"Go ahead."

"Before getting this post in B.C., I was in New Brunswick, doing general policing mostly, with a bit of an anti-organized crime focus."

"Were you now?" Winters' cop brain switched into high gear and he could guess why Farzaneh was calling. Eliza, and all their troubles, were forgotten.

"Yup. And during my time there I had occasion to run into a group out of Montreal. I saw a gentleman of my acquaintance not more than fifteen minutes ago."

"That's enough for over the phone," Winters said. "Where are you?"

"Bar at the Koola Hotel where we're staying."

"I'll be there in fifteen minutes."

He snapped his phone shut, switched off the TV, tossed the unfinished lemon chicken and fried rice into the trash, and headed for his car.

The bar of the Koola hotel was crowded on a Saturday night. It was still early; the patrons were mostly friends and family groups out for dinner. A cluster of eight or nine middle-aged women had pulled three tables together in the center of the room. One woman waved her hands over her head like a mad thing, and the others filled the room with shouts of laughter. This group came here every Saturday night, their numbers expanding or contracting depending on circumstance, the time of year, the weather, but they were always here. Jim Denton's wife, Gale, was one of them. She gave him a wave.

Kevin Farzaneh sat at the bar. He swallowed the last of his beer, put a bill on the counter, and joined Winters. "Let's walk."

"Don't know where the boss is," Farzaneh said, rubbing the top of his hairless head. "Alison's reworking some stuff in the lab now we know about Steiner's brother, the maintenance… sorry, wasn't supposed to mention that." Winters doubted Kevin Farzaneh slipped up much. There might be dissent in the IHIT team, and this was probably Farzaneh's way of letting him know they had a suspect. Other than Eliza.

"I went for an early dinner by myself," the Mountie continued. I was sitting in the window at that place, the something Grill, around the corner from the Hudson Hotel, just finishing up, and who do I see walk by, other than your delectable beat constable, but François Langois."

"And Monsieur Langois is…"

"His pride would be offended if he finds out you don't quake in terror at the mention of his name. Langois works for a mob boss name of Guy Marias. His job, unless he's been promoted recently, is enforcement. Marais operates in New Brunswick and Quebec mostly, because he's more comfortable in French, although he speaks English well enough. Maybe he's branching out into B.C. like most everyone these days. I ran a quick warrant check. Langois has nothing outstanding, more's the pity, but he does have a nice long record, assault, extortion, uttering threats."

Strange, Winters thought. *Madison hasn't bothered to tell Farzaneh that Josie Steiner is Guy Marais' daughter?*

"Did Langois spot you?"

"No. Might not matter if he did, I don't know he'd recognize me. I spent some time on surveillance, watching him, but we never came face to face."

"Thanks for letting me know." They came to a corner and waited for the light to change. "Don't suppose you know where Langois is staying?"

"He spends plenty of time in the gym, but's not the type to get exercise by going for a long walk in the spring air. I'd guess he's at the Hudson."

"He has a record you say? Then it would be well within my responsibilities to pay him a visit, and make sure he understands we're a quiet, peaceful little town and don't need outsiders causing trouble."

"That's what I was thinking. Hey, there's Molly." Farzaneh grabbed Winters' arm. "Call her over, will you, Sarge? Let her know how helpful I've been."

Molly Smith was heading toward them on the other side of the street. She was taking her time, walking slowly, her eyes moving.

He lifted a hand and waved. She looked at him and he beckoned her over.

"Great, thanks, Sarge," Farzaneh said, straightening up and brushing off the front of his shirt.

"Afraid you're too late, my boy," Winters said. "The lady's spoken for."

"That can always change," the Mountie said. "I note there is no wedding ring."

◇◇◇

Smith caught movement out of the corner of her eye and looked over to see Sergeant Winters calling her. He was standing outside Wolfe River Books with the good-looking Mountie from IHIT. She was pleased to see it. If Winters was back working with IHIT then his wife must be cleared. She waited for a break in the traffic.

Amy's brother Mike had been at the Bishop when Smith had dropped in, and upset at what she had to tell him about his sister's shopping habits. "She's working at that place that takes care of dogs during the day. Dog day care they call it, for God's sake. What's wrong with leaving your mutt with a bowl of water and kibble when you're at work? Some people have more money than they know what to do with. I can give them a couple of suggestions. No matter, it's a good job for Amy. They like her there, say the dogs get on well with her. Now she wants to get a dog for Robbie." He made a face. "That's all I need."

"What does she do with Robbie when she's working?" Smith sipped at the glass of ice water the bartender had poured her. She and Mike had pulled stools up to the bar. The Bishop and Nun was almost empty. A couple of guys were setting up instruments on the postage stamp-sized stage, and the light was very poor. A cheap bar could be a depressing place early in the evening.

"She works three days a week, for four hours at a time. The women's support center helps her out. She pays a small amount out of her salary and they supplement it so Robbie can go to a lady's house. The plan isn't to have Amy supporting herself, that's never going to happen, but to give her a feeling of independence. Her boss is already asking if she can work more hours, but I think it's enough for a start. She's so proud of earning money." He sighed. "I guess I forgot to tell her that you have to have the money in your pocket to pay for what you want, not just the promise of it coming in at the end of the week."

A loud crash and the room turned blue with swearing. One of the musicians had knocked over the drums and the other started berating him.

"Hard lesson to teach someone," Smith said, turning back to Mike, "when she must see people all the time holding up plastic cards and then walking out with stuff."

"We've got a cousin couch surfing with us at the moment. Maybe I can get her to take Amy shopping, show her how to figure out if she has enough money to pay for things she needs."

"That would be a good start."

"Sometimes I wish I was so innocent. Amy has no guile at all, and never wishes anyone anything but good."

"A nice world to live in," Smith agreed.

They arranged that Monday morning Mike would take Amy back to Rosemary's to pay what she owed. He would try to explain about the intricacies of commercial transactions. In the meantime Smith would speak to her mom. Perhaps the support center could offer some classes on basic finance.

The last car passed and she darted across the street to join Winters and Kevin Farzaneh.

"Hi," she said, "What's up?"

"I can't decide where to eat in this town," Farzaneh said. "Too many choices. I need someone local to show me around. Say dinner tomorrow, or lunch, even breakfast?"

It was nice to be asked. She gave him a big smile, before saying, "I don't date cops."

"What she means by that," Winters said with a laugh, "is that she doesn't date you. Thanks for the tip."

"All part of the job. Speaking of which…Oh, never mind, but I'll be back."

He walked away, after giving Smith a most charming grin. She wondered if he practiced it in front of the mirror every morning.

"What's up?" she asked again.

"I've had word that a known gang member with a criminal record is in town. I'm going to drop by his hotel, let him know

I'm watching him. I thought it might be nice to have a uniform beside me. Are you free?"

"For now. Not too much happening."

"If you get a call, take it, but come with me in the meantime. What? Do you have a problem with that, Smith?"

"No, not at all." She'd hesitated, considering telling him about Madison's insinuations regarding their relationship. Suppose she'd only imagined what the Mountie had been hinting at. She'd look like a fool, or worse that she was projecting. She fell into step beside the sergeant.

"Do you have a guest staying here by the name of Langois?" Winters asked the front desk clerk, showing his badge. Not really necessary, as she certainly remembered him, and Smith stood beside him in full uniform.

"Yes," she said, without checking her computer.

"Room number?"

"310"

They took the stairs.

Without words, Smith stood on one side of the door to 310 and Winters on the other. He reached out a hand and knocked.

"Yes?"

"Police."

The door opened.

The man who stood there was dressed in the trousers of a nice gray suit with a well-pressed white shirt neatly tucked in and an expensive pink tie properly knotted around his neck. He looked like any prosperous businessman, except for the size of his neck and the bulge of muscle underneath the shirt. His hair was buzzed down to the scalp and the remains of old acne scars pitted his face like a topographical map. His nose looked as if it had been broken more times than probably even he could remember, and his small black eyes reflected no light. Those eyes made Smith think of the rat she'd found impaled on her door. He smelled, very heavily, of tobacco.

His gaze, not quite a sneer but close, crossed Smith, dismissing her instantly, and focused on Winters. "What do you want?" He had a heavy French accent.

"Mr. François Langois?" Winters asked.

"*Oui.*"

"May we come in?"

"*Non.*"

"Do you want us to discuss business in the hallway?"

"I 'ave no business with you."

"I'm sure it's not a problem, François," a man said from inside the room. "Let the gentlemen in. We only wish to be of assistance."

Langois opened the door and stepped back.

Josie Steiner and her lawyer were sitting at a circular table by the window. Glasses and food dishes and papers were piled high on the table. A bottle of wine nestled in an ice bucket.

Oh boy, Smith thought, *this is awkward.* Wasn't Sergeant Winters forbidden from any involvement in the Steiner murder?

Josie opened her mouth. The lawyer waved her to be quiet. "If it isn't Sergeant Winters," he said, "As I recall you've been removed from this investigation for personal reasons. I suggest you leave or I will be forced to make a complaint."

"Unfortunately," Winters said, not sounding at all concerned, "this is a small town with a small police service. We all have to multi-task, isn't that correct, Constable Smith?"

"What? Uh, yeah, that's right, sir."

"I'm here on another matter. If you'd be more comfortable, perhaps you and Mrs. Steiner should leave."

The lawyer jerked his head toward Josie. Without a word, she got up, taking her wine glass with her. She grabbed the neck of the bottle and pulled it out of the ice, crossed the room, and opened a door. She closed the door behind her, but the scent of her perfume lingered.

"I'm here to have a chat with Mr. Langois," Winters said. "A private chat."

"'e stays," Langois said. He picked up his beer and took a hearty slug.

"I had a look at your record," Winters said. "It doesn't look good."

"Mr. Langois has paid his debt to society," Iverson said. "He can come and go as he pleases. Which, come to think of it, is more than can be said for you right now, Sergeant."

"Nevertheless, I'm wondering what you're doing in our fair town. Perhaps I can offer you some tips on the best sights to see. Skiing's over for the year, do you hike?"

"What?" Langois said, confused. He put his beer on the table and threw a questioning look at the lawyer.

Iverson peered over the top of his glasses. "François is here as a friend of the family to support Mrs. Steiner in her grief. Mrs. Steiner's father," his eyes lingered on the sergeant, "is unable to get away at this time. As much as he would like to."

Smith looked back and forth between the three men. A lot more was being said in this room than words, and it was in a language she didn't understand.

"Thoughtful of you," Winters said to Langois. "A word to the wise—we will be watching you."

He turned and walked away. Smith pulled the door shut behind her.

At the bottom of the staircase, Winters stopped and waited for Smith to catch up.

"That might have been a mistake, Molly," he said. "Iverson isn't playing in the minor leagues, and he will do whatever he can to protect his client. I don't see Mrs. Steiner killing her husband, she's been brought up to keep her hands clean, but I doubt Iverson understands that."

What Winters could possibly know about Josie Steiner's upbringing, Smith couldn't imagine. She didn't ask; he wasn't soliciting her opinion.

He stopped talking while a woman clattered down the stairs. She gave them a sideways glance and hurried away.

"Anyway, if things don't go well, I wanted you to know, Molly, that you're a good police officer. You've got a future ahead of you, if you want it."

What the hell?

She was so dumbfounded that he was out the door to the lobby before she recovered and ran after him. "John, I don't understand."

"You don't have to."

Her cell phone vibrated in her pocket and she checked the display. The station. She answered, following Winters through the lobby and onto the street.

"Thanks, Ingrid." She put the phone away. Winters waited for her.

"Fellow by the name of Frank Spencer, who lives on Station Street, called to speak to me. I questioned him the other night about the B&E across the street. He said he remembered something. It's still quiet so I'm going to try to get someone to cover the street, grab a car and pay him a visit. Do you want to come?"

He studied her for a long moment. His eyes were heavy and he looked very old. "No, Molly, you take it. I think it's time I had a talk with my wife."

He walked away. A streetlamp lit him in a circle of yellow light, just for a moment, before the darkening night swallowed him up.

Chapter Twenty-one

It was time to talk to his wife. It was long past time to talk to his wife. When he realized Iverson and Steiner were in Langois' room, Winters had had a momentary stab of panic. He could be suspended for interfering in the Steiner case after being ordered not to. Then, without conscious thought, he came to the decision he'd been wrestling with. Eliza mattered more than the job. If she were charged, even if Madison kept badgering her, he'd quit. Walk away from his career, and do everything possible to clear her.

She was sitting in the living room, in her favorite chair, holding a book to her chest, her legs curled up underneath her, her feet bare. Her hair was lifeless and her eyes puffy and red. She must have heard him arrive, his car in the driveway, his key in the lock, his footsteps on the hallway floor, but she made no move to stand up. She looked at him, and didn't say a word. A pile of tissues was scattered across the table at her elbow, beside her reading glasses. Outside, dusk was deepening, turning to night, but she hadn't turned on the reading light and her face was in shadow.

She turned back to her book and said, "Forget something?" in a tone meant to convey disinterest.

"Forgot to say I love you."

She turned a page. "Do you?"

He stood in front of her chair. "Of course I do. I always have. I always will." He took the book out of her hands and dropped it to the floor. "Come to the kitchen. Let's have some tea and talk."

"Do you mean talk, John, as in an exchange of mutually beneficial information, or just an attempt to bully me into confessing to something I didn't do. Like your Mountie friend?"

He took her hands and pulled her to her feet. "This is a mess, for sure, but we won't sort anything out if I don't let you tell me what's going on."

The laugh lines around her mouth and eyes had set into dark trenches. She'd aged about twenty years in less than a week. Her hair was dirty and uncombed, and her T-shirt had a coffee stain on it. "To show you I'm serious," he said, "I'll even make the tea."

She didn't laugh, but let herself be led by the hand into the kitchen. She sat at the table while he filled the kettle and plugged it in. A single-serving yogurt container, half-full, was in the sink, beside a piece of toast with a couple of small bites taken out of it. It was unlikely she'd had much more to eat than that for days.

He could feel her eyes on him as he busied himself making up a tray with tea pot, cups, milk, but she said nothing.

Finally the kettle boiled. He poured hot water into the pot, and put the tray on the table. He placed a cup in front of her. At last he sat down.

"Tell me," he said, "about Steiner." He poured tea.

She pulled a tissue out of her pocket and twisted it around her fingers. At first he was afraid she wasn't going to speak to him. He'd hardly blame her if she didn't. He sipped at his tea as his heart thudded in his chest. He didn't know if he could live without her.

◇◇◇

She'd been at a party with Rudy that night twenty-seven years ago. As usual, there had been lots of booze and lots of cocaine. She didn't usually drink because she couldn't afford to waste any of her miniscule daily allotment of calories, but drugs didn't make you fat. She hadn't been in the mood to party—a boring function for some magazine editor's birthday—and wasn't even in the mood for snorting coke, even though the party organizers had bought the best. She'd had a meeting with her agent that afternoon. The agent told Eliza, straight out, that she needed to be more *friendly* to the executive at the advertising agency which was handling a major campaign for a high-end European designer moving into Canada.

She didn't want to be *friendly* to any of them anymore, and she didn't want to keep taking the drugs that made it easier.

She'd been bad-tempered at the party, had a fight with Rudy over nothing much at all, and gone home. Alone, sober, and wondering why, now that she'd achieved, at twenty-one years of age, all she'd dreamed, she was so unhappy.

If she were to make excuses, explanations, the first would be easy. She'd been so young. Her mother, a housewife from Saskatoon, tried to guide the sixteen-year-old girl around the world of high fashion, so out of her depth it was laughable. Eliza's first agent might as well have been a pimp. She was, truth be told, a pimp. "Make men like you," had been her advice to the shy, awkward girl from Saskatchewan. And Eliza had somehow known what she had to do to make men like her. As she crawled up the slime-soaked ladder that was the modeling world, even once she'd been in sight of the top, she still made them like her. Although, most of the time, she didn't like herself very much. She'd discovered she had a good head for money, and began taking courses in finance, which she absolutely loved. She kept that a secret from Rudy and her agent, knowing, probably subconsciously, they both needed to keep her dependent.

She arrived home from the party to find the lock on her front door smashed, and called the police. The officer they sent was young, new. His name was John Winters. She showed him around the apartment, knowing he'd be impressed by the furniture, the art, the view. Her ass. She turned to see that his head was down as he wrote in his notebook. "Did you get all that?" she said.

"I think so." He finished writing and only then looked at her. "You should call an emergency locksmith, ma'am. I'll wait until someone comes, if you like."

She loved him, the handsome, passionate, dedicated, sexy policeman, who pushed all her erotic buttons and taught her that sex could be something more than the most boring part of a job interview. She loved him so much she stopped screwing for work. And, to her surprise, she kept getting work. She no longer needed the coke and hadn't taken a hit since. She'd pretty much forgotten about that part of her life.

When she did think of it, it frightened her to realize how different it could have all turned out. If she'd been stoned, as she usually was after a miserable industry party, she would have either not called the police about the break-in or waited until the morning. And someone else would have come.

She shook her head, chasing the memories away, and looked across the table at her husband. He looked so stricken, she wanted to reach out and kiss his face. Kiss it all over, and keep kissing until all the unhappiness had gone away.

Instead she said, "You knew I was engaged when we met. The night I met you I realized that even if I never saw you again, I didn't have to settle for the likes of Rudy Steiner. I've seen him around over the years, at functions and parties. We said hi and moved on. It seemed every time I ran into him, he was with another wife. They were getting progressively younger, at least in relation to him. I heard he'd married five times. I never doubted for a single minute I'd merely have been wife number one."

"Guy was a fool," John said with a growl.

She almost smiled. "He cornered me at a gallery opening not long before we moved here, maybe just over a year ago." John hadn't been with her. Even if he hadn't been busy—and that was the height of the infamous Blakeley case that had almost broken him—John avoided fashion parties and gallery openings almost as much as the press clamoring to know when he'd be making an arrest. "His breath was bad and he needed a bath, and he was with a woman who looked to be about fifteen. He'd been pretty high. He told me the biggest mistake he made in his life was letting me get away. I could have told him he hadn't *let* me do anything, but what was the point." Rudy had taken the breaking of their engagement badly, and had bad-mouthed Eliza for a long time after. "And that was that." She looked out the window. Rain slashed against the glass, and all was black and wet.

"Drink your tea," John said.

She picked up the cup and took a sip. He'd added sugar while she wasn't looking, but she drank it nevertheless.

"Obviously," he said, "that wasn't that."

"No. He called me two weeks ago. Said he was going to be in Trafalgar for a few days, on assignment, and would like to get together."

She looked at her husband. "I couldn't see the harm, John. A quick drink in a busy bar for old times' sake. I told him I'd enjoy meeting his wife. He snorted, I remember that, and said he'd give me a call when they got here."

"Which I'm guessing he did."

"It was Saturday night. You were working." She held up one hand. "I'm not blaming you, John. You were busy at work. That's always been okay with me.

"He had a minor germ phobia when we were together. I found it irritating, but nothing excessive. Over the years, I could see it was getting worse. At parties, he'd bring his own glass and wear white gloves. He always snagged a chair, so no one could stand in front of him and breathe on him, and if everyone went to a restaurant, he didn't usually come. When he phoned, he invited me up to his room at the Hudson House. I said no, and suggested a nice bar. He sounded so panicked at the very idea, I agreed. Foolishly." She finished her tea and looked at the water running down the outside of the window.

He poured another cup and slid it toward her. "How'd it go?"

She laughed, the sound harsh and bitter. It was so unlike any laugh he'd ever heard from her he could hardly credit that it came from Eliza. "Not exactly well. He had a good bottle of wine on a room service table, white tablecloth, red rose, very nice. I took off my coat, sat down, and accepted the glass he offered me. He looked dreadful, simply dreadful. I hadn't seen him for a year or more, and was shocked at how much he'd changed. I didn't want to lie to him, tell him he was looking good, so I didn't say anything. We chatted a while, about the old days mostly, about people we knew back then. Come to think of it, I did most of the chatting, I don't think Rudy said much at all. Which was odd, he's always been very," she paused, searching for the right word, "loquacious. Had to be the center of attention, all the time." She waved her hands in the air, "Look at me, look at me, look at me now. That was Rudy." Her hands dropped back to the table, and she cradled the cup as if seeking its warmth.

"You cold?" he asked.

"A bit."

He started to stand up. "I'll get you a sweater."

"No, John. I have to tell this."

"Okay."

"I finished my wine—it was very good—and said I had to be off. He asked me not to go. He said his life had been nothing but a disaster since the day I left him and he had one last chance to make it right. He had an idea for a set of photographs. Art photos for a coffee table book that would be his legacy. His career wasn't going well, I knew that. He hadn't done anything new or original or even very good in years. He still got work on the strength of his reputation, but I thought it a bit odd that at not yet sixty he was thinking about a legacy. I pretended some interest in the project. And then he told me I would be it."

"Be what?"

"The project. I was to be the only model in this book. He got excited talking about it. He still had many of the pictures he took of me all those years ago. He wanted to shoot new ones, in the same poses, same general background and layout, put those with the old pictures and make an art book about ageless beauty. Or some such rubbish. I didn't suggest he wait until I'm ninety before talking about ageless, but I wanted to."

She looked out the window again. It had been awful. She'd told him she wasn't interested in helping with his project, but thanked him for his interest, wished him luck, and started to leave. He hadn't cried, but came near enough. All he'd ever wanted, he told her, all these years, was to get her back. For her to be his model as well as his wife. He'd spent years searching but he had never been able to find a woman who, like Eliza, was a match for the greatness of his artistic vision. He'd married women who reminded him of her.

Eliza doubted that: she'd met his newest wife, once, on the way out of a restaurant. The current Mrs. Steiner had been an emaciated groupie.

"You've seen that thing I'm married to," Rudy said, as if reading her mind. "Nothing but a talentless wanna-be who thought I'd be her ticket to the big time. A drunken cow. That's what I'm reduced to."

"You aren't exactly a believer in the sanctity of marriage," she said, gathering up her coat. "Divorce her if you feel that way."

"I can't."

"Of course you can."

"Her father does believe in the sanctity of marriage, and... well, I owe him some money. I owe him a lot of money. He didn't approve of her marrying me, but he ensured that I can't dump the bitch."

"Good-bye Rudy." She headed for the door.

"Wait, Eliza, please. If you don't want to get back together, that's okay. We can still work together, right? It'll be just like the old days. If you hadn't walked out on me to take up with some flat-footed cop I would have stayed at the top. We were an invincible team, and we can still be."

Eliza doubted that, but it was a moot point anyway. She hadn't been interested in posing for Rudy to begin with and the intensity, the very *neediness*, of him was frightening her. She had her hand on the doorknob, but hesitated at the sound of a drawer opening.

"Look, Eliza, this is how much you mean to me. I've carried this around all these years. No matter what bitch I was married to, this is the picture I looked at at night."

It was that picture. That awful picture. She'd posed for it when they'd first started dating, trying to be alluring, tempting.

She'd been darn high. There was nothing sexy about that photograph—it was just pornographic.

She'd slammed the door on her way out.

"He wasn't trying to blackmail you with it?" John asked.

"Blackmail? Of course not. For some reason he thought I'd be flattered that's how he remembered me. When I saw you had it, that awful thing, I thought he'd given it to you out of spite, to show you he had some sort of claim over me." She shuddered.

"I don't care what you say, I'm getting you a sweater. You'll catch pneumonia."

◇◇◇

Frank Spencer answered the door to Smith's knock. He had a baby over his shoulder; one of the twins clung to his right leg. The baby screamed and the boy whined. The dog tried to make its escape through the open door. Spencer blocked it with his free leg as if he were a goalie with the Toronto Maple Leafs. He gestured for Smith to come in, and she closed the door behind her while Spencer stickhandled the yapping dog.

"Sorry," he said with a rueful twist of his mouth. "James was asleep when I called and I'd put the boys to bed so I figured it was a good time to talk. Guess I was wrong." Upstairs a loud crash, and a child began to cry.

Spencer thrust the crying infant at Smith. "Here," he said. He ran up the stairs. "Jason, what are you doing up there?"

If Jason was upstairs than it must be Jeremy watching her. He stuck his thumb in his mouth. The baby stopped crying and wide blue eyes stared into hers. "Uh," she said, "good boy." He smelled clean and fresh, of baby powder and nuzzling kisses.

"You can take him to your house if you want," Jeremy said in deep serious tones.

"Back to bed, now," Frank shouted from upstairs. "Jeremy get up here."

"Bye," the boy said.

"Bye," Smith replied. Jeremy climbed the stairs, clinging to the banister, his short legs barely making the risers. The dog ran on ahead.

Smith stood there with the baby. What would she do if Spencer decided to sneak out the back way? Not that she'd blame him.

"Sorry about that," he said, taking the child from her arms. "Marianna has one more shift on nights. Hopefully I'll live that long. Do you have any children?"

"No."

"Don't let the Spencer family put you off. I wouldn't give the boys up for anything. Well, maybe for a good night's sleep."

"Jeremy said I can keep the baby."

He laughed, a deep, rich laugh, and kissed the infant's cheek. When he looked back at Smith he was smiling. "I wanted a hockey team, but I think this one's the last. Come in. Can I get you anything to drink?"

"No, thank you. You've got your hands full."

She took off her hat as he led the way into the living room. It looked like a bomb had gone off—a bomb stuffed with toys and baby equipment. There was scarcely an inch of carpet not covered with colored blocks, balls, stuffed animals, baby bottles, dog toys. The room smelled of spilled milk, too much junior testosterone, and love…plenty of love.

"Have a seat."

She picked up a one-eyed pink dog and sat on a chair. Broken springs sagged and she had a brief memory of smugly hiding behind a door while Lucky yelled at Sam for using the couch as a trampoline.

Spencer put the baby onto the floor and handed it a blue rattle. He discarded the toy immediately and struggled to his feet. A few wobbly steps and he was drooling on Smith's pant leg.

"You said you'd remembered something, sir?" She prodded Spencer.

"Yes, I did. You were asking me about anything out of the ordinary I'd seen at night. And, as I told you, I hadn't seen anything in the night. Kind of like the dog who didn't bark. Nevermind. But I did notice something in the day time. It was about ten days, two weeks ago. Might be nothing, of course, but you said you were interested in anything going on."

"That's right."

"Around six o'clock. I'd picked up the kids and the dog from their respective day cares and was taking everyone for a walk while Marianna fixed dinner. There was a guy taking pictures of the street. I didn't give it much thought, perhaps someone thinking of buying in the neighborhood, except that there aren't any houses for sale on this street. None that have a sign up anyway. I didn't pay him much mind, as I said." He shrugged, looking slightly embarrassed. "I guess I'm wasting your time, eh?"

"Not at all," she said, meaning yes, you are. She pulled her hat away from the baby's reaching fingers. "Can you describe him?"

"Not very well. Average height, on the slight side. He wore a brown jacket and jeans, nothing special. Short hair, but not too short." He pointed to his own head of hair curling around his ears and the back of his neck. "Probably about the same length as mine, longer than yours. Sorry, Officer, that's about it."

"If you remember anything else…"

"I know where to find you."

She pried baby fingers off her knee and stood. James dropped to his well-padded bottom; small feet sounded on the stairs and one of the twins called, "Can I have a glass of water?"

◇◇◇

Eliza broke down and started crying. Through her tears and ragged breathing and stuffed nose she told her husband what had happened the night Rudy Steiner died.

She'd left Rudy's room in a towering rage after he showed her that dreadful picture. The very idea that he'd been carrying it around all these years made her skin crawl. She grabbed for the picture, but he whipped it out of the way, and she wasn't going to get into a brawl. She told him what she thought of him, and left the hotel, vowing to never have anything to do with Rudy again.

Thoughts of the picture tormented her all week. It preyed on her mind, knowing it was out there. What would he do with

it? Would he show it to someone? To her husband? He hadn't
shown it to anyone before, but she didn't trust him not to, not
after she'd told him he was a sick, perverted has-been.

All week, she debated calling him, asking him to see sweet
reason and hand over the picture.

Monday, she finally made the call. Rudy had been happy to
hear from her, said he'd been about to call her himself, but had
been busy with the photo shoot and hadn't had time. She could
come around later and pick it up. How about eight-thirty? He'd
be busy with his assistant until then.

Like a fool, she believed him.

At eight o'clock, it was raining heavily. She put on her brown
raincoat and picked up her Burberry bag and drove into town.

It had not gone well, to say the least.

She broke down and began to cry. The tea pot was refreshed,
and she clutched at the cup as if she were drowning and it were
her life preserver. The conversation had been so painful, so
frightening, it almost physically made her sick to think about
it. She tried to tell John the essence.

◇◇◇

The picture had been nowhere to be seen. Rudy suggested she
take her coat off, sit for a while. She didn't want to sit, she said.
The room was a mess. Typical Rudy, he'd pulled out all the stops
trying to impress her, but couldn't make the effort to pick up
his own underwear.

He started to get angry. Like the Rudy of old, he was going
to have a temper tantrum if he didn't get his way.

"This is my chance Eliza. My chance to show them, one last
time, that I'm my generation's greatest photographer of women. I
need you to make this work. Any woman your age would be happy
to pose for me. I put the word out what I plan to do and they'll
be begging at my door. But I can only do it with you. You, Eliza,
are my inspiration. You took my gift with you when you left me."

"I took nothing, Rudy. Please understand: this isn't going
to happen."

"I've loved you all my life. I've photographed hundreds, thousands, of women, and not one of them could make my camera sing the way you could. I married five women, knowing everyone of them was second-rate. Christ, second rate is a long way up for the bitch I'm married to now. All I want is to be with you, Eliza, to work with you, one last time."

"Please stop this. I do not want to pose for your book. Why can't you understand that? If you care so much about me, make me happy and rip up that picture, and we can be friends."

"Tell you what, Eliza. When the project's finished, I'll give back the picture."

She picked up her purse. "Good bye, Rudy."

There was a tap on the door, and he went to answer it, saying, "I ordered something to celebrate our renewed partnership."

It was room service. Pushing a table decorated with a crisp white cloth and a single red rose in a silver vase. A bottle of Champagne nestled in ice in the matching bucket, and plates were laid out with fruit, cheese, and crackers.

"Shall I open the Champagne, sir?" said the waiter, tossing a smile toward Eliza.

"Please," Rudy said.

Eliza turned her back.

She heard the cork pop, and Rudy say, "Thank you, I'll pour. Here you go." When the door shut behind the waiter she turned around. Rudy was studying the bottle. "As I remember, you're partial to *Moet*. Take your coat off and have a seat."

"You're crazy." She crossed the room.

Rudy dropped the bottle into the cooler in a rattle of ice. "Don't think you can insult me, you stuck-up cunt." Startled, she stopped with her hand on the doorknob. She looked back. His eyes blazed with anger.

And Eliza Winters remembered why she had not married this man. He could act charming and self-depreciating, but underneath there lay a layer of raw rage, ready to burst up like a volcano, spewing hate like hot lava into the air.

His eyes were small and mean, red pricks burned beneath the black surface. "You want the picture, do you? Well there's a price. I remember what you were like. Not too proud to fuck for what you wanted when you belonged to me, were you? Once a whore always a whore. I don't even want to fuck you. If you want the picture, you're going to work with me, and do what I tell you, and then you can have it. Shut up and take off your coat and sit down. Two hundred bucks for this Champagne, you're going to drink it."

She opened the door. "Keep your damn picture, Rudy."

And she left.

Eliza felt John's hand on her arm as he half-lifted her to her feet. "You need to lie down."

◇◇◇

John Winters shut the bedroom door carefully. He'd insisted on putting Eliza to bed. He'd closed the drapes and fluffed her pillows while she used the bathroom. He wrapped the duvet around her thin frame and touched her face. She smiled, and rolled over with a deep sigh.

He went downstairs. He hadn't told anyone at the station where he was; he didn't think they particularly cared what he did. These days he was just an embarrassment. Everyone either slid past, avoiding his eyes or, like Barb, tried so hard to be friendly they made him feel like a charity case.

It was close to ten, Eliza would probably sleep the night though. She needed it. So did he, but right now he didn't want to be trapped in his own head, thinking about what she'd told him.

He grabbed his keys and headed out.

The rain was coming down in sheets, cutting visibility to a few yards in front of his car. A truck passed, a big one, kicking up so much spray, Winters was momentarily blinded. The windshield wipers worked hard to clear the window. He concentrated on his driving.

As she told the story, Eliza had been crying steadily, gulping her words like foul tasting medicine, her face a mess of tears and mucus and pain. At times he couldn't make out what she'd been trying to say, but didn't want to interrupt the narrative to ask her to repeat herself.

Did he believe her?

Totally. Absolutely. Everything she'd said had been exactly as he'd expect Eliza to act. She had no more shot Steiner in the back of the head than the man had done it himself and walked downstairs to toss the gun into the dumpster before conveniently returning to the bathroom to die.

But what about the rest of it?

Did he even hear correctly?

Once a whore, always a whore. What the hell did that mean?

Chapter Twenty-two

Molly Smith finished processing a drunk who'd made himself a bed on the steps of city hall and disagreed with the suggestion to move along. She glanced at her watch. Three a.m.

She closed out her shift, said goodnight to the dispatcher and the shift supervisor, and headed for home. It had stopped raining and the night air held a touch of warmth, the slightest of hints that summer might be on its way.

The streets were quiet, not a soul to be seen. The moon was a round white ball over the black bulk of Koola Glacier. She walked down Monroe Street, the bright outdoor lights of the police station fading behind her. No cars were coming and she took her time crossing the street. A scrap of paper blew past. She turned into the alley. It smelled of garbage left outside for pickup and the lingering odors from the restaurant. High concrete walls and locked back doors lined the narrow passage, utility poles and cables forming an urban forest overhead.

As she walked, she thought about Sergeant Winters. She'd typed up a report, but hadn't called to tell him what she learned from Frank Spencer. Nothing important enough to bother him, when he had so much else on his mind. Would he end up having to resign over his wife's involvement in the Steiner case? Might well happen.

She'd left her Ford Focus in its parking space behind the bakery, as usual. Dim light from the streetlamp shone onto it.

As she got closer, her nerves twitched and her senses began to wake up. Something looked wrong. She pulled her flashlight off her belt and the alley lit up.

The car was leaning to one side. Both tires on the right were flat. Not, she noticed as she got closer, merely flat, but slashed to ribbons. As she played the light over the ground, it reflected off shards of glass, twinkling in the dirt of the alley.

The windows were smashed, and the roof and hood deeply dented.

Someone had gone after her car with a tire-iron and sheer spite.

She heard something behind her and almost jumped out of her skin. A cat dashed out of a clump of bushes and disappeared into the garbage bags at the back of the convenience store on the corner.

All fell quiet once again.

Heart pounding, she rested her hand on the butt of her gun and fingered the radio at her shoulder with her flashlight hand.

"Ingrid." Her voice broke and she swallowed before continuing. "Ingrid, I think I need…I need a patrol car at my place. Send them to the alley behind 245 Front Street, Alphonse's bakery."

"On its way. Are you okay?"

"Me? Yeah, I'm fine. Send the car, please."

She heard the siren immediately, and her legs almost collapsed under her with relief.

White and red and blue lights flooded the lane, and she lifted her hand to wave the car down. She had a moment of sheer panic, realizing she was lit up, a perfect target, but it passed. Charlie Bassing wasn't going to shoot her from a distance. He'd want to be in her face.

Dave Evans got out of the car. "Geeze, Molly," he said. "Have you been playing bumper cars?"

"Ha, ha. Very funny. I got home and found this."

He walked around the car, studying it from all angles. He said, seriously, "Have a fight with Tocek?"

"What the hell does that mean?"

"Just asking."

"If you can't handle this professionally, Dave, I'll call for a real police officer to deal with it."

"Lighten up, Smith. You've got to learn to take a bit of ribbing, you know. Not every police force is as *friendly* as we are in Trafalgar."

She stepped toward him. "Someone has vandalized my car and I have called it in. I expect you to treat this as a crime. Think you can do that, Dave?"

He started to say something, and then thought better of it. He turned away. "You see anyone?"

"No. I just got here and this is what I found."

"Looks nasty."

"You will note," she said, spreading her arms wide, "there is no other damage. Not even the garbage cans have been turned over. Does that tell you something?"

"I noticed that, thanks. Means it's probably personal. So I wondered about the boyfriend. It's happened before."

They glared at each other, Smith uncomfortably aware that Evans thought of her as a woman with relationship problems first, rather than as a police officer. He turned away and called Ingrid to send a tow-truck.

"You will be sure and secure the vehicle, right? Until someone can get out and dust it for fingerprints."

"I know how to do my job."

That she doubted, but she said nothing.

She'd hoped Charlie would give up making his childish gestures and go away. Clearly, that was not going to happen. The intensity of his threats was increasing. Her home—maybe even her body—would be next.

Chapter Twenty-three

Lucky Smith had prepared a hearty picnic lunch. It had been a long time since the Smith family had been together and she wanted to do something nice. Too bad the grandchildren hadn't come, but for a while she'd pretend it was the old days, and Samwise and Moonlight were still kids, still living at home.

That they'd have to eat the meal sitting around Andy's hospital bed couldn't be helped.

She unpacked the hamper. A thermos of soup made from last summer's home-grown tomatoes, sandwiches, fruit, cookies. Beer for Sam and Moonlight, iced tea for her.

Andy had a new roommate. An old man, all liver spots, sagging skin, rheumy eyes, and sour smell, arrived during the night. He was sleeping, at least his eyes were closed and his breathing was regular, although loud, and Lucky pulled the curtain between the two beds.

"Isn't this nice," she said, handing Andy a can of non-alcoholic beer.

"No," he replied.

Sam helped himself to a sandwich. "I spoke to Judy last night," he said. "We think it would be okay to take the kids out of school for a couple of days and bring them down for a visit when you're out of here, Dad."

Andy smiled. "That would be nice, son. I'd like to see them."

"What a lovely idea," Lucky said, "Much better than visiting when you're in hospital." Andy reached over and laid his hand over hers and stroked it with his thumb.

Sam related some story Judy had told him about Ben's science project.

Moonlight stood by the window, running her long thin fingers across the blinds. Her nails were badly chewed and a hangnail on her thumb had torn, leaving a jagged cut in the skin.

"Everything all right, dear?" Lucky asked.

Moonlight turned around. She studied her mother's face. Lucky looked into her daughter's eyes, waiting. "Actually, Mom…"

"Afternoon all." The nurse pulled the curtain aside. "What a nice looking picnic. That's not a real beer you have there I hope, Mr. Smith."

"As if," Andy grumbled.

"Everything all right here?" she asked.

"No," Andy said.

"Just checking," the nurse said, her cheerful smile fixed firmly in place. "Be sure and let me know if you need anything." She bustled off.

When Lucky turned back to her daughter, Moonlight asked Sam what Roberta would like for her birthday, and the moment for confidences was over.

◇◇◇

Winters had driven around for hours last night, with nowhere to go, nothing to do, his mind in turmoil.

He didn't know what to do; he didn't know if he could face her, sleep in the same bed with her. So he took the coward's way out and returned to the motel, telling himself that the Chief had suggested he not stay at home until this was all sorted out.

In the morning, he felt like garbage.

He was staring blankly at the TV when his phone rang. "Winters."

"Sorry to bother you at home, John," Molly Smith said. "I know you're busy these days, with other things, I mean."

"Is something the matter?"

"Perhaps I shouldn't have called. It can wait until you're back at work."

"Molly, spit it out."

"Charlie Bassing is after me."

"Where are you now?"

"At the hospital. I don't mean he's after me right now, as in breaking through the doors, I just mean…" Her voice broke. "I don't know what to do."

"I'll pick you up in fifteen."

Knowing the place would be largely empty on a Sunday afternoon, he took Molly Smith to Big Eddie's Coffee Emporium. The red velvet couch against the back wall had seen better days, but it was clean and comfortable. Old newspapers and ski magazines were tossed on the table. He carried over coffee and a mug of hot chocolate, overflowing with whipped cream. He went back to the counter and took a plate of cookies from Jolene. The soft voice of Diana Krall, perfect for jazz classics, came from the speakers at the back.

Smith accepted her drink with a small smile. He sat beside her, drank his coffee, listened to the music, and waited.

Finally she looked up. Her eyes were clear but her mouth was set into a tight line. "Charlie Bassing wrecked my car last night."

"You report it?"

"Yes. Dave had the nerve to suggest it was Adam."

"Never mind Dave. He has issues of his own. Where's the car now?"

"Taken to the body shop we use and locked up. Someone from forensics is going to have a go and see if they can find any fingerprints. When they can get the time."

"You're sure it's Bassing? Could have been someone else you've run afoul of since you've been with us."

She shook her head. Her short blond hair quivered. The haircut made her look too young, too vulnerable. He would never say so. "It's him, guaranteed. He's been following me, making hostile gestures."

"Has he said anything?"

"Nothing that could be considered threatening. I look up and he's there, watching me. He did tell me he and I have unfinished business."

"When was this?"

"New Years. The night after the Wyatt-Yarmouth case ended."

"What the hell! This has been going on for three months and you're getting around to telling me about it *now*. Are you crazy?" Not just crazy, but downright stupid. Young cops, sometimes they thought they could handle all the world's problems by themselves.

He looked up to see Jolene watching them, her beautiful black face concerned. He gave her a sheepish nod.

"I guess that was a mistake," Smith said.

"It was."

"It's just that I was worried I'd look like I can't handle my own problems."

"You were worried some people in the department will think you're a hysterical female, you mean. Which is nonsense. You're hardly the first police officer to be threatened by someone they put away. What's Adam got to say about it?"

"I haven't told him," she said in a low voice. She dipped her index finger into the whipped cream mountain on top of the hot chocolate.

"You didn't tell Adam either?"

"I was afraid he'd overreact. Do something…career limiting." She sucked the tip of her finger.

He let out a breath. "Okay, I can see that." *Another stupid young cop.*

"For starters," he said, "this is criminal harassment. We're going to lay a charge under Section 264.1 of the Criminal Code. Please, please tell me you've been keeping a record of these events."

"I started a file after the rat incident."

Winters rolled his eyes to the ceiling. "The rat incident?"

"He nailed a dead rat to my door."

"For God's sake, Molly, that's serious stuff."

"I know. Don't be mad at me, please. It's just that so much is going on. My dad, Adam fighting with the guys I have to work with, you…I mean your wife."

He put his cup down. "Let's go. Anything else you have can wait. We're going to start a complaint against Bassing. Then I can bring him in, let him know I'm watching him. The least we can do is get an order keeping him away from you."

"He won't pay attention to an order."

"Probably not, but once he knows the police are paying attention to his every movement, if we're lucky he'll leave town. Permanently."

She looked directly at him for the first time. "I'm scared, John. I really am getting scared."

"I understand. Don't worry anyone's going to think less of your professionalism because of this, Molly. Unfortunately it can come with the job. You've a right to be frightened of him."

He stood up, and held out his hand. She took it and he pulled her to her feet. He held her hand for a moment and looked at her. The traces of a smile touched the corners of her mouth. The music came to a stop as the CD ended.

"The only unprofessional thing you've done is not report it immediately."

They turned to leave. Dick Madison stood in the doorway watching them.

"Fuck," Smith said under her breath.

"Sergeant, Constable. Enjoying your days off?" Madison's face was set into a smirk.

"Yes, thanks," Winters said, brushing past the Mountie.

Smith's face had turned a brilliant red. "That wasn't good," she said.

"What?"

"There's something else I haven't been telling you."

◇◇◇

Molly Smith went back to the hospital after her meeting with Winters. She didn't care for the look on Madison's face when he'd seen them together. Winters had gone white with fury when she told him Madison was making suggestions that Winters had something to do with Steiner's death because he was possessive of his wife. And, she'd said, feeling her own face turning red, Madison was also insinuating that Winters and she, Smith, were playing games out of school.

The Steiner murder was like a poison, spreading venom to everything it touched. The Chief had earlier sent a memo around, reminding everyone they could be dismissed, even brought up on charges, for revealing confidential information. Particularly to the newspapers. Now, everyone was walking on eggshells.

Lucky and Sam had left the hospital, taking the picnic things with them. Andy sat up in bed, watching a movie on a portable DVD player Lucky borrowed. His roommate was sleeping, and they'd been joined by a third man. A young fellow with a thick white bandage wrapped around his head, cuts and scratches all over his face, and his arm in a cast. A bicycle helmet sat on his bedside table, indicating the probable cause of his misfortune.

Andy pulled out the earplugs and switched the machine off when his daughter came in. She pulled the curtains around his bed to give them some privacy and kissed his cheek before sitting down.

"All ready for tomorrow?" she asked.

"Ready as I'll ever be," he replied. He studied her face. "You don't look too good lately, sweetheart. Not worrying about me, I hope."

She tried to smile. "I never worry about you, Dad. Other things on my mind I guess." She hadn't planned to but found herself telling him she was considering looking for a city job and moving away. As well as Toronto, the city of Ottawa was accepting applications. People said Ottawa was a nice place to live, although darn cold in winter, and it wasn't too far from the ski hills of Quebec.

"Would you be okay with that, Dad? If I move?"

"Of course not. But not as upset as my mother was when I left the States and moved to a foreign county. And definitely not as upset as my father was when I not only moved but abandoned everything he thought important in life." Andy and Lucky had left Seattle to settle in Canada when he received his draft notice during the Vietnam War. "Children have to do what they have to do. If it's what you want, then go for it. Your mother won't be happy, you know that, but we can always visit, wherever you are." He gave her a big smile. "I hear they've invented this marvelous thing called a flying machine. We don't have to travel over the mountains by ox-cart anymore."

She laughed. "What will they think of next?"

"Do I take this to mean your relationship with Adam isn't too serious?"

"That I don't know, Dad. I want to be with Adam, yes, but I'm not sure I'm ready to plan my life around him. I haven't said anything to him about it."

"Perhaps you should. For all you know he's been offered a posting in Ontario but isn't taking it because of you."

She talked about Adam for a while, how conflicted she was about her feelings for him, how she thought of Graham sometimes when they were together, and felt guilty.

The nurse came in and Smith got up to leave. "You sleep well, Dad. I'll see you tomorrow." She leaned over to kiss him on the cheek. When she pulled back his eyes were very wet.

"You'll find your own way, Molly. And whatever you do will be right. I'm proud of you. Very proud. You've grown up to be a wonderful woman."

Her own eyes filled up. "Thanks, Dad." She said good night to the nurse and left.

◇◇◇

Eliza wrapped herself in a warm sweater and took her book and a cup of tea outside. A tarpaulin covered the large patio table, and she tucked a corner back before using a kitchen rag to wipe some of winter's residue away. She brought a single chair out of the storage hut and settled down.

Dirty snowbanks still lined the driveway and the paths, but crocuses were erupting in welcome bursts of purple and yellow and white and the green tips of tulips had broken through the earth. A woodpecker landed on the dead branch at the top of a pine tree. The sun was warm and she lifted her face to it, but she felt no warmth inside her. She sat for a long time, while her tea got cold. She didn't read a single word of her book.

She had told John everything that had happened that night. The night Rudy died. He wrapped her up, and led her upstairs and put her to bed and she thought it would be all right.

But when she woke, it was obvious that he hadn't joined her. His car was gone and there was no note explaining he'd been called out.

Didn't he believe her? Could he really think she had killed Rudy?

It was time, she decided, to end this. One way or the other.

She went into the house and picked up the phone.

Less than a half an hour later she pulled up in front of the worst motel in town. This was where he was staying? Her husband would rather sleep here than in their own house, with her?

He opened the door to his room before she even knocked. He looked dreadful, eyes puffy, face drawn, unshaven. Behind him she could hear the tinny voice of the TV, blaring out some stupid sports game.

He rarely watched sports on TV, although he did like to go to a hockey game when they were in Vancouver. He was a great reader, John, the sort of man who rarely watched TV or rented DVDs. He liked to spend his quiet time in the pages of a good book. He liked hard-edged action thrillers. She liked movies, light and fluffy things usually. On a normal Sunday evening they'd sit together in the family room, her curled up on her chaise lounge watching a silly romantic comedy, him in his leather chair, nose buried in a book. Apart, but somehow together. He would look up when she laughed or reach out to touch her hand as she passed by, heading for the kitchen or the bathroom, and she would sometimes sneak up behind him and plant kisses on his head.

This was most definitely not a normal Sunday evening.

"May I come in?" she said.

He stepped back. A bottle of beer was on the night table between the narrow twin beds. Another in the trash.

"We can't go on like this, John."

"It looks like we're going to have to," he said.

"How long do you plan to stay here?"

"In Trafalgar? As long as I have a job."

"You know that's not what I mean."

"In this room? I like it here, don't have anyone nagging at me to pick up my socks." She looked around. There were no socks on the floor. The place was probably neater than the maid left it.

"Is that so?"

"Paul Keller doesn't want me having any contact with you while you're under suspicion."

"You wouldn't have agreed to that if you hadn't wanted to," she said, feeling a knot of anger rising in her chest. He hadn't offered her a seat—which didn't really matter as there weren't any chairs and she was not going to perch on the end of a bed. "You are my husband, John, and I am your wife. I've been through hell this week and perhaps the worst part of it is realizing that I can't count on you to believe in me. Instead, you actually think it's possible I could cold-bloodily kill a man."

"I don't believe that," he said.

"That makes me feel so much better. Now, I know it's just that you'd rather live in this hovel than in our home, with me."

"I've my own problems with this, you know Eliza. The whispers behind my back, that fucking Madison and his smirks and insinuations."

He leaned across the bed to grab the bottle of beer and took a long drink.

She raised one eyebrow.

"What?" he growled. "It's just a beer."

"I didn't say anything."

"You don't have to. Your face is so bloody expressive. Is that why they liked you when you were a whore?"

She sucked in a breath. At last it was out. She'd been distraught, afraid she was watching her life falling into ruins around her, and so she'd told him most of what Rudy had said to her that night. She hadn't stopped to consider that perhaps she was telling John too much.

"I was never a prostitute."

"Whether money is involved or not doesn't matter in the law. Exchanging sexual services for something is called prostitution."

"Don't quote the law at me. You've no idea what you're talking about."

"What did your pal Rudy say? *Once a whore always a whore.*"

She hit him, hard across the face. He threw the bottle against the wall. It shattered and brown liquid sprayed across the floor.

"You bastard," she said, shocked at what she'd done. "You know nothing about it. I was young, I was innocent and naive, and I was living in a world where everyone, from my agent to my fiancé, was only interested in making sure I generated as much money as possible. You took me out of that. I've never, ever forgotten it. If you want to condemn me for things that happened thirty years ago, go ahead, but don't expect me to hang around to hear it. I'd move into the condo in Vancouver except your colleague has ordered me not to leave town. He's as judgmental as you."

His face was turning red, from the blow, from anger? Probably both.

"If you want to be Mr. High and Mighty go ahead, but tell me first how everything you've done in your life has been noble and honorable. Tell me when you were young and randy all the time you didn't ever try to take advantage of a girl. Or maybe you can tell me that you're a man, so that makes it all right."

She turned and grabbed the door knob. Her hand was so soaked with sweat it couldn't get purchase, and she had to use her other hand to help open it. She stepped outside, and took a deep breath.

She turned again, slowly this time.

"Oh, and John, none of this is about you. Get it? My past happened before I met you, and Rudy's death doesn't have anything to do with me, let alone you, although the police seem to want to make it so. You need to get over your hurt feelings, stop worrying that your friends are going to laugh at you as if you're a twelve-year-old, and offer me the support I have a right to expect from my husband. If you can't do that, I'd prefer you don't come home." She waved her hand at the shabby motel room. "You'll be happier living here, drowning in self-pity."

She walked to her car without looking back.

Chapter Twenty-four

First thing Monday morning the warrant to investigate Dennis Jones' financial records came though. Ray Lopez almost rubbed his hands together in glee. Conveniently, Jones kept his accounts in one bank. Lopez picked up the phone. He played poker with the branch manager occasionally.

Copies of Jones' financial records were on his computer before the hour was up. Lopez wasn't a forensic accountant, but he could read a simple bank statement easily enough. And Jones' was simple.

A small amount of money came in.

A large amount of money went out.

The guy had three credit cards maxed out at twenty-five thousand dollars each and a line of credit worth another twenty thousand. He didn't appear to own a home and drove a ten year old car. He had never been married and had no record of any children.

Earlier, Lopez had found that Jones had been given a couple of speeding tickets over the past year. One by the RCMP detachment in Kelowna, another on highway 33, heading toward Kelowna. He also had been arrested for being involved in a fight in a Kelowna bar. Lopez checked the date of the tickets and the fight against cash withdrawals on the credit cards. Bingo.

Jones was going to Kelowna, often, and taking a lot of money with him.

What was in Kelowna that Jones might find so appealing? Off hand, Lopez could think of one thing—a casino.

Passport records showed that Jones had taken a plane to Las Vegas twice in the past year. No doubt at all about what one would find appealing in Vegas.

Dennis Jones had a gambling problem. A serious one by the look of it. He was almost maxed out on his legitimate sources of funding. What would he do if he couldn't borrow from the credit card companies and the banks any longer?

Give it up?

Or find another source of cash? Like a rich brother.

Lopez glanced at his watch. It was almost noon. He was supposed to be on a diet, but he deserved a treat after that round of inspired police work. Time to order something from Trafalgar Thai, walk down and pick it up, that would count as exercise, eat lunch at his desk while reviewing his notes, and be ready for the meeting with IHIT at one.

◇◇◇

He had spent most of the night drinking beer while staring at some bunk on the sports channel, and on the way into town John Winters' mind kept calling up the fight with Eliza.

Last week they'd had what he thought of as a perfect marriage. Now? What was this doing to them? She'd never hit him before, rarely even raised her voice. She was an expert at showing her anger though a well-placed glare and a tilt of the chin. A lift of the eyebrow was the most disapproving she ever got.

She was right, and it hurt him to admit it. Somehow all of this, in his mind, had become about him, about his feelings, not about her and what she must be suffering. What had been his first thought on seeing the photograph of Eliza? He'd be a laughing stock at work.

As for his youthful antics, he'd done things he wasn't too proud of. There was that time in high school when he told the girl he was dating he wanted to marry her but first they needed to be sure they were sexually compatible. He'd bragged about his conquest to his buddies the next day.

He wondered what that girl was doing now. He couldn't even remember her name.

Eliza, his wife, was on the verge of being arrested for murder, and he was mad because of something she'd done twenty-five years ago?

Didn't she have the right to expect him to support her?

The Smith family had gathered in the waiting room outside the OR. Adam Tocek was with them, Molly's small hand folded into his big one. Jane Reynolds, Lucky's good friend, sat in a corner, knitting. A man Winters hadn't met paced the room. Lucky was sitting in an armchair, an unopened book on her lap. The room smelled of sanitizer and furniture polish, the only sound the clicking of Jane's needles.

They all looked up as he entered. "John." Lucky Smith got to her feet. "How nice of you to stop by."

"I wanted to wish you all the best," he said. "Paul Keller sends his regards."

She took his hand and held it in hers. Her eyes were very wet and the moisture made them shine like jewels. "Thank you so much."

Never one for a display of emotion, John Winters was highly uncomfortable with his hand being held. "Take a seat," Lucky said, releasing him at last. "I don't think you've met my son, Sam."

After the introductions, Winters went to the couch beside Molly and Adam. They shifted over to make room.

"How long's it been?" he asked.

"They started about half an hour ago," she said. She was dressed in jeans and a loose blue T-shirt, which matched her eyes. Her feet were stuffed into well-used running shoes and the laces on the right one had come undone.

They sat in silence for a few minutes. Jane's needles continued to move, and a soft white cloud filled her lap. From the corridor outside they could hear the sound of a busy hospital, shoes tapping, people talking, carts clattering.

Winters coughed. "Do you think your mother would mind if we talked shop for a few minutes, Molly? Someplace private."

He thought he'd kept his voice low, but Lucky heard. In a crisis in which she could do nothing, all her senses were on high. "Not at all. If we need you, we can find you."

They left the waiting room, Tocek following, went downstairs to the nearly empty cafeteria and sat at a long table in the back. No one wanted coffee. Winters and Tocek took the bench that put their backs against the wall. Smith faced them.

"I read your report on your visit to the neighbor on Station Street," Winters said.

"The Spencer Family." Molly smiled at Adam. "I was offered a baby to take home."

"That would constitute a bribe."

"More like a threat, I'd say."

They all laughed.

"This person taking pictures?" Winters asked. "Did Spencer see him only the once?"

"I think so. That's all he mentioned, anyway. Do you think it's important?"

"Probably not. Just clutching at straws. We've had five B&Es over the last six weeks. I'm going to go back to Elm Street, the scene of the last one, and do the neighbors again. I don't have much hope but maybe this guy with the camera was seen there as well."

◇◇◇

They were all there and Barb had had to gather chairs from other offices. The outsiders from IHIT, the local Mounties, Ray Lopez, Paul Keller.

John Winters' absence was like a missing tooth in the face of a grinning hockey player.

The mood in the Chief Constable's office was solemn. No one chatted about the weather, last night's game, about this and that. They stared at their notebooks and accepted the coffee Barb passed around. Before anyone said a word, Barb knew it was going to be rough.

She sat down and opened the laptop computer on which she'd take the minutes.

"I'm ready to bring Eliza Winters in," Madison said, without preamble. He had a strange sort of half-smile on his face, and Barb didn't trust him one bit.

She glanced at the Chief. He looked stunned. "You've learned something since we last spoke?"

"Nothing new, no. Just reinforcing my impressions."

"Then you've got fuck all," Lopez said. "The idea is preposterous. You bring her down here, she'll have a good case for laying a complaint."

"I'm with Ray," Ron Gavin said. "You go to court with that you'll be laughed out the door."

"You have a hunch, a suspicion, not a single thing that can stand up in court," Keller grabbed a can of coke out of the fridge behind his desk. He hadn't finished his coffee yet. "Yes, Mrs. Winters was in the deceased's hotel room shortly before he was killed. So was the room service waiter, but I hope you're not planning on arresting him too. You have no evidence. Nothing."

"I don't need your approval, Chief Constable," Madison said. "This is my investigation, and we're not going to vote on it. However, as a professional courtesy," his voice dripped with sarcasm, "I'm informing you. I intend to detain Eliza Winters, allow her to *assist us with our inquiries*. However, if it will make you feel better, I don't believe she killed Rudolph Steiner."

◇◇◇

"Frank Spencer is such an involved dad," Smith said. Her face was on Winters but she was looking at Adam Tocek out of the corner of her eyes. "Guy looks like he hasn't slept in a week. His wife works nights, here at the hospital, so I bet she comes home to a quiet house with the kiddies and the dog at day care and has a nice long sleep. And he gets them at night, after working all day."

"The dog goes to day care," Adam said, "Really?"

"Yeah, I…"

"What?" Winters said. "You've thought of something, I can see it written all over your face."

"The dog. The house on Elm Street, the one that was broken into. They had a dog too. I didn't see it, but I remember seeing a dog toy on the floor. They don't have kids. Did you see a dog when you were there?"

"No, no I didn't."

"Maybe it was still at the kennel," Adam said. "If they just got home they might not have picked it up yet."

"The first house we went to, they have a dog," Winters said. "They'd put it in that kennel on the highway as you head out of town. Houses number two and three had a dog, because one of the first things we checked, looking for something they all had in common, was if they used the same kennel. They didn't, and as I remember at least one of the families took the dog with them on vacation, so that line of inquiry closed." His mind raced. The two young officers watched him.

"This is the first I've heard of any dog day care," he said at last.

◇◇◇

"You're out of your mind," the Chief yelled over the din. Barb could think of a thing or two to say to the man from IHIT but she kept her head down, and concentrated on typing.

"That's ridiculous," Ray Lopez said.

"If you people can't keep your emotions out of it then this meeting is over," Madison said.

"It's over when I say it is," Keller snapped back.

"John Winters knew his wife was screwing around with her old flame. Hell, maybe she was thinking of getting back with him. We know the guy was dying, maybe he played the pity card."

"Maybe he played the idiot card," Lopez muttered, so low only Barb could hear. She didn't enter that into the minutes.

"Winters went to the hotel after she left and shot him," Madison continued.

"Steiner wasn't killed with a Glock," Gavin said.

"I don't think for a minute Winters is stupid enough to use his own service weapon. I've run his passport and see he went to Florida a couple of weeks ago."

"His wife's parents are in Florida," Lopez almost shouted, seeing where this was going. "Half the old people in Canada go to Florida for the winter."

"The reason doesn't matter. It was the opportunity for him to purchase an illegal weapon."

"My wife and I went on a tour to Russia last year," Keller said. "Where I had the opportunity to purchase weapons grade plutonium on the black market. I did not."

"In my experience," Madison said, "the sort of man who's most likely to resort to violence at his wife's infidelities is the one who's screwing around himself. Winters is having an affair with Constable Smith."

She was so shocked, Barb stopped typing.

Keller laughed. "Now you're right around the bend."

"I saw them together yesterday as it happens."

"I don't believe it," Lopez said. "Where?"

"That coffee place around the corner. Looking quite intimate. It was most touching."

"Intimate at Big Eddie's! Oh, yeah, if I was having a secret assignation, I'd conduct it at a place I could be sure most of my colleagues would pass through in any given day."

Everyone spoke at once, and Barb could tell the room was not behind Madison. Even the other member of the IHIT team looked unhappy.

"If you pursue this," Keller said. "I will make a formal complaint. I will state that I believe you have a personal vendetta against a member of this force and are exercising improper judgment. In light of the recent difficulties the RCMP is having with its public image, I don't imagine your bosses will be too happy about that."

Madison stiffened. "I would have thought we're all interested in seeing justice done no matter who's the perpetrator."

"Now see here." Keller began to stand up.

"See justice done, exactly," Ray Lopez raised his voice. "I'd like to talk about the brother, Dennis Jones." Keller dropped back down. He drained his can of pop, and crushed it in his right hand.

"We have motive and opportunity." Lopez emphasized the points by counting them off on his fingers, "The killer had to be someone close to Steiner. You're forgetting, Sergeant, that Steiner invited this person into his room, and went to the bathroom to be sick. Would he have turned his back on someone he didn't trust?"

◇◇◇

"Molly, get back to everyone who's had a B&E, confirm that they own a dog, and find out what they do with it during the day." Winters remembered where he was and stopped issuing orders. "Sorry, forgot. You're kind of busy right now."

"I'll be at work tomorrow, and I can do it then, if you don't mind waiting a day. I probably don't have to talk to them personally, a phone call should do it. Do you think we're onto something?"

"I've been trying and trying to come up with what these victims all have in common. So far nothing. This might be a stretch, but it's worth a couple of phone calls. Don't worry about it, I'll call them myself later. You just worry about your dad."

"Dog day care," she said, stretching the words out as if she were tasting them. "I know someone who works at such a place."

"Give me their address and I'll go around."

"No," she said. "That wouldn't work. I don't mean you can't do it, I mean it's a special case." She explained quickly about Amy and her new job. "Amy knows me, and I think she likes me. She might not open up to you."

She looked at her watch. "I'll stay with Mom until Dad's out of surgery and back in his room, and then pay Amy a visit."

◇◇◇

"Dennis Jones owes a hundred thousand dollars to credit cards and his bank. I'd guess he probably owes a lot more to sources I haven't found yet. He's a maintenance man at a hotel, not much money in that. His long-lost brother arrives in town, flashing the cash, the trophy wife, the assistant. There was already a lot of bad blood between the brothers. Jones was seen on that floor around five o'clock. He says he was replacing a broken lamp, which may or may not be true, but it's good odds he dropped in on his brother at the same time. Rudy refused to give him money, they had an argument, Jones stews about it for a couple of hours and comes back later to continue the fight. Steiner won't give in, Jones looses it, and pop. Jones wears baggy workingman's overalls and carries a belt load of equipment on him. Easy enough to hide a handgun. You don't have to go out of Canada to buy a gun, you know. They're available right here if you know where to look, and Jones is likely to know where to look."

"You're still forgetting about the sneaking up from behind part," Kevin Farzaneh said. "First, let me say I've seen Molly Smith and Winters together and if they're doing the dirty, I'll..." he touched his shiny dome, "eat my hair." They all, except Madison, laughed. The laughter was tight and forced, nothing but relief at the chance to momentarily break the tension.

Keller looked at Barb. She tried to read his mind, but couldn't. She gave him what she hoped was a supporting smile. He didn't smile back, but perhaps some of the strain lifted from his face.

"Go on," he said to Farzaneh.

"The mob angle. How we can sit here and not even mention that there is a known mobster in town, who happens to be staying at the same hotel in which the murder was committed, where the wife is still staying, I can't imagine."

"This is the first I've heard of this," Keller said. "I've read the report about Mrs. Steiner's father, and I know her father's lawyer came to town *poste haste*. Are you saying someone else from Marais' organization is here?"

"That's what I'm saying, saw him myself. What's this about Mrs. Steiner's father? You're saying he's a made man?" Farzaneh turned to Madison. "Why didn't you tell me this?"

"Because you didn't need to know. You're here to help with the forensics."

"Mrs. Steiner's father is Guy Marais," Keller said.

"What the hell? You know I worked organized crime in New Brunswick. You didn't think I might have something to contribute to this?" Farzaneh threw up his hands.

"That's neither here nor there," Keller said. "I'll let you sort out the lines of communication. Kevin's right. We have a known criminal connection. The long arm of Mrs. Steiner's father. Why aren't we paying a lot more attention to that?"

"Or to Mrs. Steiner." Alison Townshend spoke for the first time. "Rather than gossiping about who might be fooling around with who." She threw Madison a poisonous look. He didn't react. "Let's talk about who was definitely fooling around. Josie Steiner was married to a much older guy who's about to kick the bucket. She has criminal connections, no problem at all about getting a weapon, she probably found a new one in her Christmas stocking every year. The marriage was odd, to say the least, perhaps she decided to get out of it the easy way.

"What's her story for the time he died?"

"Not much," Lopez said. "That lawyer watches over her like a mother lion. She says what he allows her to say, and that's that she left Steiner's room around seven after looking at the day's photographs, and was alone in her own room, having a glass of wine, with the TV on loud, for the rest of the evening. Not much of an alibi. Room service records show she orders a bottle of wine, sometimes two, every night. The bottles are empty when picked up in the morning."

"She, above all the people previously mentioned," Townshend said with a satisfied nod, "would be able to walk up behind her husband upchucking into the toilet. I think that's one of the things they cover in the for better or for worse part of the marriage vows."

◇◇◇

They agreed Winters would head back to the office and find out if the homeowners all used the same facility for their dogs.

Molly would go around to Amy's later, unofficially, and talk to her about the day care.

"Anything I can do?" Adam asked.

"You could send Norman into the joint, undercover."

"He could sniff around, smell out the word on the street."

They smiled at each other, in a way that made Winters feel as if he wasn't in the room.

Winters wanted to find Madison and smack some sense into the creep. It wasn't easy, he knew, for women to get accepted in this job. It was in many ways still an old boy's club. Molly shouldn't have had to fear that reporting Charlie Bassing's harassment would make her colleagues think any the less of her. Whether or not it would have didn't really matter as long as she thought it would.

The last thing she needed were rumors, no matter how ill-founded, that she was aiming for promotion by sleeping with her superior officer.

"I'll say good-bye to your mom," he said. "And as for that matter we talked about yesterday, I'll be doing something about it this afternoon."

"Thanks."

"What matter?" Tocek asked.

"Nothing," Smith and Winters said in unison.

Tocek didn't look convinced.

"Anything?" Smith asked her mother when they walked into the waiting room.

"Not a peep," Lucky said.

"I'm going into work," Winters said. "If you need anything, be sure to call."

"Thank you."

The door opened and a man walked in. He was dressed in blue scrubs too long for his short legs. A woman followed him, wearing a nice business suit.

The man approached Lucky. He had coke-bottle-bottom glasses propped on the top of his head, and smelled of the human body. The woman with him had deep, serious eyes, and she was not smiling.

Lucky got to her feet, a bit shakily, her eyes round as she tried to read their faces. Jane Reynolds put down her knitting. Molly and her brother stood on either side of their mom. She was so short, and looked so frail, between them.

Adam Tocek and John Winters glanced at each other. They'd given the bad news many times, to many families. They knew that expression, the look in the eyes.

"Mrs. Smith," the doctor said. "I am so very sorry to have to tell you this, but Mr. Smith did not survive the procedure."

"What?" Lucky said as all the color drained from her face.

The woman, almost certainly a grief councilor, stepped forward. "Why don't you sit down, Mrs. Smith."

"I don't want to sit down. Is the operation over? Is Andy in the recovery room? When will he wake up?"

Adam Tocek said, "What do you mean, he didn't survive? It was a goddamned hip operation. My eighty-six year old grandmother had one and is the champion of her lawn bowling team."

"Mr. Smith suffered a pulmonary embolus, a blood clot in his leg. It can be difficult to detect and…well…when he was moved to the table it broke away and quickly moved to his heart. He went into shock, and…I'm sorry, Mrs. Smith, but despite all our efforts we were unable to get his heart working again."

Lucky swayed. Sam Smith put his arm around his mother. "Come on, Mom," he said. "Let's sit down."

Jane Reynolds' knitting needles were still in her hand. The wool had fallen to the floor. Tears ran down her cheeks.

"Dad?" Molly said, her voice catching in her throat. "Where's my dad?"

The doctor turned to her. "I'm sorry, Miss Smith. Your father didn't survive."

She moaned, a long plaintive wail. Adam Tocek wrapped her in his arms.

Chapter Twenty-five

"It seems to me," Paul Keller said, "we have a plethora of suspects here. *Good* suspects, not gut feelings or grudge matches."

Madison sat there with a sly smile on his face. *He's a weird one*, Barb thought.

"Now," Keller went on, "as much as this is an IHIT investigation, I do believe the first 'I' means integrated, as in working together, is that correct?"

Madison continued to smile. Finally Kevin Farzaneh said, "yes it does."

"This is my town," Keller said, "and once you've gone, with or without making an arrest, back to your regular jobs, I have to live here, I have to police here, and I have a department to run. Therefore, I have a few suggestions to make to the team. Good work Ray on digging up Jones' financials. Keep digging and let him know you're digging. Might shake him up a bit. The mob angle is good, very promising. As you seem to know about these people, Corporal Farzaneh, perhaps you could find out if the muscle was in town last week. And as for Mrs. Steiner, seems to me that in my days as a detective we always considered the spouse first. Are we finished here?" He looked around the room. Everyone was nodding except for Dick Madison. "Good. John Winters is still my lead detective in everything other than the Steiner murder. If that changes, I expect to know about it first. His wife will not be detained in order to force him to confess. Just a suggestion, of course."

"Of course," Madison said.

Everyone began to stand up.

"Team work," Madison said. He remained sitting, his legs stretched out in front of him. "It's all about team work. Shake things up, throw out a ridiculous idea, and you find people can quickly put their minds to coming up with a better one." He stood up. "Alison, get back to the lab. We've a lot more tests to run. Kevin, check into Langois' movements. Gavin, I need a lift to the Hudson House Hotel. I'm going to have another chat with Mrs. Steiner." He left, without saying good bye.

The others followed. Ray Lopez and Ron Gavin gave each other confused looks. Farzaneh kept his eyes on the floor. Barb closed her computer and unplugged it.

"Shut the door, will you," Keller said.

She did so.

"What a crock." He tore the tab off a can of pop.

"You don't think he mentioned John and Eliza in order to get people thinking?"

"If he did, it's about the stupidest thing I've ever heard. The guy's a loose cannon, couldn't admit he was making a mistake when all the other suspects came up, so pretended he was stringing us along. I'm going to have to mention it to his commander. I'll make sure they know I don't ever want that jackass back in my town."

"Will they listen to you?"

"Probably not."

The phone on his desk rang. "Well that was fun, back to work." He picked up the phone, listened for a moment, and said, "Thanks for letting me know."

He placed the phone in the cradle carefully and took a deep breath. When he looked at Barb his eyes were round and sad.

"What?"

"That was John. He's at the hospital. Andy Smith died on the operating table."

◇◇◇

John Winters didn't stay long. Lucky had her friend and her children; Molly had Adam. He wasn't needed.

Ray Lopez was in the office when he came in. "I heard about Molly's dad," Lopez said. "Darn tough."

"Fifty-seven," Winters said, tossing his jacket onto the hook by the door. "Too damned young. It came out of nowhere, was supposed to be a routine operation."

"Barb's taking up a collection for flowers. The department will send something, but Barb likes the personal touch."

"Good old Barb. I can't imagine they pay her enough."

Lopez stood up. He shut the office door, and turned to stand with his back to it. "I have to tell you something. The guy's out to get you, John."

Winters didn't have to ask Lopez who he was talking about. "Yeah, I figured that. I've never met him before, never heard of him until last week. I've no idea what he's thinking."

"You're not the only one in his sights."

"Molly?"

"Yes."

"Is anyone buying what he's selling? I don't mean about me, I can handle it. Her? Not so well."

"The Chief almost threw Madison out of his office, and I thought Barb was going to hit him over the head with her computer. You know as well as I do that most people in this department like Molly. She's a nice person and a good officer. But there are always some…"

"I know."

"I hate to say every cloud has a silver lining, but with the death of her dad happening so suddenly no one will want to be seen bad-mouthing her."

"What are you working on?" Winters changed the subject.

"If I was allowed to, I'd tell you I'm about to have a chat with Dennis Jones, who turns out to be the estranged brother of Rudolph Steiner, nee Albert Jones, and that I'm gathering details of his precarious financial situation so he knows I know he's in a ton of trouble. Unfortunately I can't tell you that right now Jones is the number one suspect, but only one of several, so I won't."

Winters grinned. "Thanks, Ray. I've got a few calls to make about the B&E business."

"I'd forgotten all about that. You have a lead?"

"I hope so."

They returned to their computers.

A few minutes later Lopez got up and left, presumably to visit Jones. Winters began calling B&E victims at their places of work. Only one wasn't available, but the others told the same story. They took their dogs to Debby's Dog Centre Monday to Friday during the day while they were at work. It was much better, they all said, for the dog to be exercised and in a social environment than sitting at home alone, lonely and bored.

He leaned back in his chair and thought about his next move. He'd find out what he could about Debby, whoever she was, do a record check, see if she'd ever been in any trouble. Presumably she had some staff, even if just someone to keep the books, and a partner, or friends with whom she chatted about her business. Chat about things like who wasn't going to be coming for a couple of weeks because they were going on vacation. Molly had mentioned Amy worked there part-time. He'd met Amy once; unlikely she had the organizational skills to pull off a series of B&Es.

Molly had been planning to drop in on Amy, ask a few questions about the running of the dog care business. He couldn't ask her to do it now.

He had something else to do first. He picked up the phone. "Jim, is Dawn back yet?"

"She's waiting for you."

Dawn Solway was standing by the dispatch desk when Winters got there. He'd checked earlier to see who was on shift this afternoon. Solway and Brad Noseworthy. For this job, he wanted the woman. He explained what they were after.

"Once we get in hearing range, I want lights and sirens. The whole shebang. We're going in like gang busters. I want the handcuffs on before he can blink."

"It'll be my pleasure," she said.

"The bigger the audience the better. I'll say the words, then you stuff him in the car. Lights and sirens all the way back to the station. Let's go."

"Tough about Molly's dad," Solway said, pulling into Monroe Street. They were heading for the garden center on the other side of the Upper Kootenay River. It was still only early April, but landscaping businesses were busy getting stock in, preparing for the spring rush soon to begin. Lots of heavy lifting to be done, bags of compost, mulch, potting soil, trees with roots wrapped in burlap bags, crates of seedlings and small plants. Good work for a man with muscle but not much else.

As they crossed the bridge, Solway began the sound and light show. She took the corner into the side street on two wheels. By the time they got to the parking lot, and pulled up in a shower of gravel, people had stopped work to see what was going on.

Charlie Bassing was driving a forklift, moving a couple of baby maple trees. His white T-shirt was filthy with sweat and soil and his baseball hat pushed to the back of his head.

Winters marched up to the forklift, Solway behind. "Charles Bassing," he said, in a good loud voice. "Get down from there. I'm arresting you on a charge of criminal harassment."

"What the fuck?"

"Climb down, or I will bring you down. Now."

The moment Bassing's feet were on the ground, Solway moved in. She pulled his arms behind him and snapped the handcuffs on. She took hold of his arm and marched him to the car.

"Hey," Bassing shouted, trying to twist in the woman's iron grip, "I didn't do nothing."

"You will have the opportunity to tell that to a judge," Winters said. "You have the right…" he followed, reciting the warning. Solway pushed Bassing into the back seat of the car, her hand on the top of his head. The two officers got in the front and she drove away, siren shattering the peace of the spring air. Bassing began to swear. Solway turned her head slightly, and Winters winked.

The whole thing had taken less than two minutes. He'd been particularly satisfied at the looks of open-mouthed astonishment on the faces of the onlookers.

◇◇◇

By the time they got home, to the house in the woods at a bend in a tributary of the Upper Kootenay River, Lucky's legions of friends had gathered. Tea and coffee were made, cookies and squares laid out on plates in the center of the wide, heavily-scarred pine table. A pot of fragrant stew bubbled on the stove, and the dog's food and water dishes were full.

Sylvester ran to the door to greet Lucky, his favorite person. His furry tail wagged and his wet pink tongue hung out of his mouth at the sheer pleasure of seeing her.

Lucky dropped to her knees and put her arms around him. Her whole body shook as she hugged the dog. Happy at first at the attention, Sylvester soon began to squirm and try to pull away. Sam put his hand on his mother's arm, and guided her to her feet. Her face was streaked with tears, and a few golden dog hairs had attached themselves to her cheek. Sam brushed them away.

"I have to get Norman and go to work," Adam said to Molly. "You going to be okay?"

"As okay as I can be." She turned her face up for a kiss.

"You going to stay here for the night?"

"Probably."

"I'll come by first thing tomorrow." He kissed her, very softly, and turned and walked away.

She went into the kitchen.

When the doctor broke the awful news, it had taken her straight back to the day Graham died. They'd said he was in critical condition, but she arrived at the hospital to find that Graham hadn't had a chance; he'd been dead when he'd been found. Lying in a filthy, garbage-strewn alley, a knife in his stomach. Victim of one of the druggies he'd been trying to help.

Today Adam had been so kind, so caring, she was embarrassed she'd been remembering Graham.

"Moonlight, dear?"

Smith snapped back. Jane Reynolds was speaking to her. The old woman's eyes shone with tears and kindness. "Tea is ready."

"Thanks."

Smith started to hang her jacket on the row of hooks by the door. Her hand froze. Her dad's hat was there, the one he always wore working in the yard in summer to protect his balding head. She swallowed, and turned away, and dropped the jacket over the back of a chair.

Sam had settled Lucky at the kitchen table. One of her friends had placed a mug of tea and a lemon square and oatmeal cookie in front of her. Her fingers tore the cookies into crumbs.

"Would you like to lie down?" Jane asked in a low, soft voice.

"I'm so very tired all of a sudden. Moonlight," Lucky said, "will you help me?"

"Sure, Mom."

They went upstairs, to the large, sunny bedroom at the end of the hall where Lucky and Andy had slept together for more than thirty years. Smith helped her mother take off her shoes and her pants. Lucky lay down and her daughter pulled the cover up. It was a beautiful quilt, which Lucky won in a fund-raising raffle for the Grandmothers in Africa group. It was made of tiny squares in all shades of blue, getting increasingly lighter as the squares moved toward the center.

Lucky closed her eyes. Her chest moved. "Did I ever tell you how your father and I met?"

Many times. Smith stroked her mother's hand.

"We were in our junior year at the University of Washington. He had his eye on a girl in my Medieval European history class, one of the campus organizers for the SDS. Andy didn't have the slightest interest in Medieval Europe, but he was trying to look interested in order to impress her." Lucky chuckled at the memory. "Between his involvement in the SDS and everything else anti-war, and going to classes he wasn't even taking, it's no wonder he failed his math courses. He always sat beside me, only because it had a good view of the girl. I thought he was cute, and I wondered how I could get him to start talking to me. He smoked heavily, so many of us did back then. I didn't really smoke but thought I'd try it to look mature and serious. I pulled out a pack of cigarettes and offered him one. Imagine smoking in a lecture hall. I believe that's a capital offence now." Lucky's voice was soft, but steady. "I gave the pack a little jerk to release one, the way I'd seen people do on TV, and the whole lot of them spilled out. All over the floor, between the seats. I was horribly embarrassed. Your dad picked two up, gave me one, put one in his mouth and lit mine first. Since that day, we've scarcely ever spent a day apart." Her eyes closed. Molly sat with her mother for a while, deep in her own thoughts. Mostly of her father, who she'd always adored, but also about Graham. And Adam.

When Lucky's breathing was steady, Molly gave her a light kiss, whispered, "Sleep well, Mom," and tiptoed out. She left the door open a crack and went downstairs.

Sam sat at the kitchen table with Jane Reynolds. Another of Lucky's friends stood at the sink, washing dishes.

"How is she?" Jane asked.

"Sleeping."

"That's good."

"I've called Judy," Sam said. "She and the kids will be here tomorrow. I spoke to Aunt Helen and she'll break the news to Grandma and Aunt Mary-Ann. She'll call us when they've made their flight arrangements."

"Thanks, Sam."

"We need to contact…" his voice broke, and he turned away. When he recovered he looked at his sister. "The funeral home."

"Mom'll want to be there."

"Let your mother sleep," Jane said. "I'll phone the home and let them know you'll be by first thing in the morning to begin the discussion."

"Thanks," Sam and Molly said.

Sam got up. "I'm going for a walk, won't be long. Want to come Moon?"

"No. I've got something I have to do. Will you be here until Sam gets back, Jane?"

"Of course."

Her ruined car was at the police lock up. She reached for her dad's keys from the hook by the door and felt a wave of sadness wash over her. Then she grabbed the keys and left.

◇◇◇

Lucky Smith felt her daughter's soft lips on her cheek, heard the whispered, "Sleep well, Mom," and the sound of the door moving but not quite closing. When she was sure Moonlight was gone, she opened her eyes. The curtains were drawn, but the room was still bright. She lay on her back with her eyes open.

Andy.

They'd been married for thirty years. They'd had good times and bad, and had been through a patch so rough a year ago that it looked as if the marriage might not survive. But it had held, and got better, and then, to her surprise, they found themselves falling in love all over again.

Andy. Andrew Smith Junior, who liked his eggs so over easy they were disgustingly raw and couldn't abide cooked tomatoes or red peppers in any form and tried very hard to diet but did love junk food. He left the toilet seat up and drank beer straight from the bottle and liked to cook steaks on the barbeque, medium rare. He thought he was a great handyman, but it took him hours to mend the fence or fix the plumbing and Lucky usually had to call in a contractor to repair whatever 'fix' Andy had done. He didn't read much, any more, loved the Vancouver Canucks, hated the Blue Jays, supported the Seattle Mariners. All the University level calculus and algebra he'd studied had been lost long ago, and somehow it had fallen on Lucky to balance the business' books and household accounts. He cursed and swore over the *Globe and Mail* on a Sunday morning and said the country was going to hell in a hand basket. He bragged about his son, the lawyer, fully expected that his grandson, still only five years old, would make the NHL one day, and almost burst his buttons when he told people what his daughter did for a living. Not that he would ever tell her. He phoned his mom, now drifting in and out of lucidity in a nursing home, every Sunday without fail, and mourned his father, who had died without having reconciled with the son he regarded as a traitor, to his family as well as his country.

He was a normal man, of his age, his place, his time.

She loved him to the depths of her soul.

At last she slept.

◇◇◇

Charles Bassing, bursting with righteous indignation, was charged with the criminal harassment of Constable M. L. Smith. He protested that he'd passed Smith in town a few times: it was hard not to as it was her job to walk up and down the street. He claimed to know nothing about any rat nailed to the door or the destruction of her car. Ron Gavin had taken a break from his other work, including the Steiner murder, to go over the car very, very carefully. He found no evidence of Bassing's fingerprints, which didn't surprise Winters. Without a witness, not even Smith had actually seen him, it wasn't nearly enough to hold him. Threatening gestures were always open to interpretation.

But it was enough to let Bassing know the police would be watching him and to arrange a day in court. "Your parole officer will be made aware of this," Winters said. "If you don't want to go back to jail, stay away from Molly Smith, her home, her property, her family."

Bassing sneered. He smelled of garden soil and sweat and naked aggression. "Fuckin' bitch. Go near her and my balls are likely to fall off. Like yours have done, I'd guess."

"Feel free to insult me all you want, Bassing. It's all part of the record."

He was soon swaggering down the steps of the police station. Winters watched him go. Something uncomfortable niggled at the back of his neck. He'd taken a gamble that the arrest and the charges would be enough to curb the man's behavior.

What if he were wrong?

Chapter Twenty-six

Meredith spent the weekend holed up in her apartment. She'd looked into Josie Steiner's background, and a very interesting background it turned out to be. One of Meredith's classmates was working for TV in Montreal and put her onto all sorts of stuff about the business dealings of the Marais family.

Juicy, juicy.

She sent the beginnings of a story about high fashion, aging but still glamorous models, young wives, murder, and the criminal underworld to some of the less reputable papers and leaned back in her chair with a satisfied sigh. Maybe, just maybe, getting fired from the *Trafalgar Gazette* would turn out to the best thing that could have happened.

Josie Steiner might be connected but she was as dumb as a stack of bricks. Meredith was due to meet her in the hotel bar at six. Ply her with a couple of drinks and hopefully the woman would give up the dirt, thinking she was helping with a piece on herself for some celebrity mag. As if.

Emily Wilson wasn't any brighter than Josie. The stupid girl had called Meredith earlier, all in tears because Dave Evans dumped her for talking to the reporter. Somehow, in Emily's mind it was Meredith's fault. "Here's an idea," she told Emily, "don't tell a reporter if you don't want to see it in the paper the next day." She hung up, thinking Evans wasn't all that bright either.

She started at a knock on her door. It sounded as if someone were hitting it with a hammer.

She opened the door and peeked out. "Yes?"

In Trafalgar plenty of people didn't lock their doors, and almost no one checked to see who was there before opening up. By the time Meredith realized her mistake, it was too late.

The man pushed her out of the way and came in, kicking the door shut behind him. She reached into her pocket for her cell phone but it wasn't there. She'd put it on the kitchen table to recharge. The man was short, but stocky, with a neck as thick as his head. His hands were like hairy baseball gloves. Incongruously, he was dressed in an expensive suit, perfectly clean and sharply pressed. She took a step backwards, and prepared to scream.

He grabbed her arm and lifted one finger to his lips. "Not a sound, Madame." He had a strong Quebec accent, and smelled of men's cologne, heavily applied. "I am not 'ere to 'urt you."

She swallowed. Her arm throbbed under the pressure of his hand. He squeezed it a bit harder. "Unless I 'ave to."

Still holding her, he looked around the room. His eyes rested on the computer, her notebook beside it. "Writing, Madame?" he said.

He waited a moment. "I asked if you are writing?"

Her mouth was so dry, and her tongue so heavy, it was difficult to get the words out. "I'm a journalist. I write...I write for a living."

"You write about small town things, eh? 'ockey score. What's on at the movies. Police corruption."

She nodded.

"That's good. A good job. You do not write about people who have lost their 'usband to a random murder, do you?"

He waited a moment, and then gave her arm another squeeze. "It is not polite to not answer a question. I said, you do not write about these things that are not the business of you or your town."

"No."

"That is also good." He looked around her apartment. It was small, but comfortable, and she'd taken care to decorate it with things important to her.

His other hand shot out and he picked a small china figurine off the table. Shepherdess with a crook. It was old-fashioned and ugly and chipped but it had been cherished by Meredith's grandmother, the one for whom she had been named. The man looked into Meredith's eyes as he held it. She heard a crack and the shepherdess fell to the hardwood floor.

"Madame Steiner will not be joining you for dinner. You will make no more telephone calls to Montréal. Understand?"

She nodded.

"I asked if you understand."

"Yes." She forced her lips to move but no sound came out.

He let go of her arm. "That is also good. And so I can say *Au revoir*, Madame."

He opened the door. She took a deep breath, but it caught in her chest when he turned around suddenly. "You should put the chain on when you do not know who is calling. Some people are not as reasonable as me."

He shut the door quietly behind him.

Meredith dropped to the floor. Sobbing, she gathered up the pieces of her grandmother's shepherdess.

◇◇◇

Molly Smith phoned Winters as she drove into town. "I should be the one to drop in on Amy," she said. "We have a rapport, although tenuous, from when we were in school." First time she'd considered that an advantage. "I spoke to Mike, her brother, about it just the other day."

"Don't you think your mother needs you?"

"She's sleeping. Sam's with her, and her friends. John, I need to do...something."

"Let me know what you find out. I've charged Bassing with criminal harassment. Had to let him go, but we'll get him into court this week. I'm hoping this'll be enough to have his parole revoked."

"Thanks, John."

"Just doing my job."

Mike and Amy lived in the top floor of an old house broken up into apartments. Smith climbed the stairs at the back. They had a spectacular view across the rooftops to town. The sun shone on the sparkling waters of the river, and the buds of the trees in the yard were beginning to swell. Mike waited by the open door, dressed for work in dark pants and a black T-shirt with the logo of the Bishop and Nun. He didn't look pleased to see her.

"Is this going to take long? I have to eat dinner and get to work. We went around to Rosemary's earlier and settled up. I haven't had time to call your mom about some counseling."

"My mom. She won't be at the center for a while. Ask for someone else."

He looked at her, and the defensive tone in his voice faded. "Are you okay, Molly?"

"Yeah, Mike. I'm fine. I'm not here about that business with Rosemary, and I promise I won't be more than a couple of minutes."

Amy's son Robby ran toward them, shrieking. He grabbed Smith's legs and held on, yelling something indecipherable. His face and hands were sticky with blueberry jam and when Mike pried him away, there were blue stains on her khaki pants.

Amy stirred a pot on the stove. It smelled great, of garlic and tomatoes and herbs. She said, very formally, "How nice of you to call, Moonlight. Will you join us for dinner? We're having spaghetti. Mike likes spaghetti."

"Thanks, Amy, but no. I need to ask you a couple of questions about the place you work, is that okay with you?"

"Yes."

Mike sat down. The table was old, cheap wood, badly chipped, but it, like the rest of the kitchen, was impeccably clean. A trace of the scent of skunk mixed with coffee—pot—lingered in the air. Smith ignored it.

"Mike, if you wouldn't mind giving Amy and me a few minutes…"

He looked dubious.

"I have a couple of simple questions about the dog center where Amy works, that's all." Smith watched Mike's face. He didn't show any signs of being particularly concerned when she mentioned the dog place. That was good. But what did she know, she wasn't a detective.

She gave him what she hoped was a reassuring smile, and he got to his feet with some reluctance. "I'll take Robbie and wash his hands." He scooped up the little boy, tickled him under the chin, and carried him out slung over his shoulder. Robbie waved at Smith, and Mike closed the door behind them.

"You work at Debby's Dog Centre, right?" Smith asked Amy when man and boy had gone.

"Yes." Amy continued stirring. "I like it there."

"I'm glad. Do you get mostly the same dogs every day?"

"Some of them. Some come once in a while, when their owners have an appointment or something."

"Tell me about the ones who come every day. They don't actually come every day, would that be right?"

Amy's face scrunched up. She paused with the spoon held over the pot. Red liquid dripped from it.

A floorboard creaked and Smith knew Mike was listening. She liked Mike a lot, thought he did a good job looking after his sister and her son. She didn't think he was behind the thefts, but you never knew what people would do when the responsibilities got too big and the bank account got too small.

"No," Amy said at last. "The regulars don't come on the weekend."

"What about when people go away, like on vacation?"

"Then they can't bring their dogs, can they, Moon?"

"I guess not. Do they tell you when they're going to be away?"

"Yes. Debby told me it's important to know when the regulars aren't coming. So she can manage the cash flow." Amy grinned. She was obviously reciting the term, and pleased with herself for remembering. "Like I have to manage my cash flow and not buy things when I don't have money. Mike told me that."

"Do you like working there?"

She smiled. Amy was not pretty, her complexion was poor and her hair lifeless and badly cut, but when she smiled her eyes filled with a joy that lit up her face. "Oh, yes, it's wonderful. The dogs are so nice. Debby says I have a way with dogs. That's good, right, Moon?"

"Very good." Winters would no doubt soon be paying a call on Debby. Smith had seen her around, talked to her a couple of times when walking the beat. She was in her forties, and full of enthusiasm about her new business. Strange that she'd risk it all by breaking into clients' homes when they were away. Unless that had been the plan all along.

"That's about all I wanted to know. Thanks for your time, Amy. Say bye to Mike for me." Smith started to turn toward the door. Then she stopped. She looked at the kitchen table again. It was laid with three place settings: knife and fork and spoon and a folded square of paper towel tucked under the knife. Robbie wouldn't sit to the table: his plastic bowl, decorated with a picture of brightly colored balloons, was on the tray of his highchair.

"Amy, when you know someone's going to be away for a while, on vacation, do you, well, tell anyone?"

"That's confidential information." She mispronounced the words slightly as if repeating what she'd been told.

"Thanks. See you around."

"Diane said it's okay to tell her, though. She'll keep it confidential, too."

"Who's Diane?"

The door off the kitchen opened.

"Diane is our cousin," Mike said. "She's staying here for a while. What are you getting at, Molly?" Robbie had the right ear of a stuffed pink rabbit in his mouth. He toddled over to his mother and tugged at her leg.

"I'd appreciate it if you don't tell anyone about this discussion, Mike. Amy, can you keep it a secret?"

"Sure," she said, picking up Robbie.

Smith doubted that, but she only needed enough time to get to Sergeant Winters.

"Catch you later," she said. She ran down the stairs so fast her running shoe slipped on the step and she managed to keep her footing only by grabbing at the peeling wooden banister. A splinter broke off and imbedded itself into her right thumb. She ignored it and was almost at her car when a woman came around the corner. She was dressed in loose clothes, and had a camera bag tossed over her shoulder. Smith averted her face and scurried across the street. The woman passed without giving her a glance.

Smith had been in uniform when they'd met. The uniform her brother said made her look tough, not like any young woman going about her business in a residential street.

She nipped behind a walnut tree and watched the woman turn at Mike and Amy's apartment and head for the back stars.

Diane, the cousin.

Diane Barton. Rudy Steiner's assistant.

Chapter Twenty-seven

Ray Lopez went back to the Hudson House Hotel, one more time. He had a gut feeling about Dennis Jones. Then again, perhaps he shouldn't have had the extra spicy golden curry for lunch. He stifled a burp.

Dennis Jones was waiting in the conference room, looking out the window. The hotel was beginning to treat the police like staff: no more coffee, sandwiches, cookies, just an empty table.

When Lopez came in, Jones threw himself into a chair. He had a purple-gray circle around his right eye, and his knuckles were scratched. Lopez openly studied the man's face. "What happened to you?" he said at last.

"Walked into a door," Jones said. He glared at the detective with an expression as dark as the bruises on his face, then lowered his head to study his hands. He began picking at dirt lodged under his fingernail. Lopez made a mental note to check the shift reports for the last couple of nights.

He sat down and threaded his fingers together. "What did your brother say when you asked him for money?"

Jones' head jerked up. Lopez watched him, saying nothing further. He was only guessing, had no reason, other than his gut instinct and his reading of the handyman, to believe Jones had confronted his brother.

Finally Jones shrugged. "He lied. Said he'd help me out if he could, but he was dead broke."

"You didn't believe him?"

"'Course I didn't." Jones jumped to his feet. He crossed the room to stand at the window. It had a view only of the back alley and the rear of the building opposite. "Look at the way he lived. Look at the wife. Think a woman like that would stay with him if he didn't have money coming out of his ass?"

It wasn't Lopez's place to tell Jones that his brother had, in fact, been telling the truth. "What time did this happen?"

Jones turned, and stared into the detective's face. "I don't remember," he said.

"By your own account, you were on the second floor around five-ish." So far no one had come forward to report seeing Jones later in the day. To hotel guests, he probably blended into the woodwork. They would take as much notice of the scowling, overalls-clad man as they would a chambermaid's cart. "Did you drop in on your brother, say hi? Ask for a handout?"

"Didn't want any fuckin' handout. I want nothing more than what I'm owed. I'm the one stayed in Sydney all those years to look after our mother. I was the one took care of her when she took sick. Dad couldn't do it, too drunk, usually. Anyway, it was him made her sick, most of the time. I went to Alberta once, got a job in the oil patch. Good job, real good money. Then Mom fell down the stairs, broke both her legs. She couldn't work, couldn't take care of Dad or the house. Someone had to go home, someone had to look after her. It sure wasn't going to be Mr. *Steiner*." Jones' voice dripped with contempt. "He sent her a magazine when she was in hospital, a flash fashion magazine full of the sort of women I couldn't have in my wildest dreams. Mom didn't even know why he'd sent it to her. But I knew. His name, his fake name, was in it. He'd taken some of the pictures. Greece. Blue water, white buildings, expensive women with bored faces and no tits, wearing blue and white bathing suits and come-fuck-me shoes.

"He hadn't sent the mag because he thought Mom would be pleased. He'd sent it because he knew she'd show it to me and he could rub my face into it. He sent her presents some times, for her birthday and Christmas. An ugly scarf from Paris, a purse from Italy, jams and jellies from London. Never any money, never anything that would actually help us out.

"I told him it was time to pay up. Time to pay me for all the money I'd lost over the years, taking care of our parents, *his* parents."

Jones shook his head. "And he sat there and told me he was dying and didn't have a penny to his fake name."

Silence stretched though the room. Finally, Lopez asked, in a very low voice. "What did you do then?"

"I left. I walked out. He was a pathetic creep. He was lying when he told me he didn't have any money, but I figure he was telling the truth about dying. He looked like he was dead already."

"What time was that?"

"Five-thirty."

"Next time you saw him?"

"There was no next time. And now there won't be. I'm not expecting to get an invitation to the funeral reception." Jones looked at Lopez. His eyes were dry and his face was angry, but he spoke in a low voice. "Before I left, for the last time, I told him what I thought of him. I told him that our mother died, wondering why he hadn't come to see her. Her last words were something like, Albert was always so selfish. He was never as strong as my Dennis. You might think I killed him in revenge, but I didn't need to. That was all the revenge I needed."

Jones walked out. The door shut quietly behind him. Lopez let out a long breath and sat back in his chair. *Did he believe the man?* Yeah, he did.

Deep in his pocket his cell phone began to vibrate. It was John Winters, telling to get back to the station ASAP.

◇◇◇

Smith was so excited, Winters could barely understand what she was trying to say. "Hold on, Molly. Take a breath."

She didn't take his advice. "We have to move fast. Mike knew what was going on, and I don't know if he'll protect his cousin. At any rate, Amy'll let the cat out of the bag soon."

"I'm glad Mike knows what's going on, because I don't. Where are you?"

"Turning into Monroe Street."

"We'll talk about this when you get here. I'm in the office." He hung up and waited for her.

She was out of breath when she ran into the GIS office. Her face was flushed and her eyes wide with excitement. She'd temporarily forgotten her grief over her dad, but it would be all the harder to handle when it came crashing back.

"Take a seat," he said.

Full of nervous energy, she remained standing. "Diane Barton, one of the women we arrested in that street brawl, is Amy and Mike's cousin. She's staying there. Amy tells her when clients at the dog day care book off for a period of time. Which they do when they're going on vacation."

"Careful, Molly, don't get too excited. We have a link, but it's thin, and I don't think the time frame's right." Diane Barton had arrived with Rudy Steiner, to take photographs of the Kootenays for a travel magazine. They'd come to Trafalgar less than a week before Steiner's death, but the B&Es had been going on for at least six weeks.

"Oh." Smith's face collapsed in disappointment and she dropped into Ray Lopez's chair.

"Hold on," he said. She perked up again, and he almost smiled. She was as enthusiastic as an untrained puppy. What had Barton said when he interviewed her—when he was still allowed in the murder investigation. That she'd arrived in Trafalgar ahead of her boss, to scout out locations.

"Phone the Hudson House," Winters told Smith. "Ask them for the date Diane Barton first checked in." Smith dove for the phone. When Steiner was alive he paid for his assistant to stay at the hotel. Once he died, she was on her own tab and moved in with Mike and Amy. No reason to assume she didn't have contact with her cousins no matter where she was staying.

Winters pulled up his file on the B&E to refresh his memory.

"Thanks," Smith said into the phone. She hung up. "March fifth."

Winters skimmed his notes. The first B&E was March twelfth. "You might be onto something, Molly, good work." He read the most recent entry. "Frank Spencer saw a photographer on the street a day or two before the break-in across the road."

"That doesn't help us, that was a man."

"Did Spencer say it was a man?"

"Let me think. He said he saw a guy taking pictures."

"A guy, as in a male, or a guy, as in a generic person of not much interest?"

Her blue eyes opened wide.

"I would have thought you'd be aware of the dangers inherent in sexist language, Molly."

"He said the guy." She made quotes in the air with her fingers. "Was about average height and slender, with short hair. Average height for a man is around tall for a woman. Barton always dresses in sloppy, generic clothes. She could pass for a guy—I mean for a man—at a distance."

Winters stood up and took his jacket down from the hook. "I'm going to pay Ms. Barton a visit." Smith jumped out of her chair. "Unfortunately, you can't come with me. You're not in uniform and you're unarmed."

"I can borrow a gun."

"You most certainly can not. You're a uniformed officer, not a detective.

"Go home, Molly. You've done a good job and if this pans out, you'll get the credit. But right now I think your mother needs you more than we do."

She deflated as quickly as a popped balloon. "My mother. I actually forgot for a while there."

"I'll give you a call, at your mother's house, when I have something to report."

It was almost six o'clock and the Chief and Barb had left for the day. Winters took the back stairs to the parking lot two at a time and called Keller. "I have a lead, a promising lead, in the B&E business."

"Glad to hear it."

"There's a complication."

"Isn't there always."

"I'm bringing Rudolph Steiner's assistant, one Diane Barton, in for questioning. Obviously, there's likely to be some overlap with the IHIT investigation."

"You can bring this woman in. Sit her in the interview room, but don't start questioning her until you either get the go ahead from Madison or he joins you."

"I'm not going to let him take over. He doesn't know a thing about the B&E case."

"Agreed. It's your show. Good luck with it."

Winters didn't take a uniform or a patrol car to pick up Diane Barton. This was just going to be a friendly little chat. Smith had given him nothing but conjecture. Conveniently Barton had the charges of assault and creating a pubic disturbance stemming from that fight with Josie Steiner hanging over her, which would give him a welcome amount of freedom in handling her.

He followed Smith's directions to Mike and Amy's place. When he knocked on the door, Amy answered. She was holding her young son, squirming like a bucketful of eels, and gave Winters a shy smile. "I remember you," she said. "You're with the police."

"That's right, Amy, and I remember you too. May I come in?"

"Sure." She stepped back. "This is Robbie."

"Hello, Robbie."

She put the child down. "Mike's not here. He's at work."

"I'd like to talk to your cousin, Diane Barton, is she here?"

"She's here." Barton got up from the kitchen table. Short-haired, tall and lean, dressed in an oversized sweat shirt and loose pants she could be mistaken for a man by someone not paying much attention. "I don't have any business with you. My court hearing is on Thursday."

"I want to talk to you about another matter. I don't want to disturb Amy and Robbie so I'd like you to accompany me to the station."

Behind her glasses, the corner of her right eye twitched, and she shot a glance toward the open door behind him. "And if I don't want to?"

"It will be mentioned at the hearing."

Amy's face was pinched in concern, sensing the tone, if not understanding the meaning. Robbie picked up a pink rabbit and waved it over his head.

"You've got the power," Barton said, spreading her arms. Her hands were shaking and the twitch in her eye was getting worse. "I'm all yours."

Winters put Diane Barton in an interview room with a cup of coffee, checked the audio and video recording equipment, and went to his office to wait, without much patience, for Madison. He started the ITO for a warrant to search the place at which Barton was staying. Unlikely, if she were the thief, she'd store the computer equipment and DVD players at Mike's small house. He'd have to find a storage facility somewhere. If he were lucky, she might have kept some of the jewelry or smaller electronics such as iPods with her own possessions.

Lopez came in, followed by Kevin Farzaneh. "Got a call from the Chief," the detective said. "What's up?"

"Where's Madison?"

"Talking to Mrs. Steiner," Farzaneh answered. "In the presence of her lawyer. He said I can sit in on this interview."

Winters explained what he'd learned about Diane Barton's possible involvement in the recent spate of B&Es.

The three men walked into the interview room. Barton had made an ashtray out of her coffee cup, and a couple of butts floated on remains of the dark liquid. "No smoking in the building," Lopez said.

"Arrest me," she replied. Her dark eyes, magnified by thick glasses, skittered about the room, between the three men, to the door, her hands, the coffee cup. They sat down, and Lopez switched on the recording equipment. Winters stated the date and time and the names of those present. He told Barton she was not under arrest; they just had some questions for her.

"Do I need a lawyer?" she said.

"Up to you."

She leaned back in her chair. "Go ahead." Her left leg was twitching, the foot beating out a tattoo on the wooden floor. Seeing Winters' eyes on her, she pressed her hand onto her thigh and the movement stopped.

"Why are you still in town?" Winters asked. "Your job here is obviously finished."

She attempted to shrug, but the movement didn't cover her nervousness. She wiped her hands down the front of her pants. "Maybe I like it here. Actually, that's a lie. I don't like it here. My job, as you put it, is over because someone bumped off the boss. Definitely terminated, not only the job but my expense account as well. I would very much like to go home, except the bitch of a wife has my photographs. Besides, in case you've forgotten, I have to appear in court on Thursday."

"You can come back for the court appearance."

"Travel costs money. Some of us can't afford to criss-cross the country whenever we want."

"Short of money are you, Miss Barton?"

"If it's any of your business, yes. I'm unlikely to get paid for not only the last week of work, but all my expenses as well, and I'm out the proceeds from my photographs unless her ladyship decides to give them back. Which will happen about the time hell freezes over."

"You've been staying with your cousin Mike Stanford?"

"Can we hurry this up? You know perfectly well where I'm staying considering you found me there."

"When did you first arrive in Trafalgar?"

She leaned back in her chair, and chewed at the nail on her index finger. "March fifth." The leg began moving again.

"Have any contact with Mike or his sister, Amy, between then and when you came to stay with them?"

"Sure. They're my cousins. I called to say hi."

"Is that all?"

She looked at him through narrow eyes. "Why are you asking me about them? Mike didn't know Rudy and far as I know they never met."

Winters thought. So far no one had mentioned the dog day care or the B&Es. Should he let her think he thought Mike was implicated in the death of Steiner? She was obviously anxious and trying to hide it, but that meant nothing. Lots of people, with absolutely nothing to hide, got jumpy at police attention.

"Let me repeat the question, Ms. Barton. Did you visit your cousins since coming to town before moving in with them?"

"Yes, I did. Amy's a retard but she's an okay person. I went over for dinner once."

"Once?"

Her eyes jumped between the men. "Once. Twice maybe."

"What did you talk about at dinner?"

"I didn't tell them they'd find Rudy alone in his room in the evening and they could bump him off, if that's what you're asking."

"That's not what I'm asking."

"We talked about family mostly. Who's doing what. Jobs, children."

"Jobs?"

"Yes jobs. My sister Fran's a law clerk and she got a new job in Toronto. If you want the address of the firm I'll get it for you."

"Did you talk about Amy's job?"

It was almost imperceptible, but Diane's face relaxed and she lost some of the tension in her shoulders. She lowered her glasses over the bridge of her nose and rubbed at her eyes.

"Amy's job?" she said, when she could see again.

He said nothing. Farzaneh looked confused, but Lopez almost grinned in understanding.

Barton's eyes slid to one side. She glanced at the camera mounted on the wall. "Amy's a retard. She doesn't have a job."

"Amy might be slightly *mentally handicapped*," Winters said, "but I've found her to be bright and engaging. Some people, people others might make fun of, have no need to deceive. They tell the truth, when asked, because they have no reason not to."

"Yeah, well, some people make things up too."

"So they do."

"You know what I think? I think this is a way of getting at me for that fight the other day. It wasn't me who bopped the blond cop. You should be talking to Josie, but I guess you don't want to bother her. After all, she's staying at the hotel, not on the couch of a relative's cheap apartment." She placed her hands on the table. The shaking had stopped, and her leg was still.

"The matter of the altercation between you and Mrs. Steiner isn't our concern right now. Nor is the death of Mr. Steiner."

Something moved behind Diane's eyes, and Winters' nerves stood to attention.

"I'm asking you," he said with great care, "if Amy told you about her new job."

"Now that you mention it, she might have said something. She's so proud of some stupid minimum wage gig, you'd think she hit the jackpot."

"Perhaps for Amy her job is good enough."

"Whatever." Barton waved one hand in the air. She'd relaxed, and as he spoke Winters' thoughts raced back over the conversation.

"Tell me what she had to say about this job."

"She walks dogs and picks up their shit. Fun, eh? She babbled on like the moron she is about how important it is to clean up after the dogs because you don't want to dirty the park."

Winters could imagine what had happened. Barton had paid a courtesy call on her cousins because her mother told her to. That done, she wouldn't have given them the time of day again, except for something that Amy let slip about her job.

"She talk about the clients?"

"No. Just the dogs. How much they like her."

"Ms. Barton, Amy told one of our officers that you asked her about the clients' schedule. Specifically who was going to be away for an extended period of time. Can you tell me what interest you have in that?"

"Making polite chit-chat, pretending I give a fuck."

"Not." Lopez spoke for the first time. "The sort of thing I'd ask just to be friendly."

"I really don't care what you'd ask."

"Ms. Barton. Why did you ask Amy Stanford about the vacation schedules of the regular clients at Debby's Dog Centre?"

"No reason," she said.

Winters stood up. "Diane Barton, I am arresting you for breaking and entering 702 Station Street on April 7th. It is my duty to inform you…" He finished the statement. "Do you have anything to say?"

She looked at him. She mouthed the words, "Fuck you." Her eyes were dark with anger, but there was something missing, and he almost hesitated.

"Detective Lopez, take Ms. Barton downstairs and meet me in my office."

Winters walked out, Farzaneh following.

Chapter Twenty-eight

Winters was standing at the window when Ray Lopez walked into the GIS office. Diane Barton had been checked in and a legal aid lawyer called.

Winters turned. "We're going to have to move fast on this. I don't have much more to hold her on than my suspicions. General chit chat amongst relatives about someone's new job is unlikely to stand up in court and the minute that lawyer arrives, he's going to realize it."

"You're sure she's guilty?"

"Absolutely. The timing is right and you can be sure she didn't ask Amy about the job to be polite. I doubt if she knows how to be polite unless it's to get her something. Go around to Frank Spencer on Station Street and get a proper description of the person he saw taking pictures. Get a warrant for Barton's camera, her computer, and for her room at Stanford's place. And get it fast. Then go around to the other neighborhoods and start asking if anyone saw someone taking pictures. I'm guessing that once Amy told Barton who was going to be away for a few days, she checked out the house pretending to be snapping pictures of the street."

"Got it," Lopez said. The game was on, and his heart was racing. He knew why Winters needed to move fast. If the lawyer could get Barton out of jail, she'd be erasing everything on the cameras and ditching the stolen property.

"I'll get out of your hair," Farzaneh said, "as this obviously has nothing to do with the Steiner case."

"Don't be too hasty. Take a seat," Winters said. "Ray, I started the ITO, work on it while you're listening to this."

Farzaneh and Lopez exchanged glances. The Mountie sat in the spare chair and wheeled it across the room. Lopez activated his computer, found the ITO and started to type.

"When I went around to get Barton, she had the look of the mouse being sized up by the cat. Too bad we can't convict people because of the look in their eyes. It would save us a lot of time and bother."

"You got that right," Farzaneh said.

"She was nervous and frightened, and I figured right then we could get her for the B&Es."

Lopez turned around. "We know that, Boss."

Winters stretched out his legs. He ran his thumb across the face of his watch, and Lopez knew he was thinking. Farzaneh lifted one eyebrow in question, and Lopez could only shrug in return.

"But, as soon as we got down to the brass tacks, she relaxed. Notably."

"They all try to act casual," Farzaneh said, "some get weepy in disbelief that we could possibly be thinking of blaming them, some get super defensive, and some try to sound all cocky and not bothered. That was her."

"Agreed," Winters said. "That was her. At first. But when she realized where I was coming from, that we were talking about the B&Es, she didn't just pretend to be not bothered. She *was* not bothered."

"What? You said a moment ago you knew she was the one, and now you're not sure?"

"I'm sure all right. She's up on charges for assault and causing a public disturbance, and now she's arrested for a B&E. Judges don't like to see someone using the courtroom door as if it revolved. So why would she not be too concerned at the possibility of charges?" Winters looked at Lopez, waiting for an answer.

"Maybe Langois threatened her for fighting with the boss' daughter, and she thinks jail's a good place to spend some time while he cools off," Farzaneh said.

"Possible," Winters said. "But she wasn't happy to see me at first, as she would have been in that scenario."

"Why would someone be happy to be charged with a B&E?" Lopez said, very slowly.

"Because they're guilty of something a lot more serious," Winters answered.

"Steiner?" Farzaneh said. "You think she did Steiner?"

"Yes, yes I do. She thought she was being questioned again about the murder of Rudy Steiner, and when she understood I wanted to know about a reasonably minor series of B&Es she relaxed considerably."

Lopez had abandoned the ITO. "Sorry, Boss, but it won't wash. You've been out of the loop, remember. I checked into Barton's activities that night. She's in the clear. Has an alibi."

"Alibis can be broken."

"She was having dinner at eight-thirty, and stayed at the restaurant for a good long time. Trafalgar Thai. The waitress remembers her."

Winters turned to Farzaneh. "You're still sure of the time of death?"

"Pretty much. Steiner was seen by the room service waiter at 8:38 in the company of…uh…of…"

"A woman, yes, I do know that."

"Estimated time of death is 8:38 to eleven, but the witness who heard a shot puts it just before nine."

"Time for Barton to abandon her dinner and get to the hotel?"

"It would be very tight. Too tight, I'd say. The waitress said Barton had several beers and lingered over her food. She's sure of the time. It was getting dark when the woman arrived, and sunset these days is just after eight."

"Okay. Let's work on making sure that B&E sticks. Meanwhile, I'm convinced Barton has something to hide about the murder. We'll keep trying to break that alibi."

"Sergeant Winters," Farzaneh said. "Sorry to have to remind you, you're not to be involved in that case."

Winters smiled without humor. "Got carried away there."

"I'll tell Madison I have a gut feeling about Barton."

"Thanks."

Ray Lopez worked on the warrants after Winters and Farzaneh left. The Mountie to update his boss, Winters to call on Frank Spencer to get a description of the person he'd seen taking pictures. When Lopez finished, it was getting late, close to eleven o'clock. Too late to make random calls on neighbors, but tomorrow they'd re-visit everyone in the vicinity of the B&E's. With luck, that might not be necessary. Barton might still have some of the stuff in her possession, and there was a good chance she'd have kept the shots of the neighborhoods on her camera. She'd have trouble explaining to a judge why she happened to have pictures of houses that had later been broken into.

Lopez pushed the keys to send the ITO on its way. Hopefully they'd have the warrants first thing tomorrow. Tonight Barton was tucked up in the cells; the lawyer would be arriving in the morning. He took off his gun belt and locked it in the office safe, and then called home, knowing someone would still be up.

Madeline answered.

"I'm finishing here, and I'll be leaving in a few minutes. Need me to pick up anything?"

"No thanks. I made beef stew for dinner. You know it keeps well," she said. He knew.

"Becky's quite upset about tomorrow," Madeleine said.

"Why?" He put on his jacket and turned off the office lights. The corridor was dark and quiet; a glow came from the lights in the entrance and over the dispatch area.

"The trip's been cancelled."

"That's too bad." Lopez's youngest daughter had been looking forward to the club's first kayaking trip of the season. "Why'd they cancel it?" He glanced at the bank of TVs monitoring the cells. Diane Barton lay on her back on the highly uncomfortable metal bed. "Is she still up? I'll say something comforting."

"You can speak to her in the morning."

"Why'd they cancel it?" He mouthed "good night" to Ingrid and headed for the door.

"Weather. Heavy rains expected to move in tomorrow afternoon. This lovely spring sunshine isn't going to last for long. It's going to be as bad as last week."

Lopez stopped in his tracks.

"Ray? Are you there?"

"Put the stew back in the fridge. Tell Becky I'll take her out on the river once it clears up." He punched the red button on his phone to disconnect and immediately called up another number.

◇◇◇

"Did you sleep well, Ms. Barton?" John Winters asked.

"Perfectly well, thank you," she replied. "Not that you give a fuck." She leaned back in her chair. Her clothes were rumpled, looking and smelling as if she'd slept in them, which she had. Her hair was mashed flat on the left side and the fine skin beneath her eyes was as dark as a spring storm.

It was 7:15 on Tuesday morning, and Barton had been roused with coffee and breakfast and the news that Sergeant Winters wanted to speak with her.

"Only two of you this time," she said, pretending to yawn. "Other fellow still in beddy-bys?"

"A lawyer has been contacted at your request," Winters said. "She is due to arrive at ten o'clock. If you wish, we can wait until she gets here."

Barton waved her hand. "Let's get this farce over with. I don't know anything about any job of my cousin Amy's, other than what she told me, or any clients she might have. Can I go back to bed now?"

"Soon," Winters said.

He could see Madison out of the corner of his eye. The man's dark face was set in its usual angry expression. Winters didn't know how long the Mountie would be able to keep his fat mouth shut.

They'd met last night in the Chief Constable's study. The Chief had hastily pulled on track pants, splattered with paint the color of the study walls, and a Toronto Blue Jays sweat shirt. His wife, yawning with more believability than Diane Barton was now doing, brought in a tray of coffee and packaged cookies.

Against orders, Lopez had called John Winters to report what he'd learned.

"I dropped the ball on this one, Boss," he said. "Barton told me she got to the restaurant around eight-thirty. When I spoke to Lynne, the hostess at the Thai, I came right out and asked her if Barton had been in around eight. She said yes. She said she was sure of the time because Barton was sitting by the window and it was almost dark out."

"And…"

"Think back to last Monday. Big storm charged in late in the afternoon. High winds, lots of rain, and very, very thick black clouds."

Winters remembered Eliza getting home. She'd taken off her rain coat at the front door and it had dripped all over the floor and she said she was looking forward to spring in San Francisco. She'd been very tense, angry at he knew not what, said she had a headache and went upstairs without another word or even wiping rainwater off the floor.

"I'll check the airport," Lopez said, "but I'm betting it was dark as night by five, six o'clock."

"Which means," Winters said, "Barton could have finished her meal before eight, leaving her plenty of time to stew in her resentment and get to Rudy's room around nine, just after Eliza left. Good thinking. I'm calling the Chief and asking for a meet right now. You get Madison. I hope he's sound asleep and we can shake him out of his dreams."

Sure enough Madison had been in bed when Lopez called. Winters contacted the Chief Constable, who agreed to an unusual impromptu meeting.

Madison hadn't been at all happy, but Keller convinced him to play along.

Winters smiled at Diane Barton. She did not smile back. He went over yesterday's conversation, about dinner with Mike and Amy, Amy's job.

"When Amy babbles," Barton said, "I don't pay much attention. Who the hell cares what she's doing with her miserable life. Like I said, she's a retard. If she told me something she shouldn't have about some people I don't know who are away on vacation, that's her problem. Unless the law changed while I wasn't looking, you can't charge me with the crime of not listening."

"I expect to receive a search warrant this morning authorizing me to search your belongings, in particular your cameras and computer," he said.

Her eyes twitched, but she didn't react. She must have known he'd be interested in her things.

He was playing a dangerous game. It had been a hard sell, first to the Chief Constable, and then to Madison. If it didn't go well, if he failed, his career would be on the line. Madison would make sure of that.

"You were seen, you know," he said.

"Seen where?"

"On Station Street for one. Taking pictures of the street. Of one house in particular."

"So? It's not a secret I came to your pleasant town to take pictures. I am a photographer's assistant, as well as a damn good photographer in my own right. Taking pictures is what I do. Like brow-beating women is what you do."

Madison shifted in his chair. Burton turned her attention to him. "And as for you, I thought you were here to investigate Rudy's killing. Did you get demoted or something?"

There it was—out in the open. Winters circled. "The death of your employer must have been upsetting for you."

"So upsetting, I decided to break into random houses? Try again." She pointed to the camera. "That was a rhetorical question, I'll have you note."

"Noted."

"No, Rudy's death did not particularly upset me. He was a jerk, and, other than the fact that I'll probably never get paid what I'm owed, I don't much care."

"Why was he a jerk?" Winters asked, his tone conversational, just wondering.

"He hadn't produced a piece of work worth mentioning since something like 1902. His hands shook and his eye was bad and all the taste he had left was in his crotch. And damned little of that." Her mouth pinched with anger and for a moment it looked as if she were going to spit on the floor. She leaned across the table, her shoulders braced, her eyes dark with rage.

It is said that every person is capable, given the right circumstances, fear, hatred, self-defense, of killing another human being. John Winters didn't know if that was true, but as Diane Barton looked between him and Madison, he had no doubt this was a woman able to kill. And to justify it after.

"I took the job with him 'cause I admired his earlier work. I thought I could learn something. Then I saw the crap he was producing these days." She threw up her hands. The overhead light shone off her glasses. "I could learn more from a kindergarten class, or from my fuckin' cousin Amy."

"Why did you stay with him then?"

"Job offers aren't exactly falling all around me, you know. I lost the job I had in Toronto, lugging around equipment for a food photog. She fired me, the creep. Said she didn't like my attitude, but it was jealousy, pure and simple. She started a whisper campaign against me, saying I was a problem." Barton snorted. "So I decided to leave Toronto." Winters made a mental note to locate this previous boss and find out what had really happened. He said nothing, sat back and let Barton vent all her rage. *Give them enough rope...*

"Even when I realized what a washed-up has been Rudy was, I figured he could help me out. Introduce me to the right people, you know, show some of my pictures around." She laughed, the sound so harsh and brittle it made the hairs on his arms rise up. You could use that laugh to frighten small children into going to bed on time. Winters stole a glance at Madison, willing the man not to make a sound. Barton was talking to herself, justifying everything she did. If she remembered they were there, where she was, it would all be over.

"I should have realized what would happen. Instead of showing my pictures around, letting people know about me, he started saying they were his, that he'd taken them." Blotches of red rage were breaking out on her face and neck.

Winters heard Madison's chair squeak. Outside in the hallway a man laughed. Barton picked up her coffee cup. Her fingers picked at the cardboard rim. He thought she'd clammed up, but she began talking again.

"When I finally realized what was going on, I figured I could talk some sense into him. His fifteen minutes were over and there was nothing he could do about it. Stealing my pictures wasn't going to help him get his career and reputation back."

She abandoned the cup and rubbed at her face. It had gone quiet in the corridor, and silence filled the room.

Winters waited, scarcely daring to breathe. "Sounds sensible," he said at last.

"Of course it was. But he wasn't. The fuckin' jerk." She looked up, and stared straight at him. Her eyes were clear and intelligent, and she knew full well what she was saying. "He dared to laugh at me. I made sure he wouldn't laugh again."

Madison let out a long breath. "How did you do that, Miss Barton?"

"He was a real weirdo, had an incredible phobia about germs. When I got to his room he was holding a glass of water. There was champagne in a bucket and some food on the table, but he didn't offer me anything, stuck-up bastard. I told him I knew he was stealing my pictures, and he said I didn't have enough talent for him to want to use anything I'd done. He was lying. I said I'd take him to court, and he laughed. He put the glass down and went to the bathroom. When he got back he started snapping out orders for the next day, as if nothing had happened. He drank out of the glass of water and it was my turn to laugh. I told him I spat in it when he was out of the room. That freaked him all right. He ran into the bathroom with his fingers stuck down his throat like a model at a dessert party. It was absolutely pathetic. I didn't really plan to, I was just wanting to give him a scare. But when I saw how easy it would be I decided it was time to put an end to his misery." She lifted her hand so suddenly, Winters started. "And bang. It was done."

"Where did you get the gun?" Madison asked.

"Picked it up in Toronto. For protection."

Chapter Twenty-nine

He found Eliza in bed with a magazine. Her eyes were red and a snowstorm of crumpled tissues were scattered across the duvet. It was her habit to get up early during the week, to be at her computer shortly after the markets opened in the East. That she was still in bed at ten o'clock was not good.

He sat on the edge of the bed and lifted her hand. He kissed it and stroked the palm. Tears ran down her face.

They said nothing for a long time. Then she spoke, her voice very soft. "I didn't kill Rudy, John."

"I never thought, not for a minute, that you did. I was angry and jealous and scared, and yes, worried that people would laugh at me because of a thirty year old photograph. You were right, Eliza, I did think it was all about me, and I left you alone to fight this. All I should have been thinking about was how to support you. Can you ever forgive me?"

She used her free hand to stroke his cheek. "As long as you believe in me I can face anything. That man, that Madison, he's making threats. He said it would go easier on me in court if I turn myself in."

Winters felt a knot in his gut. "And what did you say to that?"

"That I am certainly not going to confess to something I didn't do."

He wiped a tear off her cheek. "You won't be hearing from him again. We arrested the one who did it less than an hour ago. Madison is doing the paperwork and telling everyone what a hot-shot detective he is."

"Then it's over?"

"It's over." Before coming home, he'd gone for a walk along the shores of the Upper Kootenay River. He tore the old photograph into shreds and threw the pieces into the water.

"Since the day we met, John, you've always been the only one." Eliza gave him a small smile and wiggled under the covers. She was wearing a turquoise satin nightgown with thin straps and white lace trimming the deep neckline. The tears had stopped. "I hope you know that. You've been out of this bed for too long. Get in."

She gave him a wink, broad and bawdy, yet tinged with sadness.

He didn't need to be asked a second time.

Chapter Thirty

"Five-one?"

"Five-one here." Molly Smith answered the radio. It was ten days after her father's death. The funeral was over, the home-made casseroles and plates of squares had stopped coming, Andy's mother and sisters had been and gone, Sam had taken his family back to Calgary, and Lucky had reopened the store. Smith didn't think her mother was coping all that well, but she had the support of her vast circle of friends and work was better than hanging around the house with only Sylvester for company.

Smith had gone back to her apartment and back to work. Today was her first shift since the funeral. She felt guilty at how nice it felt to be at work and away from the drama of her family.

"911 hang up. 34 Redwood Street," Jim Denton said over the radio.

"Five-one. Ten-Four." She stuck her arm out of the window, to warn the car behind her she was turning, and did a U turn in the middle of Front Street. Someone had called 911 and put down the phone without speaking. The police always answered those calls—it could be a child in trouble, a battered woman afraid of being overheard, a hand reaching across and taking the phone.

Smith unfastened her seat belt as she rounded the corner. A boy was doing wheelies in the middle of the street. He dropped the front wheel of his bike when he saw her and turned sharply to head in the opposite direction.

It was early afternoon and school had just let out. Parents were walking small children home. Weighted down by backpacks almost as large as them, the kids looked like turtles carrying their houses on their backs. A cluster of teenage girls dressed in tight jeans and short skirts and colorful tops giggled and preened as they strutted their stuff. Across the street from number thirty-four an elderly lady raked up winter's debris from her small patch of garden.

Smith notified dispatch that she'd arrived, switched off the engine and got out of the car. The yard of the house she was interested in was a mess of weeds, broken bikes, and abandoned furniture. Plywood covered the bottom right window. The porch steps creaked under her boots, but there wasn't a sound from inside the house. She knocked on the door. "Police. Open up."

The door opened a crack. A woman peered out, blinking against the light of day. Her face wasn't much more than a skull with a bit of skin stretched across it. Her pupils were black pinpricks in red eyes. She wore a dirty white T-shirt and faded jeans and a line of blood dripped out of her right nostril.

"Did you call 911, Ma'am?" Smith asked.

"Yes," the woman said, her voice very low.

"I'm coming in. Stand back, please."

She put her hand on the door and it swung open. The woman stared at her with frightened eyes and Smith took a step forward. Her fingers moved for the radio at her shoulder. "Are you alone, Ma'am?"

Out of the corner of her eye she saw something moving toward her. She ducked instinctively and began to turn. She felt a sudden, blinding pain in her left shoulder, and staggered backwards. A hand wrapped itself around her arm, her own hand was pulled away from the radio, and she was jerked forward. She stumbled into the house, stars dancing in front of her eyes, her shoulder screaming. She made a grab for her gun, but before she could get a grip, her left ankle gave way in a shower of pain and she dropped to the floor.

A great weight settled across her back.

"No," Charlie Bassing said. "She isn't alone."

Chapter Thirty-one

"Sergeant Caldwell, I might have a problem," Jim Denton said. "Smith went to a 911 call on Redwood Street. She notified me when she first arrived at the scene, but hasn't said anything since, and now I can't raise her."

"Where's Dave?"

"Couple of kids were overstaying their welcome at Big Eddies and he's gone to sort it out."

"Get him over to Redwood Street immediately. Keep trying to raise Smith. Her radio might be wonky. Tell Dave I'll be joining him."

"Problem?" John Winters came out of the legal office, carrying a stack of papers to do with the pending trial of Diane Barton for the murder of Rudolph Steiner. Dick Madison had returned to his unit to receive high praise for a job well done. Winters was perfectly happy to let the Mountie have all the credit. That way he didn't have to spend as much time in court. He and Eliza had finally been able to have their vacation in San Francisco. It had been nice to see the California sun putting some color in her face and bringing a smile back to her lips. Although the smile was small and rarer than it had been, and he knew it would take time before her faith in him was fully restored.

"Potential problem," Caldwell said. "I've got an officer out of contact. Join me?"

"Glad to." Winters handed the papers to the passing law clerk. "Who is it?"

"Molly Smith."

Winters turned to Denton. "Locate Charles Bassing. He's on a vendetta against Molly." He grabbed a radio from the dispatch desk.

"Got it," Denton replied.

Winters and Caldwell took the back stairs to the cars, moving fast. "You think this has something to do with Bassing?" Caldwell asked.

"Wouldn't put it past him."

Smith's patrol car was parked neatly on the side of Redwood Street. There was no sign of the officer who'd driven it. The door of number 34 was closed and the curtains were drawn. As Winters got out of the vehicle, a second police car turned the corner.

Caldwell spoke into his radio. "Jim, have you heard from her?"

"Nothing. I tried her cell phone, but no answer there either."

The officers looked at each other. Caldwell walked around the car to stand with Winters on the far sidewalk. "Let the Chief know what's happening," Caldwell said, "then contact the Mounties and ask them to send some help. Until I know otherwise we have a situation here."

A woman was working in her garden. At a word from Evans she abandoned her tools and quickly went indoors. Four teenage girls watched the police from the veranda of a gentrified house. Evans spoke to them, and they also went inside.

"Four-Two," Caldwell said. "Secure the street."

Evans moved his vehicle a few yards down the road, where he parked it in the center of the intersection, lights flashing.

Radio. "Charles Bassing isn't answering his phone, Sarge," Denton said.

"Send someone around to his residence and place of business. If he's not there, put a look out for on him," Winters said, "Have him brought in if he's found. Get a car to the corner of Redwood and Pine to block that end of the street. Evans has Fir blocked."

"Ten-four. Horsemen are sending two cars."

"This is your show," Winters said to Caldwell. "How do you want to play it?"

"If Molly is in that house, and we have to assume she is, she'll be well aware she should have heard from dispatch. Therefore, we have to assume she isn't responding because she can't."

"Agreed."

People came out of their houses to see what was going on. Evans sent them back indoors. An RCMP car, with the logo of three stripes and a horseman carrying a lance, arrived and moved into position to block the intersection to the west. Caldwell told them to send the next car into the alley behind the houses.

"We'll phone first." Caldwell leaned into the car and used the computer. He read the phone number for the house to Winters, who punched the numbers into his cell phone. In the quiet street, they might have heard the sound of a phone ringing inside the house, but no one picked it up.

"Can't stand here all day," Winters said. "I'm going to knock on the door."

"Are you wearing a vest?"

"No."

"I've got one in the trunk. Put it on first."

They'd kept the car between the house and their bodies. Except for the police, the street was empty. Curious faces peered out of windows. An ambulance quietly pulled up behind Evans' car.

Winters slipped the Kevlar vest over his jacket and adjusted the Velcro straps. He took a deep breath. "Guess I'm ready. I hope to God she's having cookies and milk at the kitchen table and doesn't realize her radio is off."

◇◇◇

"Not so tough now, are you, Molly?"

"What the fuck are you playing at, Charlie. Get off me."

She lay face down on the dirty floor; pain coursed through her shoulder and the back of her left leg. Bassing straddled her hips and his hand moved along her side. It stopped, for just a moment, to caress her buttocks. The touch as light as a lover's.

She kicked and wiggled, trying to escape, to get out from under his weight. She felt like one of Frank Spencer's red-headed toddlers, scooped up to be carried to bed. But instead of warm kisses and tons of love, Bassing, she knew, had nothing to offer but pain and humiliation. He laughed, the sound so mean it made her blood run cold. His hands began to move again, fingers reached between her legs, seeking the sweet spot. But she wore thick trousers, and the probing fingers moved on. They reached her gun belt, and she knew what he was after. Tucking her arm tight up against her holster, the way she'd been taught, she bucked harder, trying to toss him off. But he was heavy, very heavy. Her hands were jerked up behind her back, and Bassing shifted to trap them beneath his weight. Laughing, he ground his crotch into her body. Hard. Probing. Bile rose. She fought against the gag reflex.

"Nice, eh?" he said in a low voice. "There's plenty more to come."

In the corner, the woman whimpered.

"First things first. You learn lots of useful things in jail," Bassing said. "Like how to get one of these things free."

He pulled at the clips, gave the gun a twist, and yanked it out of the holster. His weight moved and Smith was clear. She flipped onto her back and looked up. Charlie Bassing stood over her, his legs apart, on either side of hers. He held her weapon and pointed it down at her face.

"Gotcha," he said with a smile that froze her guts. The room was dark, the heavy curtains pulled tight. It smelled of sweat and tobacco and pot, unwashed clothes, food sitting out too long. And fear. Fear emanating from her. The baseball bat he'd used to bring her down lay on the floor beside him. She'd played ball in University and knew a Louisville Slugger when she saw one. A good bat—tough and unyielding. Eyes focused on his face, she slid backwards, out from under his legs, and sat up.

He weighed maybe fifty pounds more than she did. She was runner-lean, a near-Olympic class skier, young and fit, but he was solid muscle. Without her gun, she was as good as dead.

For some reason Molly Smith thought of her mother. They'd just buried Lucky's adored husband; it would destroy her if her daughter died so soon after.

Her radio crackled. Denton trying to get her to respond, tone rising with every request. His voice brought her back to the present, to this room. To Bassing. To survival.

"Throw that into the corner," Charlie said.

Smith hesitated. He swung the gun and pointed it at the woman who'd opened the door. She stood against the wall, hands over her mouth, eyes round with shock. Blood had leaked into the deep crevices of her face; a crooked red river ran down the side of her mouth.

"You said you wanted to play a game," she whispered. "You said it would be a laugh."

Bassing ignored her. "I said ditch the radio, Molly. You have two seconds, starting now, or I shut that one up the easy way."

Smith unfastened the radio and tossed it into the air. It fell to the floor with a thud as Jim Denton called "Five-One! Smith! Come in, Molly."

"You're out of your mind, if you think you can get away with this." Her voice broke and she coughed in an attempt to clear her throat. "Assaulting a police officer is a serious offense, Charlie."

"Assault," he said, with the sneer Smith knew so well, "is the least I'm going to do. You and me, we're going to have some fun. Before you die." He lifted the gun so it pointed directly between her eyes. She could see all the way to hell. "My car's out back. We're going for a little ride before your friends get here. Stand up."

"Charlie," the woman said, "Can I go now? You said there wouldn't be any trouble when the cops arrived."

"Get into the bedroom and stay there."

Smith heard footsteps cross the floor, the sound of a door closing. There would be no help from that quarter.

"Four-Two," Caldwell said. "Secure the street." The radio transmission was full of static. People who weren't used to it couldn't make much sense of it. Hopefully, Bassing wouldn't be able to either.

"Get up," Bassing repeated. He gave the bat a kick, and it rolled across the floor. Out of range.

"My ankle really hurts, Charlie. I think it's broken."

"Use the other one."

She put all her weight on her right leg and, gripping the back of a chair for support, pulled herself upright. She stifled a groan of pain.

He waved the gun at her. "Out the back. Move."

"Please," she said, her voice cracking. "Let me go, Charlie. I'm sorry if I've upset you."

The sneer broadened. "Damn right you've upset me. Now you can make me happy. Before we settle the score."

"You won't be able to get away. They'll be searching for me, everywhere. Look, I'll tell them the house was empty when I got here. Is that your girlfriend, Charlie? She'll back me up."

"Girlfriend? Hardly. Just another junkie bitch who, with a little persuasion, will do anything for a fix. No different than you, Molly, except power's your fix, isn't it? Well I've got the power now, so shut the fuck up and move. Plenty of time to talk later."

Her eyes filled with water. "Please, Charlie, don't hurt me." She felt her body deflating, getting smaller. Her shoulders hunched and she dropped her head. "I'm sorry Sergeant Winters arrested you. I asked him not to."

His face tightened with anger. A vein throbbed in his temple. "After I've sorted you out, that fuckin' bastard's next. Move!" He screamed the last word.

She stepped away from the chair. Her leg buckled and she gave a small, high-pitched cry as she pitched forward. Instinctively Charlie reached out with his free hand and grabbed her arm. "Goddamned useless bitch, can't you even walk straight."

She pulled her collapsible baton from her belt and extended it with a flick of the wrist. Knowing her fate would be decided here and now, that there would be no second chances, she brought it down, putting every last bit of strength she could find into the hit. The baton crashed into Charlie's gun arm. She twisted out of his grip. He yelled, in pain and surprise, letting go of her, but didn't drop the weapon. Smith pivoted on her left leg and brought her right foot up to smash it into his knee cap. He howled as his leg gave way and he dropped to the floor. The gun went off. She heard the bullet strike the wall. The woman in the bedroom started to scream.

Bassing swung the weapon around so it pointed at Smith's chest. She had only one chance left, do it now or die. Praying that the Kevlar vest would give her sufficient protection, she closed in. Before he could fire again, she brought the baton down with both hands, going for the spot she'd hit before. It connected. Screaming abuse, roaring with pain, Bassing fell to his knees and dropped the weapon. The gun skidded across the floor. No choice but to turn her back on him. She swooped on it, fumbled for it, put her hand on it, closed her fingers around it, felt for the trigger. Got it. She swung around to face him.

Charlie Bassing's face shone with rage and sweat; his eyes were so full of hate they scarcely looked human. While she scrambled for the gun, he'd managed to grab the baseball bat and pull himself to his feet. He stood there, swaying but upright. His eyes were black pools in a red face. Spittle ran out of both sides of his mouth. He held the Louisville Slugger high, as if he were about to hit a home run. He gasped around pain. "You fuckin' bitch."

He took a step toward her.

Molly Smith fired at the same moment John Winters came through the door.

Chapter Thirty-two

Meredith Morgenstern ran for the phone. Her hair was wrapped in a towel and she only had half of her face made up. She glanced at the number display as she answered. Area code 416—Toronto.

"Ms. Meredith Morgenstern, please."

"Speaking."

"Ms. Morgenstern, good morning. This is Daniel Levenstein from the *Toronto Planet*. I've been reading the piece you sent us on the late Rudolph Steiner and his wife."

Meredith rolled her eyes. What a waste of time that whole exercise had been. Not only had she been threatened if she didn't stop investigating Josie Steiner, it turned out there hadn't been anything to investigate. After the arrest of Diane Barton, Josie hadn't even had the courtesy to speak to Meredith, instead made a phone call to a Vancouver paper expressing her satisfaction at an arrest in the "cowardly murder" of her beloved husband. Then she, her high-priced lawyer, and the hired muscle left Trafalgar.

This guy from the Toronto *Planet*, a highly popular muck-raking tabloid, must be getting his news by carrier pigeon he was so out of date.

"I'm sorry," she said, "I can't tell you much more about that case. It's been resolved and Mrs. Steiner returned to Vancouver." Josie would be back, to face the charge of assaulting Molly Smith. Meredith planned to sit in the front row of the courtroom, taking it all down. Hopefully she could get a good shot of the grieving widow being led out in handcuffs. She would need something, if she was going to crawl back to Joe Gessling and beg for her job.

"I know that, Meredith. I'm calling because I like the story. It's far too incendiary for us to use," he laughed, "but I like the way you write. We're looking for a new reporter on the city gossip desk. You're an out-of-towner, so you won't have the contacts, but we might be able to offer you a probationary position. If you're interested, we'd like you to come to Toronto for an interview. How about next Wednesday?"

Meredith didn't have to check her calendar to know she was free.

Chapter Thirty-three

Molly Smith placed a small plastic vase full of yellow tulips on the fresh grass. Andy's grave was neat and tidy—Lucky came every day, to pull weeds or clip the grass around the headstone or tidy the small hosta she'd planted in the shade of a leafy maple. But mostly she came just to sit on the lawn, wrapped in silence and her own thoughts.

The sun shone hot on Smith's bare head and the trees burst with blossoms and new leaves. Mounds of tulips and daffodils lined the pathways crisscrossing the cemetery, and the newly mowed grass was the color of emeralds. High in the branches of a cottonwood a hidden bird chirped, and the air was heavy with the welcome scent of spring.

She'd stopped here before going into work, wanting to talk to her dad about her future. Over the past weeks, she'd had a lot of time to think about the direction she wanted for her life.

She and Adam had gone to Whistler for a few days of late spring skiing and quiet nights around the fireplace. She'd considered talking things over with him, but held back. She was only twenty-seven years old, Adam was thirty-four, and she'd come to the difficult decision that, at this time in her life, building her career was more important than finding a mate. Watching her mom trying to be strong, but breaking down at Andy's funeral, Molly finally admitted to herself that she just wasn't able to commit herself and her entire life to Adam in the powerful, all-encompassing way her parents had to each other. She'd send her resume off to Toronto, put some feelers out to other big cities, and if she got a bite, well then she'd just have to tell Adam she needed to leave and let things fall as they may.

When they got back from Whistler, she gathered her courage and went around to the house in the woods to tell her mother she was going to look for a job outside B.C. But before she could get the words out, her brother Sam called with the news that he'd been offered a big promotion, requiring moving his family to Scotland for two years.

Smith swallowed her own words. She couldn't leave Lucky alone, not yet.

Plenty of time in the years to come.

She'd been investigated for killing Charles Frederick Bassing, and found to be acting in self-defense. Case closed, no further action. She was seeing the psychologist the department used, and thought she was putting up a good front of getting over it, but in her own head she wasn't ready to let the matter go.

Did she have to kill him? She didn't know.

She'd gone over the scene in her mind hundreds, thousands, of times, watching it play out from every angle. What else could she have done? What else *should* she have done? Bassing had been armed with only a baseball bat; the autopsy showed that his right arm was broken so he wouldn't have been able to wield the bat with any accuracy or force. The police were in strength outside; John Winters and Sergeant Caldwell were in the house, guns drawn, before Bassing hit the floor.

Charlie had been coming toward her. His ugly face still sneering, irate, full of self-justification, fury, hatred. Hatred of her, hatred of women, hatred of anyone who got in his way. In her mind she'd seen Christa's battered body being loaded onto the ambulance, seen the rat impaled to her door, her car trashed.

No more, she'd thought, and she pulled the trigger.

"Talk to you later, Dad." She leaned over to run her fingers across the fresh carving in the cool headstone, then straightened up, put her hat on her head, and walked out of the cemetery.

To receive a free catalog of Poisoned Pen Press titles, please contact us in one of the following ways:

Phone: 1-800-421-3976
Facsimile: 1-480-949-1707
Email: info@poisonedpenpress.com
Website: www.poisonedpenpress.com

Poisoned Pen Press
6962 E. First Ave. Ste. 103
Scottsdale, AZ 85251

4